Heavenly Places 2

Heavenly Places 2

Solus Deus

John Kowalski

Acknowledgements

God has blessed my life in ways that I could not have imagined before I knew him, but I can clearly see now that I am His!

*"For if while we were enemies we were reconciled
to God by the death of his Son, much more, now
that we are reconciled, shall we be saved by his life.
Romans 5:10 (ESV)*

All glory, for this book and anything else I do, goes to God!

To my wife, Wendy, son Richard, and daughters Camryn, Devin, and Aubree, you are all my inspiration!

To the staff at the House of Providence in Oxford, Michigan who do the real-life work of serving the "least of these" by providing safety, love, and healing for children in the foster care system as commanded in Matthew 25:40. Support their work at www.thehofp.org "Until Every Child has a Home!"

Finally, to the group of stalwart adventurers who play-tested the game that became these books. Wendy, Aubree, Meredith, Tony, Bryce, Megan, Kaytlynn, Kaiden, Tabitha, Ariel, Krestian, Isaac, and Sarah thank you for allowing me to pour out my crazy ideas. Your creativity, humor and faith have brought life to these characters and this world!

Foreword

Growing up in a Christian household, I had always been keenly aware of the rift between fantasy and faith. Games like *Dungeons and Dragons* were often considered "Satanic," while stories with magic and dragons were called "evil." Yet didn't Jesus tell stories, or "parables," of his own to make his point? As a kid, it left us wondering: what was the real difference between miracle and magic? A talking donkey seemed pretty fantastical to me, anyway. So, I often wondered, what was the problem? Was it because one was true, and one was make-believe? It made me feel as though there was no room for the imagination in the Christian life. But, if it was wrong, why were fantasy stories so compelling? Why was there this need to journey through fantastical realms of the imagination?

> *"I have claimed that Escape is one of the main functions of fairy-stories, and since I do not disapprove of them, it is plain that I do not accept the tone of scorn or pity with which "Escape" is now so often used: a tone for which the uses of the word outside literary criticism give no warrant at all. In what the misusers are fond of calling Real Life, Escape is evidently as a rule very practical, and may even be heroic. In real life it is difficult to blame it, unless it fails; in criticism it would seem to be the worse the better it succeeds. Evidently, we are faced by a misuse of words, and also by a confusion of thought. Why should a man be scorned if, finding himself in prison, he tries to get out and go home?*

J. R. R. Tolkien, On Fairy Stories

In this challenging world, fraught with interpersonal struggles and petty divisions, it at times becomes necessary to step outside our own identities and take on a role more heroic, more befitting our immortal souls than the mundane, often tedious, details of our daily lives. The desire to slough away the drudgery of the human condition, however briefly, is inherent to our species. Fantastic stories have always been our comfort and dearest work since the dawn of our civilization. The Epic of Gilgamesh, after all, is nearly four thousand years old. Though it is the oldest story extant, at least according to our limited knowledge, it certainly isn't the first story man has ever told, springing impossibly from the cradle of human life fully formed, like Athena from her father's head. It's simply the first time, so far as we can tell, a story made it from the oral tradition into writing. With such a propensity for storytelling seemingly ingrained into our very genes, it begs the question: Surely, we were made for something more?

After visiting the words of Tolkien, let us add to it the following insight:

vii

duckling wants to swim; well, there is such a thing as water. ... If I find in myself a desire which no experience in this world can satisfy, the most probable explanation is that I was made for another world. If none of my earthy pleasures satisfy it, that does not prove that the universe is a fraud. Probably earthly pleasures were never meant to satisfy it, but only to arouse it, to suggest the real thing. ... I must keep alive in myself the desire for my true country, which I shall not find till after death; I must never let it get snowed under or turned aside; I must make it the main object of life to press on to that other country and help others to do the same."

C. S. Lewis, Mere Christianity

With this in mind, we understand that fantasy and escapism must play a crucial role in nourishing the human soul, offering a sanctuary for imagination, creativity, and the exploration of profound truths about our existence.

Fantasy creates a space where the impossible becomes possible, and the mundane becomes extraordinary, serving as a powerful tool for dealing with the complexities of real life. It invites us into worlds where dragons soar in the skies, where magic is as real as the air we breathe, and where heroes we always knew we could be can finally embark on epic quests. These narratives are not just idle amusements; they echo our deepest desires, fears, and values. They allow us to confront, in a safe environment, the very issues we grapple with in our daily lives, like good versus evil, courage and sacrifice, and the search for meaning and identity. And perhaps, in some small, human way, it echoes the longings in our hearts for our true home, a nearer heaven, one we can hold in our hands, however briefly.

To those who feel escapism to be the realm of children, we must remind them of the transformative power of fiction. From the sci-fi novels of H. G. Wells and Jules Verne inspiring real-world technology to the social movements affected by Charles Dickens and Upton Sinclair, the books that transform us can also inspire us to change our surroundings:

> *"Fiction can show you a different world. It can take you somewhere you've never been. Once you've visited other worlds, like those who ate fairy fruit, you can never be entirely content with the world that you grew up in. Discontent is a good thing: discontented people can modify and improve their worlds, leave them better, leave them different."*
>
> *Neil Gaiman*

As readers, these fantastical worlds provide us with mental and emotional respite and solace from the mundanities of life. They stimulate creativity and problem-solving skills, offering a playground for the imagination and catharsis for our most profound emotions. This imaginative exercise is not a trivial pursuit but a crucial aspect of human creativity and innovation. The realms of fantasy and escapism are not just frivolous or childish pastimes but are essential to the human soul. They offer a space for reflection, creativity, and emotional release, helping us better understand ourselves and the world around us. Our favorite stories serve as mirrors reflecting our deepest desires and fears, as windows into worlds where our spirits can soar freely, unencumbered by the limitations of our physical existence. The ones that truly move us connect us with the divine, affirming our faith and supporting us in our spiritual growth.

From this perspective, John Kowalski has given us a doorway to enter a wholly new world within these pages: one where fantasy creatures and prayer are not divided, where magic is a God-given blessing used to aid and heal, and where adventure serves both Heaven and humans.

Some books take you on an incredible adventure. Some books teach you something profound and universal, whether about morality, human nature, or simply to see life in a new light. Some books encourage your spirit and foster your relationship with the divine. The rare books that do all three are a balm to the soul.

In the tradition of Tolkien and Lewis, Heavenly Places combines fantastic adventure with courageous faith, where the power of prayer is the most potent magic. Now let's continue Jonah, Willa, and Wren's fantastical journey through the world of Aeramor.

Audra M. Portman
Author *Legends of Andolin*

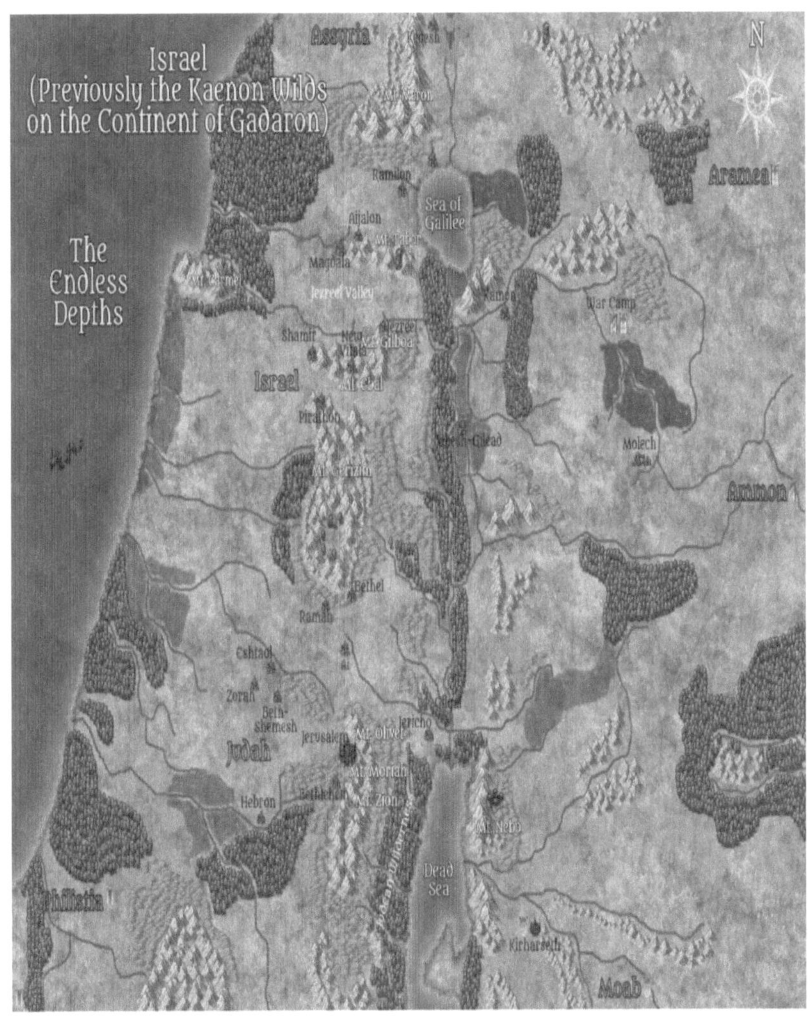

N
Israel
(Previously the Kaenon Wilds
on the Continent of Gadaron)
The
Endless
Depths
Assyria
Kedesh
Mt. Aaron
Aramea
Ramlon
Sea of
Galilee
Aijalon
Mizraim
Magdala
Jezreel Valley
Ramea
War Camp
Shamir
New
Jezreel
Gilboa
Israel
Mt. Ebal
Piral Sea
Jabesh-Gilead
Molech
Mt. Gerizim
Ammon
Bethel
Ramah
Eshtaol
Ai
Zorah
Beth-
shemesh
Jericho
Jerusalem
Mt. Olivet
Judah
Mt. Moriah
Hebron
Bethlehem
Mt. Zion
Mt. Nebo
Dead
Sea
Philistia
Kirharseth
Moab

Prologue

E lowen stepped through the portal as the angelic being who opened it had instructed. She was instantly moving at incredible speed. Surrounded by endless white, she could see pinholes of gold and black ahead that flew past her randomly as she flew. She could move freely, as if weightless, though the slightest movement sent her into a spin. It took her a moment to stop and re-center. By then she had realized she couldn't breathe. She wondered how long it had been since her last breath as she began to panic. Her lungs began throbbing, begging for precious air. Just as she was about to lose hope, she saw something ahead. It looked like a hole in the endless white backdrop. As she soared toward it, she noticed it was growing. Tears were freely flowing down her face leaving trails of moisture behind her as she hurtled toward the hole. She could see grass and trees through it now. There was what looked like a road below her. Massive beasts moved along it, with strange lights guiding their way. They seemed to be racing toward each other at high speed, barely missing what could only be devastating collisions. In the distance she could see what looked like a shining city glowing against the night sky. She had seen nothing like it in all her travels on Aeramor. She wondered where in the world she had been sent. Nothing about this place seemed remotely familiar. Could it be this wasn't even her world?

As that thought resonated in her mind, she felt a shift in the way she was moving though this portal. Her momentum slowed as if the environment grew thicker or heavier. She began to feel as if she were moving in slow motion. Elowen burst through the hole but still felt as if something was wrapped around her preventing her from skidding across this stone road into the forest beyond. Like a rubber band it stretched until her momentum slowed then it snapped, and she was standing still.

The young druid looked around confused, desperately trying to catch her breath. She found herself in the middle of the road she had seen from the portal. A sudden wave of nausea overwhelmed her causing her to fall to her knees and retch. She had barely finished releasing the contents of her stomach when she heard a deafening roar. She looked to the left and saw lights like the ones on the beasts she had seen earlier. They were so bright she could barely see the outline of the massive creature behind them.

She rose to her feet trying to gauge its speed as it bellowed, bearing down on her. From behind her a second creature began to screech. It was like nothing she had ever heard before. This creature had lighted eyes as well but was much smaller than the first. This one's head bowed down as it screamed toward her, making Elowen think it was trying to stop and avoid hitting her. She decided to try to fly over the smaller one that was stopping. She ran toward the woods on the smaller one's side and focused on being a bird. She leapt into the air but didn't transform. Airborne, it was too late to change the plan now. Elowen braced for impact. As the lights passed her, she could see that this was no beast. It was a conveyance of some sort, large and fast. Inside was a human passenger. Their horrified face was the last thing she saw before slamming into the glass front. The impact knocked her unconscious, her momentum flung her twenty into the woods where she landed on the long grass, unmoving.

The roar and the screech had both stopped, though Elowen couldn't have heard them anyway. The riders from both conveyances ran to the broken woman. They seemed distraught at the events as they tried to help the stranger.

The light was far too bright for Elowen. She tried to move her left hand to block the sun, but her limb wouldn't respond to her request. She blinked furiously, wondering why her arm felt restrained. As her vision cleared, she began to see the room around her. There was so much white everywhere, no wonder she couldn't see. To her left she heard a voice, kind and soft. Looking over she saw the blurred outline of a woman, reading from a book.

The woman read aloud in a soothing voice, "He sent out his word and healed them, and delivered them from their destruction. Let them thank the LORD for his steadfast love, for his wondrous works to the children of man! And let them offer sacrifices of thanksgiving and tell of his deeds in songs of joy!"

"Am I dead?" Elowen asked, her dry voice cracking.

"Nurse! She's awake!" The woman leapt from her chair and was instantly at Elowen's side.

A second woman, in pink, rushed to her other side. "Well, hello beautiful! We have been looking forward to meeting you." She pulled down Elowen's lower eyelids to look into her eyes. Then placed the end of a metal object, connected to her ears, on Elowen's chest. The woman seemed pleased with the results of her examination, "Do you know your name?"

Of course she did. What kind of silly question was that? "My name is El... uhm... Ell..."

Seeing her frustration the other woman spoke, "It's ok. We can just call you Ellie for now. I'm Claire. Drink some water, you must be thirsty."

Elowen complied, though the clear liquid didn't taste like any water she had ever had.

"I'm Tiffany," the nurse added. "Claire is right. It is not uncommon to suffer temporary memory loss after a trauma. You have been here unconscious for more than three months. Just take it slow, your memory will return." She looked at Claire, "I'm going to tell the Doctor she's awake, will you be here for a bit?"

"Yes," Claire replied. "Sofia is coming in an hour or so to sit with Ellie for a while."

Nurse Tiffany, pleased with the response, left hurriedly.

A week later Elowen's memories had not returned but she was healthy enough to go home. Still having no idea where she might live, Claire offered her spare room. Elowen had come to like both Claire and Sofia in the time they had spent with her, so she accepted. She occupied herself with books and hiking while her friends were at work. Their social activities were mostly faith related. Hopeful that any reminder might jog her memory she went along. They spoke of the Father, the Son, and someone called the Holy Spirit and how they were three parts of the same God. She found the concept confusing but somehow still compelling. On Wednesdays they went to their church's youth gathering to serve as leaders. She was amazed at how much time these two women spent dedicated to serving their God and his people. As the weeks passed Elowen started to engage and found that serving people was therapeutic in a way she was not expecting. When Claire and Sofia asked her to go with them to a youth conference across the state she didn't hesitate. The ride across the state was enjoyable. Their conversations were engaging and funny. She had grown to care for these two women deeply and they shared the feelings completely.

The trip was uneventful until their GPS malfunctioned dropping them in front of an old farmhouse on a tree-lined street. Neither their phones nor the car connection would give them proper directions, so they went to the house to ask for help. As they passed the barn-like garage they heard an odd noise and saw strange lights.

"What in the world is that?" Sofia was transfixed by the purple, black and gold swirl seemingly hovering in the air.

Claire shrugged having no idea either.

Elowen's reaction was altogether different than her friend's. She saw something familiar about it. Her eyes focused and unblinking, she heard a voice.

"It is time to go home Elowen. Your people need you; all my people need you."

Elowen walked steadily forward, ignoring the protests of Claire and Sofia. She managed only, "I have to go home." Then she stepped through the portal.

Claire and Sofia were terrified as their friend disappeared from their sight. They looked at each other for a moment, their eyes welling up with tears.

"Whatever this is, we can't let Ellie do it alone, can we?" Sofia asked, never looking away from the glow."

Claire grabbed her friend's hand, "God we trust that your hand is in this, and we surrender to your will."

With that said they stepped through the portal following their friend.

Table of Contents

Chapter 1   The Hunt Continues 1
Chapter 2   Valley of the Shadow of Death 4
Chapter 3   Curiosity Kills. 31
Chapter 4   Creature Comforts 37
Chapter 5   Natural Consequences 45
Chapter 6   Mayhem in Magdala 50
Chapter 7   S.O.S. 65
Chapter 8   Showdown in Aijalon 68
Chapter 9   "Gods" and Monsters 78
Chapter 10   Out of the Frying Pan 98
Chapter 11   You Can Go Home Again. 122
Chapter 12   The Scenic Route 129
Chapter 13   The Depths of Corruption 143
Chapter 14   Wedding Day Woes. 154
Chapter 15   Fierce Princess 178
Chapter 16   Aftermath 185
Chapter 17   Home Stretched 194
Chapter 18   Mission Drift 208
Chapter 19   A New Day Dawning 218
Chapter 20   The Least of These 238
Chapter 21   The Fruit of the Spirit 261
Chapter 22   To The Mountain 274

Chapter 1

The Hunt Continues

Elmore was a pleasant sight for so many around Haven. His unlikely and miraculous rescue by Moonbow and his Duskhunters had become such a reminder of the power and providence of Adonai. The nearly eight-foot tall, red-haired firbolg was regaining his strength every day. He had resumed his studies and had even started teaching others the basics of his cantrip magic and its faith inspired innovations. Today though, he was on an entirely different mission. Walking down the north hallway between the clergy and military quadrants, Elmore greeted a couple clerics heading the other way. Once they passed and he was alone, his form wavered and changed. He was suddenly a human man in plate mail and the white tabard of a Templar Knight. He turned left at the next corner and entered the first door. He knew these four knights were away on duty, so he would be alone in the small dormitory room. Elmore went right to work looking through the drawers in the small desk. In it he found documents written by three of the room's residents Kehn, Jarryd and Theon. He pulled a piece of paper from his tunic, causing his illusory image to waver briefly. He held the paper up to the samples, quickly noting that none of them were close to a match. There were only three of the four though. The knight known as Galad had nothing in or on the desk for comparison. Elmore paused for a moment as he heard footsteps and voices in the hallway. When they had passed, he moved to the footlockers. On the third try he found Galad's. In it were neatly folded clothing, shoes, toiletries and standing in the corner a scroll. He unrolled it. It was a letter from his sister who lived far to the north in Kedesh. Rolled up inside was the beginning of his response to her. Elmore found himself relieved that this sample was also not a match to the writing on the note believed to be penned by a traitor inside the Haven underground.

Putting everything back the way he had found it, he moved back to the door. Listening intently for a few seconds he decided that no one was nearby so he went out. As he was closing the door a female, wearing the blue tabard of a paladin, turned the corner to the south and walked toward him.

"Hey Kehn, you're back already?"

Elmore waved over his shoulder and walked briskly north to the next intersection. As he turned the corner to the east, he saw no one approaching so he dropped the illusion, spun on a heel and went back the way he had come.

The paladin, named Barabae, was intent on catching up to Kehn, "Good morning, Elmore. Did Kehn go by you?"

"Hello Barabae," the firbolg responded, looking back over his shoulder. "He seemed preoccupied, barely acknowledged me." The hedge wizard hated lying but the traitor had to be found, lives were at stake.

"Weird," she mused, stopping next to Elmore and looking up at him. "I'm so glad to see you back here. Are you doing well? They didn't hurt you, did they?"

"No, despite the name, Perdition Spire was well-kept," he replied. "The guards were professional. I'm pretty sure the Warden is a believer, possibly one of the Unseen, though I have no idea how she got that position."

Barabae knew that Elmore was referring to the missionaries who had spread across the world after the razing of Bethel. They found communities, got jobs that connected them with people. They would then use those positions to share the word of Adonai and protect other believers.

"I'm glad to be out of there but it could have been much worse," Elmore admitted.

"We were praying for you every day," the young paladin assured him with a hug.

"I know. I felt every one of them." Elmore's square jaw and wide nose exuded strength but in this moment, it was his eyes, glossy with tears, which showed his true feelings.

They parted with the usual pleasantries and went about their day. Elmore needed to update Moonbow. Four more knights being ruled out as traitors was great news, but it also meant that the real traitor was still here somewhere.

Chapter 2

Valley of the Shadow of Death

Jonah, Willa and Wren were bone tired. They had been traveling north for days since the Assyrian army passed by them south of the Sea of Galilee. Sleeping in the day and traveling by night provided some safety but also major drawbacks. They moved slower in the dark and slept far less in the daylight. Avoiding cities, mostly in ruins, forced them to sleep in whatever cave or hole they could find and make suitable.

They were relieved to learn from Moonbow that the army they had passed had turned west toward the Mediterranean Sea then south apparently heading toward Philistia or Egypt. They knew that this was a temporary reprieve at best. The fact that they had avoided Judah was good news, but the Assyrians had marched across Israel with impunity, attacking, looting and ransacking towns along the way. Their actions were very clearly speaking to their future intentions toward the region. Moonbow also told them that a few days ago the Aramean and Ammonite army they had sabotaged had finally moved. They had force-marched due south, staying well east of the Jordan river. At last report they were approaching the northern border of Moab. Moonbow showed deep concern when he related that Judah and what little was left of Israel would soon be surrounded.

The further north the family got, the fewer people they met. While that offered some safety it was also terrifying. They couldn't help thinking about how many were left dead in those cities and towns in the wake of the passing army. They prayed often for God to give them peace of mind and guidance in navigating such morbid thoughts. They trusted God's plan and were confident that he was with his people especially in their most desperate moments. They pleaded with the Lord often that he might lead them to survivors so that they could convince them to head south. If nothing else there may be safety in numbers. Near midnight on the fourth day heading north, they arrived in Kedesh.

Jonah watched the seemingly vacant town while they ate and rested. There were no armed encampments, patrols or scouts, but they did see signs of life in several houses. The people in them were quiet and used no lights, but occasionally they could hear wood creaking under foot, or see a curtain move or a shadow pass a window. Jonah told his family to be discreet and pretend they didn't notice. He wanted to delay making contact until morning, and after some rest. They found a small home away from the few occupied ones and made it their refuge for a rest. Once inside Jonah secured any interior doors and sat with his back against the main entrance keeping a clear view of the back door. Willa completed her four-hour trance and took the second watch, Wren and Leo took the third. The druid was getting pretty good with her lockpicks and decided to give the box from the war camp another try. She twisted and turned gently feeling tumblers move through her tools, then to her surprise the lock released. She had finally opened it after all this time. Before she could inspect the contents the doorknob on the back door jiggled, then turned. She moved quickly to the door jam, pressing herself hard against the wall and drawing her scimitar. She motioned for Leo to hold his position. He obeyed though she could hear the low growl he was emitting. The door opened slowly. A figure stepped in, then a second. They were hooded but shorter than Wren. As the second figure passed her, she grabbed them around the neck covering their mouth. As she grappled with her intruder, she softly whistled, sending Leo into action. He pounced on and pinned the other intruder. Jonah and Willa were instantly on their feet, weapons in hand. The morning light was enough that they could see that these two subdued home invaders were children, a male and a female.

Wren whispered to her captive, "If I let go of your mouth are you going to scream?"

The young brown-haired girl shook her head, warm tears running down her face into Wren's hand.

Wren released her mouth, "Who are you and why are you here?"

"Please don't hurt us," the girl could barely speak through sobs. "We were just looking for food."

Jonah commanded Leo to release the boy and helped him to his feet, while Willa closed the door. "We're not going to hurt you. Please sit down." The two children, maybe eight to ten years old, obeyed the request. "Wren, can you make some food for all of us?"

"Where are your parents?" Jonah sat cross-legged in front of them to be less intimidating.

The girl spoke, "Mother died two years ago. Father went out scavenging a month ago and never returned."

Willa couldn't hold back, "You've been alone all this time?"

The boy spoke up this time, "The others who stayed behind have helped us when they can. Food is becoming scarce, so we try to fend for ourselves and even provide for others. We don't want to be a burden to the elders."

"Admirable," Jonah admitted. "Where are my manners? I am Jonah, this is Willa, my wife and our daughter Wren is…"

"Right here with food and water," she was extra enthusiastic out of guilt after threatening the girl. "Take two berries each and a bowl of water. Eat only one berry, save the other for tonight. They will be spoiled by tomorrow."

"Thank you," the girl managed after eating the berry. "I am Netty, and this is Oren." The boy had eaten both berries and was already regretting the decision. Netty shook her head at her younger sibling, "Can I ask why you are here?"

Jonah motioned for Wren to explain, "We are looking for something nearby. We came a long way and needed rest, so we stopped here. It looked abandoned."

"Almost everything is abandoned. Most of the townspeople left days ago, a few didn't want to leave. We stayed in case abba returned." Netty was feeling more relaxed already. A thoughtful look crossed her face, then she sprung to her feet. The sudden move startled Leo who jumped up and growled.

"He's on his guard," Wren explained as she calmed her wolf. "Sudden movements set him off, especially by strangers."

"Sorry, sorry," Netty apologized. "I just realized Kalin and Lukas have been here forever. If you're looking for something in the area, they may have information about it."

The kids led them to what used to be the general store. There was no sign of activity inside in the early morning light. Netty knocked on the door three times, then once, then three more times. They heard the audible click of the lock and the door creaked open.

An older elven man peered out his eyes widening when he saw Jonah and his family behind the two kids. He closed the door quickly but carefully, trying not to make a lot of noise.

"Moreh Kalin, they are friends," Netty implored. "They have not harmed us."

The door opened more quickly this time, the elven man now behind it. "Get inside, quickly." He almost closed the door on Leo, "Is he with you?"

"Yes, Leo won't be any trouble," Wren answered in assurance.

"Come in then Leo," he said, closing the door behind the waist high gray wolf. "So, children, why have you brought these strangers into my home against all instructions?"

Oren burst out with words, "We were scavenging, and they were in a house, and they didn't kill us, but they almost did because we broke in on them and then they told us…"

"Oren, stop please," the elder elven man, gray haired and gaunt either from hard years or malnutrition, sat down at a table and beckoned the others to join him. "Why don't you and Netty get something to eat and make our guests some tea. I think they should speak for themselves."

Oren rubbed his belly, still full and aching from overeating the berries. Netty grabbed his arm and dragged him to the kitchen.

Jonah waited for the kids to leave the room then began to tell their story. He introduced his family, sharing much but leaving out the parts about where they were from. He did emphasize their mission from Adonai. He included more detail when he got to the dream about Shamgar as it was the main reason the kids had brought them to Kalin's home.

The man took it all in without a word. He pondered for a moment before speaking. "May I ask a few questions?"

"Of course," Jonah replied, "anything."

There were a lot of rummaging sounds and harsh whispers coming from the kitchen where Netty and Oren had gone. Willa stood, "Excuse us. I think we should help the kids before they destroy your house."

"You make a strange family," Kalin offered, "but there is no doubt you belong together."

"Yes, we must look odd," Jonah chuckled. "God brought us together despite incredible odds, who are we to argue with his will?"

"You are very different from many of your kind," Kalin seemed surprised, "but that is not my question. First, we are not quite as clever as we thought in staying here. You seem to have spotted us easily."

"I was a soldier, trained to notice dangers," Jonah replied. "The armies coming through will not care to wait and spot you. They will pillage everything of value. If they don't find you, they will likely burn you out. If they do find you it will be much worse."

Kalin winced and nodded understanding Jonah's meaning. "Those remaining will not travel well, but that is not your problem."

Jonah held up a hand to interrupt Kalin, "No, it is not Adonai's way to leave people to their fates. Do you know Him?"

"I know of your God, Jonah," the elf admitted, "but only through some who claim to follow him. A few even lived here in Kedesh. They left quickly with little regard for who was left behind."

"I'm sorry Kalin," Jonah seemed deeply concerned with the man's story. Jonah's greatest fear was that his actions would be an obstacle to the faith of others. "Please don't judge God by the measure of the people claiming to follow Him. Many hide their lack of true faith behind walls of self-righteousness."

"You're right," the man agreed as Willa, Wren and the two kids delivered tea and some kind of pastry. "People do not cause my distance from Adonai. There are things I don't understand about God's actions."

Jonah was intrigued, he did love a good debate, "Give me an example." He wasn't a tea drinker but didn't want to be rude, so he accepted a cup.

"Ok, I'll share, but forgive me if I get passionate," the elf paused for a moment. "I have lived hundreds of years, and I have seen many horrible things that people have done to each other. I understand that their actions are their own as, I hope, will be their judgment. What I don't understand is how God treats people like you and your family."

Jonah was taken aback by this statement, "Interesting, I didn't expect your question to go there. Please explain, how has God mistreated us?"

Kalin continued, "Perhaps mistreat is not the right word. You say you were sent here by God, to this war-torn land, with your family. If he truly loves you as you say he does, why would he risk sending you here?"

Jonah pulled his chair right in front of Kalin's. He smiled broadly and placed both hands on the man's shoulders. "That is really two questions so I'm going to give you two answers. First, God is risking nothing by sending us here. He called us for a purpose and gave us everything we needed to complete it. I… no we, believe that if we surrender to his will for our lives we cannot fail. If our purpose is to get to a certain point and be called home to him, we are happy to be of service. Death is not a barrier to Adonai; it is but a means to an end."

"Interesting," Kalin admitted, "your faith is inspirational."

"We are simply obedient," Jonah admitted. "The glory for anything we carry out while doing His will goes to Him. Now, the answer to the second part of your question is quite simple. God sent us, his treasured children who He loves dearly, into the lands of the enemy because he loves you just as much."

This statement hit Kalin like a slap. He lifted his elbows onto the table burying his head in his hands and began to sob uncontrollably.

Willa, Wren and the kids came to his side. Jonah stood and placed a hand on his shoulder, the others followed suit. Jonah prayed to God for continued clarity for this man and these children and any others here in Kedesh. He prayed that God would fill this man with the Holy Spirit to give him the enlightenment only He can provide. When the prayer was finished, they allowed Kalin time to compose himself.

Kalin wiped his eyes, and his voice wavered a bit, "You have given me everything today and I'm afraid I cannot return the favor. I know little of Shamgar except that there is a memorial to him in a nearby cemetery. There is a caretaker there, perhaps he can aid you further."

"That is plenty my friend," Jonah responded. "We will seek him out. I will ask one more thing of you."

"Anything!"

"I'm so glad you said that." Jonah chuckled then became serious again. "Get the kids, the smithy, the elderly human couple and anyone else left in town packed up and ready to leave by the time we return."

"That is everyone," Kalin stated, now unsurprised. "You really did scout us well. But what if they won't go?"

"You have God on your side now," Jonah explained. "Pray about it, then say the words He gives you and make them understand that staying here is death. Death without God is eternal separation. We need time to convince them. Once we complete the mission we were sent here for, we will return to escort you as far south as we can."

A couple hours later the odd quartet that had become known as Coram Deo arrived at the gate of the Kedesh Necropolis. This place was nothing like the burial mounds or tombs they had seen previously. This resembled the cemeteries they were used to back home on Earth. The gate was open and very rusty. They doubted that it could even be closed anymore. Just inside the gate was a map of the place, carved in stone. Wren made a quick drawing of the map while her parents studied it. At one time this must have been a site of some renown or at least regular visitation. Willa spotted the building marked caretaker in the lower left corner of the map. Jonah and Wren had long since accepted Willa's mysterious ability to read Hebrew. In unison they looked to their left and could see the small building. As they approached the house, they noted that it was the only building that seemed to be kept. It was clean and painted nothing like the condition of the rest of the cemetery, which was overgrown and dirty.

Jonah knocked hard three times and heard an immediate, and startled movement.

The door opened and a balding halfling peered out, "Yes?"

"Hello, I am Jonah, this is Willa and Wren." Jonah's voice was calm and measured.

"I'm Davel, the caretaker," the man opened the door more, letting down his defenses a bit. Robbers didn't usually introduce themselves, after all. "How can I help you?"

"My family has been sent here to seek out the ox goad of Shamgar," Jonah explained. "The people left in Kedesh suggested we come here. Can you help us in any way?"

Davel looked surprised by the question, "Hmm, never thought this day would come. Wait here." The short pudgy man trudged off into his home. The inside was as immaculate as the outside. It was clear that this man had stopped caring for his work and had taken to only caring for himself. He returned a minute or so later with an envelope. He handed it to Jonah, "This was passed to me by my predecessor years ago. He said someone would come to ask about the ox goad and that I should give it to them. I didn't open it."

Jonah opened it but it was written in Hebrew, so he handed it to Willa.

The pink-haired elf translated it aloud,

"Begin where rests the one who is the greatest of all beings.
He lived before God and the world and even the kings,
He rules the underworld and the world of the living,

Wren answered without hesitation, "Nobody is greater than God, but why would you bury nobody?"

Davel couldn't resist listening since Willa had read it in front of him. He simply said, "Akeldama."

"Field of blood?" Willa translated.

"It is the place where we bury criminals, the poor and the unknown," Davel replied.

Willa understood, explaining to the others, "It's what we call a Potter's Field, like where Judas was buried."

"I don't know of any Judas buried here," Davel looked up and left as he accessed his memory.

Jonah responded, "Oh yes, he's not buried here."

Wren looked at the map and pointed to a large area in the upper middle labeled 'akeldama'. "Here it is."

Jonah replied, "It looks like we are on a scavenger hunt." He turned to the caretaker. "Thank you for your help Davel. You should know that armies come from the north and east. You're not safe here. We will be heading south with the few people left in Kedesh when we are done here. You are welcome to join us for the trip."

Davel barely gave the offer a second's consideration, "I live in a graveyard. It is not likely anyone will come here, but if they do it's as good a place as any to die."

Willa was deeply saddened by the response, "God has more for you in this life. If you change your mind, find us."

Davel nodded half-heartedly and softly closed the door.

The cemetery was even more desolate than it seemed from the entrance. It was dirty and unkempt, and it gave the family a feeling of uneasiness. There was little feeling of life in this place, not even a flower from a recent visitor could be seen anywhere. The grass and trees were gray and lacked sustenance. The sounds and shadows combined to make for the most eerie feeling. Leo was feeling it too as he moved only tentatively into this place, but with Wren's prodding and comfort the shih tzu turned wolf soldiered on with his family.

They took the main path leading north from Davel's house. As they passed the odd-shaped central building they could see the walled off section labeled 'Akeldama'.

"There," Willa pointed, seeming anxious to be done with this task.

As they approached, they saw marker after marker with no names on them. They wondered if the few markers with names marked where the criminals lie. In the very back of this area dedicated to the lost was a large marker with a Hebrew word.

"What does this say, Mom?" Wren was scraping debris from the engraving for a better look.

"It means unknown." Willa seemed saddened by the very thought.

As she was cleaning it off, Wren noticed that there was a small fracture around a symbol. She cleared around it some more then pressed it in with both thumbs. It recessed more easily than she expected, and a small drawer protruded from what she had thought was a simple underline of the word. In the drawer was a small scroll case. She handed it to her mother, "It's probably in Hebrew."

Willa gently opened the case, finding an old scroll. As she unrolled it, she expected it to be brittle, but it wasn't. She read it slowly, translating to common,

"After the rain Noah sent a raven to scout around.
Then a dove flew near and far to find a patch of ground.
He waited seven moons and sent out a third
to gauge the water's cease,
that very eve with this leaf of hope returned the bird of peace."

"Genesis 8," Jonah mused.

"The bird of peace is a dove," Wren added.

Willa's eyes moved as she read it again silently. "Yes, but I don't think the answer is the bird. It clearly names the raven and the doves. I think the answer is the leaf. It says, 'this leaf of hope' but doesn't name it as the Olive leaf."

Wren pulled out the simple map she had copied at the entrance. All the words she copied were in Hebrew. She showed it to Willa.

In the lower right corner Willa found the word Hebrew words for 'olive tree'. "That has to be it." Willa rolled the scroll back up and returned it to its spot. She studied the map, matching the markings to the buildings and structures they were passing, as Jonah led the way to the next clue.

It took Wren only seconds to find the next scroll in a notch in the strangely vibrant olive tree. It was a vision of life amidst the death of this place. Reading it aloud it said,

"It was high in the sky but also firmly on land.
It's very accomplishment, bringing ego so grand.
Seeking Heaven without God was the ultimate doubt,
so, the Lord confused language and cast them all out."

"The Tower of Babel," Jonah answered at once. "We won't need the map for this one." Jonah pointed to the west at a huge tower reaching toward the sky.

Leo became skittish as they crossed the cemetery, especially at the enclosures nestled into the angles created by the cross-shaped central structure. The wolf lost control at the second such structure, just west of the southern spine of the cross shaped building. He stopped and stood at the entrance barking.

Wren approached trying to calm him to no avail. As she stood at her companion's side, she noticed an odd shadow that seemed to float in the air. She squinted to make sense of what she was seeing. It was the shadow of a man in black tattered robes, "Mom, something is in there."

Willa moved closer, she didn't see the robed shadow at first, but she did see what looked like apparitions of a woman and child huddled in fear near the back of the area. She moved her focus closer and found the shadow Wren had seen. The figure floated in front of the apparitions as if on guard. Willa tore her eyes from the sight as she noticed a carved stone to the left of the entrance, with the Hebrew word 'Mishpakha', which she knew meant family. "I think he is protecting them. Let's not disturb these poor souls."

Jonah calmly walked to the open gate. It took some effort to break it free of the rust, but he managed to close it. He wiggled the latch until it moved. As he clamped it shut the mother and daughter faded away. The spectral guardian looked directly at Jonah and nodded, then dissipated into nothingness.

Shivers went up each of their spines at the strange nature of the encounter. "Is that the fate of all who don't believe?" Willa wondered, hating the thought of anyone eternally separated from God. She knew that salvation was offered to all who accepted it and that universalism, the belief that everyone goes to Heaven, was just another excuse to sin without consequence. Though their decision had long since been made, Willa prayed for that family just the same.

Arriving at the impressive monolith depicting the Tower of Babel they noted that it dwarfed the nearly fifty-foot spire nearby. Willa translated the Hebrew words on the stone carving as 'Tower of Babel'. Just under those words was an underline. She noticed that, like the one in the potter's field, it seemed separate from the main structure, so she pulled. It came loose, releasing a small container. Inside was the next note. Willa translated as she read it aloud,

"It kept him steady and others away,
it kept them all safe and showed them the way,
Once thrown on the ground,
a hiss it gave sound,
When struck on the rock as was instructed,
water for all, from that rock erupted."

Wren was looking over Willa's shoulder at the map she held under the scroll. "That one is easy, its Moses's staff." She looked at her mother for the location.

"Northeast," she replied pointing at it on the map. "Right there."

The area they arrived at was more of a memorial than a burial site. There were large statues of various accomplishments of Moses on the four corners and a large fountain in the middle depicting Moses with the staff standing over the rock that clearly once produced water for this fountain.

There were benches all around for people to sit and pray. The family gladly accepted this opportunity to reach out to God.

Jonah led the prayer, "Father God, we owe you so much. We don't know why we were chosen for this mission, but we surrender to your will for us no matter where you send us. Protect us and guide us to do your will. We know that only you can see us through this."

Willa spoke as Jonah trailed off, "Thank you, Lord, for giving us true sight to see when to fight and when to use your word as the weapon. Continue to give us clarity to speak truth and use the weapons of war only when absolutely necessary. We honor your name in all things. Amen."

Leo tensed up and huffed, turning to the west.

"What is it, Leo?" Wren followed his eye line but saw nothing.

Jonah remained alert, thinking that their pursuer, Illya, may be near again. He watched their surroundings with Leo while his wife and daughter found the next clue.

Wren always had great attention to detail. After a few minutes of inspection, she found a loose piece at the bottom of Moses's staff. It came off, releasing a scroll case. She turned to hand it to Willa and noticed Leo and Jonah were no longer behind them. "Dad?" She called out. There was more fear in Wren's voice than her mother had heard in weeks.

Willa turned to look just as Leo and Jonah appeared from behind one of the four outer statues of the prophet with a third figure. It was Davel.

Jonah led him to Willa and Wren, "He was watching us from back there. I told him he was welcome to join us. His presence could be helpful."

"I'm sorry for spying on you," he explained ashamedly. "I'm not great with people, but you three are not like anyone I have ever met."

Willa didn't hesitate, "That is not us, It's the spirit of God in us!"

"May I come along?" His face now alit with hope. "I would like to know more."

"Of course," Willa assured him as she opened the next scroll. Reading aloud,

> *"It can be carried but never touched by the skin.*
> *It has angelic adornments and ten instructions within.*
> *It was revered as it was sent and kept in a tent.*
> *It was lost and then found; it came home but soon went."*

As Willa read to the point about the tent in the poem, Jonah and Wren said, "The Ark of the Covenant," in unison.

Davel was more than impressed, "How do you all know so much about Adonai?"

Wren answered, "Where we come from God's words are written and available to all for reading and study. My parents here insisted on me reading it daily. As I got older, I realized I had stopped doing it for them and just kept doing it for me." Both parents smiled at her admission. Davel nodded and seemed inspired.

"See, you are different, like I said." Davel moved north a bit then turned back. "The Ark of the Covenant replica is this way."

As they approached the large ark replica Jonah noticed a pile of refuse to the east, "Davel, why is all of that there?"

"I'm ashamed to say I gave up on my duties here." He looked down at his feet as he spoke. "When people stopped coming, I stopped caring for the place. I left that pile of old flowers and gifts there to rot."

Jonah bent to get to eye level and put his hands on the man's shoulders, "God has a word for you on that as well, my friend," Jonah's voice was soft and not judgmental. "And whatsoever you do, do it heartily as to the Lord, and not unto men."

"Colossians 3:23?" Wren whispered quietly. She knew this was the right scripture but was surprised that Jonah was quoting the New Testament.

Jonah caught the meaning and nodded at her.

"Yes, you're right," Davel admitted, having no understanding of the exchange between father and daughter. "Adonai knows I have lost my way."

Willa was already on her way as she said, "No better time than now to fix it. "She sloshed into the muck and picked up handfuls walking them through a small gate in the north wall dropping them in the compost ditch, where they were likely meant to go. The others joined in, and they made short work of the pile.

On her last handful Wren noticed that something fell from the pile to the ground. She saw that though it had been buried in refuse it was perfectly clean. She set aside the trash and picked it up. It was a beautiful pearl-white spindle stone. She held it up to the light of the sun to get a better look. Suddenly it flashed; she could feel that it no longer had any weight in her hand. It slipped free from her fingers, but it didn't hit the ground. Instead, it circled her head slowly moving just above her brow line.

Willa noticed as she picked up the trash Wren had dropped, "What is that?"

"No idea, but I think it wants to stay."

"Does it hurt?" Jonah asked.

"No," Wren wrinkled her brow as if the effort may jog it loose. "I actually feel better, more energetic."

Davel stood nearby mouth agape in amazement, "Different indeed."

Returning their attention to the Ark they found the next note wedged under the heavy top. Jonah and Willa lifted it slightly with no small effort as Wren retrieved the scroll case and Willa translated.

> *"It was a gift to the one and the envy of the others,*
> *It was a favored sign but brought fire from the brothers.*
> *Some say it brought him nothing but pain,*
> *But God's providence used him to bring them all gain.*
> *It was stolen and then torn,*
> *and became something to mourn."*

Willa knew instantly it was Joseph's dream coat. She so loved the story of Joseph and how God used even the worst circumstances created by sin and the enemy for the good of his people.

Davel had come to the same conclusion and was already moving, "This way." He was starting to feel more comfortable with these people of faith.

As they headed south down the main path Willa noticed an enclosure with Hebrew words carved above it. "Davel, doesn't that mean 'the dead'? Why would someone note that in a necropolis?"

Davel's pace seemed to quicken as he answered, "Notice there is no visible gate to access the area? The dead there are not ready to rest. Do not go in there."

Willa understood but was visibly shaken by the answer. She prayed silently for God to release those poor souls. Jonah and Wren put their hands on Willa when they saw her stop to pray. Davel bowed his head unsure what he should do in this situation.

The next crypt had a placard that Willa translated as "Joseph, Favored Son."

Wren searched around the three-dimensional relief depiction of Joseph in his dream coat, finding a note in the strangely functional coat pocket.

Willa read the note aloud,

"He had more locks than any, but God could ever number.
Vows were taken at birth to refrain from its sunder,
He was a symbol of strength but never acted with tact,
when he was shorn, he lost the spirit as he had broken the pact."

"Samson!" Willa, Jonah and Davel exclaimed almost simultaneously. "This way my friends," Davel said, now reveling in this quest though it took him mere steps from his home. "I'm sure you know that Samson's vow, taken by his parents at his birth, was that of the Nazarenes." He regaled them with more information about the Nazarene order while they walked north, then west. They listened intently, having no desire to squelch the man's newfound enthusiasm. Soon they were in front of a small, gated area. Davel released the latch and led them inside.

Willa approached the central structure, noticing the placard on it which translated to "Memorial to the Nazarenes." The stone slab had four pillars on it that had collapsed on the central figure, which appeared to have once been Samson chained to the pillars.

Jonah found it ironic that this memorial art piece was imitating life as the columns had fallen in on Samson as they did when he collapsed the Philistine building on them and himself in Judges.

Wren searched the remains of the sculpture, but it was Willa who noticed that the placard could spin horizontally revealing another message in Hebrew. This one translated to, "Enter near where the dead refuse to rest."

"We were just there," Davel reminded them.

"But you said there was no entrance to that place," Wren recalled.

Willa, still crouching near the message, rubbed her hands on the raised letters. "It says 'near' where the dead refuse to rest."

They arrived back at the entrance-less area of the restless dead. Jonah looked around and saw the Moses fountain to the north, Joseph's memorial and the olive tree to the south, and to the west he saw three buildings. The middle building of the three was the right arm of the large central building. He hadn't noticed that it had a door the other times they passed. "There," he pointed.

The door was unlocked and opened easily. Jonah entered first.

Wren followed behind him. She muttered, "Let there be light," causing her amulet to light up the space. None of them really needed the light except Davel, but they were still not used to having dark vision. The space was twenty feet wide and about fifty feet long. Burial shelves lined both sides with ancient, wrapped bodies in them. Near the back wall was a sarcophagus on a stand in the middle of the floor. Above it was two longswords crossed over a shield with a vibrant green tree painted on it.

"Let's try to disturb as little as possible," Willa suggested. "Davel, you may want to wait outside."

He responded in a hopeful voice, "If I stay out of the way, can I follow behind?"

"It's up to you, but it may be dangerous," Jonah conceded.

Wren took the lead, staying clear of the sarcophagus. As her light hit the back wall, she could see that there was no other exit from this room. She found it odd but was distracted by a splash of color she noticed on the sarcophagus. There was red, like blood between the lid and the main container. She got closer, careful not to touch anything, "why would there be blood here?"

Jonah circled around just in time to see an eye pop open on the lid and teeth begin to form along the seam of the lid. As the hideous maw opened, he yelled, "look out!"

It was too late. A pseudopod tongue lashed out grabbing Wren just above the left elbow pulling her toward the slobbering mouth.

Leo leaped to her defense, latching onto the appendage and shaking his head violently.

Willa was instantly praying, light forming in her hands as she asked Adonai for aid. She extended her cupped hands toward the creature launching a bolt of radiant energy. It struck the creature causing it to emit a shriek and rear back a bit.

Seeing an opening Jonah leaped forward, sword in hand, swinging down hard on the pseudopod holding Wren, careful to miss Leo. His strike nearly cut all the way through the tongue-like appendage, allowing Wren to break free of its grasp.

Davel had followed too closely behind Jonah and was now wedging himself into the northwest corner of this chamber in terror. He had never seen anything like this before and he had none of the training of the others. He scrambled along the wall in fear. As he reached the corner something gave way and he fell headlong into a concealed doorway leading north falling hard on the earthen ground in the space beyond.

Jonah and Wren were facing away from Davel, but Willa saw him suddenly disappear, "Davel found a secret door behind you."

Jonah fought the urge to look, as the dangling pseudopod lashed out at him. It grabbed him near his knee, but it had very little strength left. He easily severed the remaining tendons. The creature wailed again and slammed shut its huge maw. Wren seized the opportunity grabbing a sword from the wall above the false sarcophagus and driving it down through the creature pinning its mouth shut.

Jonah saw this and repeated the process with the other sword from the wall. The creature shuddered, then fell still. No one moved for at least ten seconds waiting for the obligatory 'horror movie post-death reanimation'. It didn't come.

Willa was next through the secret door into the passageway. Davel was regaining his feet as she arrived, "Are you ok?"

"Yes," he responded, dusting himself off. "I wasn't expecting the wall to give way but oddly I was hoping that it would. What was that thing?"

"I think it was a mimic," Jonah said as he stepped through followed closely by Wren. "They are a lot scarier than in my imagination playing D&D as a kid."

"D&D?" Davel didn't understand the reference.

"Dungeons and Dragons," Jonah explained. "We pretended to be mighty warriors fighting hideous beasts for treasure and glory."

"This is what you did for fun?" Davel asked incredulously.

"Yeah, it definitely seems weird considering our current situation," Jonah admitted as he walked north in the narrow curving passageway. After about twenty feet he came to a door. Wren and Leo positioned themselves opposite Jonah as he opened the door. Jonah knew this had to be the northern section of the large structure. He saw nothing moving inside so he stepped in. This chamber was like the last one, only smaller. There was another sarcophagus at the northern end. Above it, on the wall were two crossed daggers. "Wren, check behind me for a concealed door, there shouldn't be anything to the north based on what we had seen from outside. We should avoid the coffin if possible."

The cat-girl followed instructions and found the door easily. Jonah retook the lead and guided the group to the left arm of the building. He used the same logic in avoiding the sarcophagus there as well.

Wren found the next concealed door and Jonah repeated the rest of the careful process, now heading south. The next door opened into another chamber much like the others. The only difference was that this time the weapon was emblazoned on the sarcophagus itself. Above it on the wall was a tapestry depicting Shamgar and his father tending their fields with an army approaching in the background.

"Looks like we found the end of the road," Jonah's tone was confident.

"We may have to open this one," Willa offered, equally unsure.

"Ok," Jonah screwed up his courage. "All of you back to the hallway."

Willa approached her husband and said a quick prayer of guidance over him.

Jonah felt a surge of strength that he knew was the spirit of God. He made sure everyone was safely back in the hallway, then took two deep breaths and pushed. There was a moment that he thought nothing would happen but then the lid moved a bit, then more. When it was turned enough to see inside, he stopped pushing.

There was no body in the container, only a twisted mass of wood the length of the coffin. It was like four branches braided together by divine power, coming to a hook-shape at the top with gold rings at intervals holding the braids together and a yellowish gem centered in the hook. Jonah was so transfixed by its beauty that he didn't hear the grating sound of a secret door opening behind him next to the door to the hallway.

Wren saw two hulking figures lumber out of the secret room toward her father, "Dad! Behind you," she cried.

The paladin spun around; the ox goad held defensively in front of him. His eyes went black again, spectral wings appearing on his back, and radiant energy engulfing his arms and the weapon, as the two monstrous skeletons approached with giant axes at the ready.

Willa and Wren both began to pray but were seconds behind the action.

When the two skeletal guardians reached the center of the room the gem in the oxgoad flashed brightly. The eyes of the undead creatures flashed back. They instantly stopped advancing, turned to face each other, and pointed their weapons blade-first at the ground leaving the massive hilts in front of their chests. There they remained frozen, as if they had always been just statues.

Jonah exhaled in relief as everyone except Davel ran to his side. Jonah made eye contact with the terrified man.

"W-what are y-you?" Davel was clearly shaken at the sight of Jonah's Aasimar visage.

"I am of the aasimar race," Jonah explained, trying to remain calm as his heart still raced. "We are partly celestial and have some frightening looking abilities, especially if seen without warning. I am sorry, Davel."

Wren's curiosity got the better of her. She had already entered the room the skeletons had come from. "Hey guys, in here."

Jonah followed Willa into the circular chamber with a domed ceiling. In the center was a dais with a single scroll case on it. Engraved in the face of the dais were Hebrew words that, as usual, Willa translated to common. They said, "He judged a moment between Ehud and Deborah. six hundred Philistines fell to his herder's tool."

Willa unrolled the scroll. She read a little from the top, then skipped to the middle. She seemed very enthusiastic as she began rolling the top to pull more from the bottom without the delicate material touching the floor. Her eyes welled up as she read near the end. "This scroll is the entire Pentateuch," her voice cracked. "This is all of the writings of Moses."

The small group carefully left the building the way they had come. They chatted sparingly on the way back to Davel's home. The pudgy man asked them questions about themselves, their abilities, and even about Adonai. When they arrived, there was an awkward silence.

Jonah looked at Willa, then Wren. They both nodded at him in encouragement. He knew what he had to do. "Davel, go pack what you need. You are leaving this place and coming with us."

"I can't," he stammered, struggling to find an actual reason. "Who will look after this place?"

"A great man once said, 'let the dead bury the dead'. You are not dead. You are finding new life in Adonai." There was no lack of confidence in Jonah's voice. "We are not asking. Now, what can we help you pack?"

Two hours later the family, their wolf, and their new-found friend, arrived in Kedesh. Kalin met them near his house with two full carts and the six remaining townspeople. Jonah introduced Kalin, Oren and Netty to Davel. Kalin then introduced Lukas the half-orc smithy and Moshe and Lissa, an elderly human couple, to everyone. Davel put his gear in one of the carts and the small caravan set off for the south.

Chapter 3
Curiosity Kills

Draco had changed a lot since the underground had broken him out of the jail in Jericho. Using the information given to them by Daneel, Willa and Wren, Moonbow sent a team in and freed fourteen believers and some other prisoners willing to help. During the escape and evasion, the young halfling had seen some incredible things. He had developed an insatiable curiosity about Adonai and the seemingly unreasonable faith of his followers. Upon their arrival Draco had been assigned to share quarters with another freed from the Jericho jail, a shadar-kai elf named Rake, and two members of Moonbow's Duskhunters, a human named Przeclaw, pronounced 'preetz-lawv', and a purple Tiefling named Nakano. The latter two were away on a mission so Draco and Rake had the place to themselves.

Rake decided to go get some food before heading to Ramah for supplies. His seven hundred plus years did not deter him from taking a monthly jaunt to the small nearby town to get books and writing materials for his studies. Haven often had plenty available, but Rake thought it better to go get what he needed while he still could. He knew the time would come when he would have to leave such work to others, but this was not that day.

As soon as he left the room Draco looked up from his reading. His eyes wandered to Rake's backpack, then back to the door, then back to the pack. He had seen Rake handle the three scrolls on many occasions, each time increasing his curiosity. Ordinarily Draco wouldn't be interested in reading, but these scrolls were different. They were sealed with black wax and though they looked old, yellowed with age, though the seals were unbroken. That was simply too much for the delicate sensibilities of the young halfling. He found them quickly and considered resisting the urge for a mere second and a half before giving in to his desire.

The wax seals were all variations of the same design. Each had a family crest of a shield overgrown by vines. The difference was that in the center of the shield, behind the vines, were numbers in elvish. One had the number twenty-five, one had fifty and the last had one hundred. He carefully pried at the bottom of the seal numbered twenty-five trying to pop it loose from the scroll at the seam instead of breaking it outright. It worked well; Rake may even think it popped loose on its own. He unrolled the aged parchment and a wave of warmth passed through him. Draco ignored the feeling and read the scroll intently.

It was addressed to Rake Anomandaris, kin of Valan Mystralath, with the added qualifier, "Upon your twenty-fifth nameday." The letter then said,

> *"You have been blessed by your bloodline and the*
> *Raven Queen herself. Your family line traces to a*
> *prophecy that will, in time, result in the return of*
> *the Raven Queen to the Prime Material Plane. The*

Intrigued, and maybe a bit frightened, he repeated the process again on the one labeled fifty. Again, a mysterious warmth passed through him as he unrolled the scroll. This one read, *you and aided you in any need you may have had. Your gifts should be clear by now though they will still need honing to maximize your ability to perform your part of the ritual of summoning that will bring our Mistress, The Raven Queen, to our plane." A chill ran down Draco's spine as he continued reading, "As one of the three chosen to usher in her return you must be physically, mentally and spiritually ready for whatever the summoning ritual will demand of you. This second season of your life will ensure that through trial and demand. You will now go out into the world to make your name. Your name will be Rake the Raven Son. You will use your abilities to bring light to the name of the Mistress and aid to followers of her cause. You will be challenged in trials of pain and suffering but fear not as one of the prophesied ones we know your survival is assured. Your connection to the Raven Queen will grow as will your skill in using the powerful magical abilities she has granted to you. On your one hundredth nameday open the third scroll and follow its instructions. Be of steadfast heart as your success is assured."*

This time the missive was signed, "Yours in burgeoning assurance, Omen Caller Muninn, Shadar-kai Unkindness."

Even more frightened, but still undeterred, Draco opened the final scroll. Barely noticing the warmth this time. Unblinking, he read, "Rake Anomandaris, kin of Valan Mystralath, Upon your One Hundredth nameday." Draco paused as he heard a noise outside. Quickly convinced it was nothing he continued,

"Rejoice, for the day has arrived! The prophecy of the return of the Raven Queen is fulfilled and the three chosen are prepared for the ritual of summoning. It is time for your journey to the aerie where we will finally meet the mistress in person and bring forth the prophesied time of her ascendance. Worry not, prophesied one. Nothing will be allowed to prevent you from your anointed pilgrimage. The Shadar-kai Unkindness will converge on your location and aid you in every way to ensure your prompt attendance. No enemies or bystanders will be allowed to interfere in your mission. The Unkindness will kill or die for you to secure your presence. Once you arrive at the aerie the Conspiracy of Elders will lead you through the ritual. Rest and do what is needed to conserve your strength. Allow the aid of your Unkindness to protect you on the journey. Refrain from using your abilities or your escorts will take measures to ensure that you do. We understand your desire to be of service as it is your ultimate destiny, but it is not your role in this season. Conserve and be ready for the ritual you were born to enact."

The signature changed slightly again saying, this time, "Yours in anxious confidence, Omen Caller Munin, Shadar-kai Unkindness."

Draco nearly vomited after reading the third scroll. The words 'prophecy', 'the Raven Queen', 'converging on your location' and scariest of all 'kill or die to secure your presence' repeated in his mind. A noise in the hallway snapped the rogue back to reality. He quickly rerolled the scrolls, tied them back together with the red strings and placed them back in Rake's backpack. He dove into his bed as Rake re-entered the room.

"Are you up for a journey to Ramah with me today?" Rake threw his pack over his shoulder. "Filipina and Sappy… Sapin…"

"She prefers Gadget," Draco corrected.

"Yes, thank you, they're both coming," Rake said.

"Yeah, I'll go. I'm not training with Jericho until this evening." Draco grabbed his own small backpack, dagger and crossbow.

"Excellent," Rake nodded. "Let's go."

The halfling followed the elf out of their room. He couldn't take his eyes off his friend's backpack, nor could he stop thinking about the scrolls.

Chapter 4

Creature Comforts

The small caravan traveled through the night, though at a much slower pace than the family had kept on their own. Wren had scouted for a safe camp site and just after daybreak she found a secluded clearing well off any roads. They set up camp and ate. The elder couple and the kids were asleep almost instantly. Kalin and Lukas offered to take the final watch so their protectors could get more sleep.

Wren stepped away from the group to check in with Moonbow during Willa's watch. She updated him on their progress and the people they had taken on while heading back south. He offered her the good news, bad news choice. She chose bad news first thinking she knew what it was. He informed her that they had a false alarm on a suspected mole. One of the paladin's had their family kidnapped from a nearby town to get him to give information. His supervisors misconstrued his strange behavior as spying, when he was simply trying to find his family. Nakano followed him and called in a team including the centaur fighter, Filipina, the sea-elf paladin, Liathana, and the two eladrin, Azure and Elowen to affect a rescue. After an intense battle with some demons, they were victorious. Everyone survived, including the hostages, but they were very banged up for their efforts. On the good news side, he told her that many refugees had started to arrive in Gilgal claiming that Coram Deo had encouraged them to go there. The town's new leaders were handling it well. Wren was also ecstatic to hear that Galen, Ariadne and Joss had been a huge help in getting people settled there. She praised God for the work He had done in the hearts of the three former Bael worshippers and for protecting the paladin's family who had been kidnapped. The ranger wished the family a safe journey, telling Wren he had to get back to planning the necropolis mission with Xof's team. Today was the day of the raid.

From that comment she knew that it must be the twenty seventh day since her family had arrived on Aeramor.

She returned quietly to the camp and reached for the box Jonah had taken from the war camp. She realized at once that she had already picked the lock but forgot all about it when Netty and Oren tried to enter their hiding spot in Kedesh. She ran over to Willa to celebrate quietly. They opened the box with the anticipation of children on Christmas morning. The contents included a spyglass, four smooth white stones and an envelope holding a note. It was addressed to Commander Gargax, the commander of all forces in the war camp. They read the message intently,

> *"The adversary is heading your way. Be on the lookout for their interference. If you spot them, do not apprehend them. Instead follow them and alert my people. Do not be subtle, we want them to know they are being followed. Worried people make mistakes."*

It was signed, *"Cairncross."*

The handwriting and the seal were the same as they had seen before in Ai. So now they had a name for the mole, Cairncross, but it wasn't familiar to either of them. It seemed whoever the mole was they were well placed, clever and had an endgame for their family that was, yet, unclear. They presented their findings to Jonah who insisted on telling Moonbow first thing in the morning. He then took the next watch so Wren could try to get some rest.

℘

This time sleep took them easily. So many prayers had been answered and despite the many questions still nagging at them, they found peace in knowing God was at work in their lives and the lives of the people of this world. They drifted into the dream and saw a newborn, but not just any child. This was a child destined to do the work of the Lord. His parents were instructed not to let him drink spirits, eat unclean foods, or cut his hair as was the custom of the Nazirites. He was born in Zorah and would be called Samson. The dreamers watched as he was given all the teaching and support needed by one of his birthright. Still, he grew to be a stubborn and foolhardy man. He violated many rules of his sect, including taking a Philistine wife and eating honey from the skull of a lion he had slain.

He toyed with rivals and enemies alike, enraging all who knew him. He thought he was clever in creating a riddle to prove his superiority, but it was ruined by impatience with his manipulative wife. In his anger he went to Ashkelon and slew thirty men for their clothes to pay off the debt his folly had incurred. While gone his wife was given to another man. Again, Samson's heart burned with anger and as punishment for the slight he burned all their fields. The cycle of retribution continued as the Philistines killed Samson's wife. Samson refused to relent, claiming vengeance again by killing all involved before fleeing to the cleft of the rock at Etam in Judah. The

Philistines followed Samson into enemy territory and attacked the Judahites thinking they were harboring their foe. Judah's leaders, wanting no part in the feud, gave up Samson to stop the assault. Samson fought back against his Philistine captors, killing a thousand men with a jawbone from a donkey. The vision faded then returned as Samson could be seen dehydrated from the prolonged battle. For once Samson prayed instead of going his own way and God answered, quenching his thirst. Samson learned nothing from this encounter with God and gave in to his whims once again.

He married another Philistine woman. His enemies learned of this and used her to betray his weakness to them. Samson's impatience once again eclipsed his physical strength and though he resisted for a time, he eventually gave in to the nagging of his wife and revealed his weakness. She told his enemies who then captured, tortured and blinded him.

The vision faded once again as a jailed, bald and blinded Samson wallowed in a prison cell. When it returned, he was in an arena full of Philistines. They were mocking him and his God and using him to embolden their evil desires. In a rare act of vulnerability, Samson prayed once more to Adonai. He begged his Lord for the strength he had squandered to return for one last act of divinely inspired obedience. As always God answered his prayer, filling him with the spirit one last time. Samson didn't miss this opportunity as he broke the support columns with his bare hands, dropping the building on himself and the Philistines. The judge whose pride had brought him to ruin had died committing an act of ultimate faith. As the spirit of God left the body of the broken man, the dreamers awakened.

The next two days were relatively uneventful as the party moved slowly south. They avoided a few patrols and were pleased that they had seen no sign of pursuit since turning north after Jezreel. The small caravan had grown by seven people and three carts as other refugees in need were met along the way. Of the seven, Brace and Marilyn were best armed and seemed capable of defending themselves. The rest pitched in on the work happily and offered their personal rations to bolster the group's stores. They ate the food that would soon go bad first. Wren and Leo hunted to make up the difference in feeding everyone, sparing the non-perishables for an emergency. Jonah and Willa taught anyone willing to listen about Adonai each night before they slept and prayed with the group for guidance, providence and hearts open to the truth.

The next night around midnight, as they moved slowly and carefully through the moonlit wilderness, they came upon a town. Jonah referred to his maps and decided that it must be Ramilon. The northern outskirts of the town were dark. They watched for a while but saw no movement. Brace, Marilyn and Kalin joined the family in scouting the town while the others hunkered down in a stand of trees. Soon, several of them converged on a large building that was likely once a storehouse. There were even stables in the alley, though they decided that their animals should be brought inside the warehouse with them so they could remain hidden from passersby. The abandoned building was big enough to house everyone for the night. The carts were stowed in the stables and covered for security. Kalin, who had ventured deeper into the town, returned a short time later with word of an Inn in the center of town that was in full operation. The thought of sleeping in a bed was enticing for everyone but understandably too risky. Jonah did, however, think that a warm meal might improve morale and strength. He asked Brace and Kalin to join him while Willa, Wren and the others got everyone settled in for the evening.

The Blue Recluse Inn was bustling when they arrived. The music and voices could be heard from well down the street. Jonah decided to enter the place alone with the others watching from the door and window to see if he caught anyone's attention. Jonah went straight to the bar. He thought it was odd that almost all of the patrons were seated on the left side of the place and only a single table was occupied on his right. He glanced only briefly at the occupants of that table, as he passed, seeing four well-geared mercenary types. The gray-skinned dwarf seemed to be doing most of the talking, while the others, two blue-skinned tieflings and a woman with green skin, ate quietly with their hoods up.

"Good day." Jonah greeted the barkeep cordially. "Our group is passing through and in need of a hot meal, there are twenty of us."

"We can certainly accommodate you," the man seemed preoccupied by the tree symbol of Adonai etched on his shoulder guard. "Be careful flashing that around here." His eyes flicked to Jonah's chest then to the table occupied by the mercenaries behind Jonah and to his right.

Jonah resisted the urge to look. He said in a low voice, "Is there a back door out?"

"Yes," the bartender answered.

"Fill these and give them to the two men who will be waiting out back." He handed the man two baskets for the food and ten gold pieces. "Enough?"

"Too much," he responded, eyes widening a bit.

"Keep it. Thanks for the warning." Jonah turned away from the table of mercenaries and moved toward the hallway with the back door. He made a circular motion with his head hoping Kalin and Brace understood to meet him out back. As he entered the hallway he could see the door at the end, but he also saw stairs to his left and another set back by the door. He decided to try to elude any pursuers and give himself a head start. Up the stairs he went at a normal pace. When he reached the top, he sprinted down the hallway quickly. He could hear footsteps on the stairs behind him. He made it to the second set before the other person got into the hallway. He knew it could be nothing, but he couldn't have anyone following him back to the warehouse. Out the back door he went running. He turned left and left again into the alley by the inn's stables.

He saw Kalin and Brace coming. He whispered, "Hide in the stables. If anyone is following me, I'll lose them and double back to the camp. You wait until any pursuers are gone and get the food. The innkeeper will take it to the back door. Make sure you aren't followed. Set double watches when you get back, but from the inside. I don't want anyone visible from outside the warehouse." Instructions given, Jonah took off down the alley turning south, away from their camp.

Kalin and Brace hid in the shadows of the stable. Moments later the dark-skinned dwarf from inside turned the corner. He quietly looked east down the alley, then north, west and south. Brace was a mere foot from the dwarf behind the stable gate. He could see a piece of loose parchment under the dwarf's belt at his hip. The dwarf tilted his head as if listening for noise in any direction. Then he turned to go back inside. As he did Brace reached out and snatched at the parchment it released from the dwarf's belt, but the movement also pulled it from Brace's hand. It floated gently to the damp ground. Kalin was shaking his head violently from the other side of the stable, but stopped when it was clear the dwarf hadn't noticed Brace's theft.

When they were sure the dwarf was gone, Brace grabbed the note. The two men remained quietly hidden until the food came. Once the food was retrieved, they carefully headed back to the warehouse camp, making certain that no one was following them. It was just after daybreak when Jonah returned to the warehouse. Everyone was so thankful for the sustenance that they didn't let Jonah, Brace or Kalin take a shift on watch that morning allowing the trio a well-earned sleep.

Jonah had a hard time sleeping after reading the note Brace had snatched. This one outlined all of Coram Deo's movements including some that hadn't happened yet. They weren't all in the right order, for example the note said the group might be heading to Jezreel now instead of days ago, before they headed north, when they actually went there. Still, whoever this mole was, they were well informed and too close for comfort.

As the day waned, bringing the comfort of darkness, the small caravan prepared to travel again. Jonah decided to send the caravan out a half-hour ahead of them. He and his family would watch their back for pursuit. They waited thirty minutes and saw no signs of anyone following, so they set out to catch up with their friends.

As they disappeared down the street out of town, a figure stepped out from an alley across the way. It was the dwarf again, his three hooded companions behind him. "Gotcha," he said quietly as he motioned the others to follow. "Stay back until they rejoin the caravan. After that we make our presence known as ordered."

Chapter 5
Natural Consequences

The road to Ramah was uneventful. The four companions kept a brisk pace and were fortunate that no trouble arose on the road. Filipina the centaur, as she often pointed out despite its obviousness, took point. Sapientia, the forest gnome artificer, rode on Filipina's back fidgeting with the various half-finished gadgets that had prompted her nickname. Rake walked behind them pensive as always. Draco was unusually quiet, bringing up the rear. His focus was on Rake, his backpack and the ominous scrolls within. He felt a little guilty, but it was easily overwhelmed by his curiosity about what the scrolls meant and why Rake had never opened them.

They arrived in the small town before anyone except the hyper-vigilant centaur realized it. Gadget went scavenging for doodads and thingamajigs to use in her inventions. Rake excused himself and headed to 'The Emporium'. The magic shop was run by an elderly elven woman. Rake preferred to go there for the components and materials even though there were plenty of places he could get such things, even in Haven. He might not admit it or even realize it, but he really went there for the company. Taniala, the proprietor, reminded him of his mother, and home. It was a lifetime ago, but the memories of his parents still lingered. Somehow today they were stronger than ever. He quickly found all the supplies he needed, and a couple impulse buys to aid in his research. Then he spent an hour just talking with the elderly shopkeeper. He helped her straighten and organize the shop while they discussed family and home. They came from very different parts of the world, but Elven culture was somehow always familiar and comfortable.

Draco quickly realized that he had no reason to be in Ramah and worse he was alone with Filipina. She was his opposite in almost every way. He kept to the shadows, trying to remain invisible. She was boisterous and always front-and-center. It wasn't lost to him that her personality allowed him to thrive in his ways. That said, he never had any idea what to say to her. Today was different. He knew something no one else in the group knew and he was freaking out about it. The words 'Prophecy', 'Raven Queen', 'converging on your location' and 'kill or die to secure your presence' echoed in his mind again. He couldn't bear the weight of it alone any longer.

"Fili," he rasped, his voice raw from hours of silent thought. "I did something I shouldn't have, and now I know something I have to share."

"Well out with it," the former gladiator was never one to mince words.

"I looked at something belonging to Rake that I shouldn't have…" He began hesitantly.

"Okay, before we get into this, we need to have an understanding," Filipina interrupted.

"Uhhh," was all Draco could manage before she continued.

"Speak plainly and don't lie to me," she continued. "If you're going to tell me half the story, why tell me at all?"

Draco breathed deeply a couple times before speaking again, "I looked at the three scrolls in Rake's backpack. I think he's in big trouble and we may be too."

"There, was that so hard?" Filipina seemed unfazed by the information. "One person I know is in trouble is you. You are going to tell him what you did, and we will work it out together as always."

"Yeah, yeah," Draco reluctantly agreed as Gadget returned carrying what appeared to be junk, scrap metal and spare parts. Filipina and Draco fell silent on her approach.

"Awkward much?" The gnomish woman announced, still focused on her find. "You two up to something?"

"Well, one of us is," Filipina quipped.

Draco sighed audibly but said nothing.

"Alright then," Gadget changed the subject. "Rake's not back yet?"

"No not yet," Filipina answered, "You know how he likes to dawdle at The Emporium. We can meet him there. Hop on, Gadget."

The trio walked up the busy market street toward the magic shop. About halfway there Filipina, a head taller than most people, saw Rake coming. They made eye contact and he nodded at her. As she nodded back, she saw two black cloaked figures bump into her friend pushing him into an alley and out of her sight.

"What the..." she managed. "Gadget, hold on tight, something's wrong. Draco, head east, cut them off," she looked over as she spoke and the halfling was already running full-speed east down the alley. Somehow at just over three feet tall the halfling had seen the whole thing.

Fili galloped forward and turned right down the alley where the two assailants had pushed Rake. At the other end she could see two people completely clothed in black carrying the limp body of their friend. She caught movement to her right just as a crossbow bolt whizzed by glancing off her shoulder guard. She continued at full gallop as she re-focused to find her attacker. "On the right, low," she yelled back to Gadget.

The halfling had already packed away her finds for the day and retrieved her own crossbow. It was an odd-looking weapon that seemed cobbled together in a mechanical fashion. She called it the clockwork repeater because it could hold six bolts at a time and would occasionally fire two in succession on one trigger pull. She aimed and fired with practiced precision despite the movement of the centaur beneath her. The first bolt caught the attacker square in the chest. As her first bolt caused the robed man to fall back, losing the cover of the crates he was hiding behind, her second shot hit him square in the forehead just above the creepy looking beaked mask he was wearing.

Filipina rode past the man as he slumped to the ground, slowing only slightly to make the next tight right turn. As she came out of the turn, she saw two more black-robed assailants trying to pin Draco to the ground. One of the two was bleeding badly. The halfling was deftly avoiding their blows, but she knew that couldn't last much longer. The centaur charged, hitting the two assailants hard. The bleeding one flew ten feet into a stone wall with a loud crack and stopped moving. The other one rolled to a stop a few feet away.

Draco was on him instantly slashing feverishly with the dagger he had found so long ago in his father's belongings after he disappeared. "I got this! Go!" He yelled to Filipina who had broken stride after the collision.

She nodded in acknowledgement and was back to full speed in seconds. She took the next left which was the only choice. As she took that turn, she saw nothing. The two men and Rake were gone. There were no other assailants, just a few startled residents. "Black robes and beaks, where?" She looked down on an older dwarven woman sitting on a stoop mending some clothing.

She pointed north.

Filipina took off again, yelling to her rider over her shoulder, "Watch the side alleys on the right, I've got the left." She went a hundred feet until the alley ended and saw no sign of their friend or his abductors. She doubled back to check again. About halfway back she spotted Draco looking down a side alley heading west.

"He's gone," she said, breathing heavily.

"I found his backpack here but no sign of him." Draco had blood spatter all over his clothes.

"Any of that blood yours?" Gadget asked, concerned.

"Some, I'm fine," he responded, then started backtracking. "Let's check the bodies for clues."

When they got back to where their assailants had fallen there was no sign of the bodies or even blood in either alley.

"Does this have anything to do with those scrolls you mentioned?" Filipina asked Draco.

Draco removed them from Rake's backpack and held them for his companions to see, "Yeah, probably."

"What scrolls?" Gadget asked.

Filipina, "Both of you mount up and hold on, we need to get back to Haven."

Chapter 6
Mayhem in Magdala

Jonah led the small caravan southwest. They needed to get to Aijalon and felt it was safer for the civilians they were protecting if they remained together for now. They stayed off the roads as much as possible but couldn't get very deep into the trees with the carts in tow. This slowed them considerably but with so many to protect they felt it a necessary precaution. About halfway through the night, judging by the position of Lunastré, the larger of the two moons, they began to hear raised voices. There was a strange orange glow to the southwest and the air began to smell of burning wood. As they continued south, ash floated to the ground around them, like at a campfire, but significantly denser.

"Something bad is happening ahead," Jonah said. "Let's get everyone out of sight and go check it out."

Willa and Wren agreed. They escorted the caravan to just within sight of the north-south road, instructing them to stay hidden. Just as they were about to head southwest toward the commotion a family of three ran right into their hiding spot. They were terrified of something behind them and out of breath from running.

"P-please don't hurt us," the man said, putting his body between his family and these strangers.

"You're safe here," Willa assured them. "What happened?"

"Creatures attacked in the night," the man was nearly hyper-ventilating.

Willa tried to get the man to calm down, "Take it slow, breathe." She didn't know it yet, but her Boots of the Gospel had a calming effect on the family. Another of their abilities meant to help with the spread of God's word.

"They were orcs and goblins and some larger creatures we had never seen before. I don't think they were alive. They had open wounds, exposed bones, but only dried blood. It was a nightmare."

"Did any of them follow you?" Jonah interjected while never taking his eyes off the southwestern direction.

"I don't think so," the man was calming a bit but still clearly agitated, "and I don't want to find out."

"Alright, plan B then," Jonah's mind was already adjusting. "You all take the road back north to the last crossroad we passed that went east. Stay on that road until you reach the Jordan, then head south all the way to Gilgal. You'll be safe there for as long as you'd like. We will see if we can get an escort to meet you along the way. Stay together."

Willa looked at the man and his family, "You are welcome to go with them at least to Gilgal for safety. Someone will send word there if we can stop whatever is causing this attack."

Jonah gave the maps and the note they found in the war camp to Kalin with instructions to pass it to Luc, the temple cleric in Gilgal. After brief goodbyes to their newfound friends the small caravan was back on the move. Jonah waited until they were out of sight then turned to his family, "Are you ready for this?" They nodded. "Lord God be with us as we try to do your will and protect your people from whatever the enemy has used against them this time. We know you and trust you with our lives. Guide us tonight as you have every other night. In your name we pray. Amen."

Their movements had become precise and practiced. They zig zagged through the trees, staying quiet and out of sight until they could see the threat. They quickly guided anyone fleeing the melee north and east toward their friends and kept moving south toward town. As they reached the first buildings two large ones on their right were fully engulfed in flames, the two on their left were not. They looked a little like a S.W.A.T. team as they moved from cover to cover along the alleys. They hugged the buildings on the left, which opened into an alley. As they entered the area, they were met with swords and spears.

"Whoa, we're friendly," Jonah exclaimed, stepping in front of Willa and Wren.

The men holding the weapons relaxed a bit but kept weapons at the ready. There were six men here, four in uniform. Jonah noted that this small convergence of alleys had narrow exits to the north, where they had entered, south and southeast. There were two men at each of the openings. The men to the southeast were actively fighting something they couldn't see from their vantage point. A large building was on fire further south behind the attackers, the light from it making it hard to see anything in that direction.

One of the two men stabbed forward with his spear, then yelled, "There are more circling west, coming your way."

The two men in the south opening instantly sprang into action. One took a claw to the shoulder opening a wide gash.

Jonah stepped forward unsheathing his sword, "We can help. Willa, Wren support positions. Send Leo to any breaches but keep him in this alley."

The men were surprised by the forceful move but made no attempt to stand in the paladin's way.

Jonah put his shield hand on the shoulder of the injured man, uttering a quick prayer of healing. The bleeding stopped and the wound all but closed. The man nodded in acknowledgement but still had his hands full with his attacker.

Jonah, steadied by having his left hand on the man's shoulder, came across right to left with his sword, driving it through the attacker's temple. It fell to the ground, but not before Jonah got a good look. The creature had green skin, though much of it was missing. It had two tusks on its bottom jaw and sharp teeth between them. It had a wide flat nose and a large square jaw line. Its body was clearly once heavily muscled judging from the sag of the remaining skin. He could only guess this was an undead orc. The man in uniform to his right finished off another attacker as did the southeast group with aid from the ladies and Leo.

The respite in fighting allowed for conversation, "I'm Jonah, this is my wife Willa and daughter, Wren. What is this town and what in the world is going on here?"

The first soldier, a human of about thirty-five years, answered, "I'm Remme, the guard captain. This is…was… Magdala. We're not sure what happened. A patrol sounded the alarm, but the creatures seemed to be everywhere by the time they were noticed. Most seem to be undead orcs and goblins, but a few bigger ones have been spotted."

Two more guards and an injured civilian woman arrived with creatures chasing them. One of the approaching guards ran directly to Remme while the other teamed with the alley defenders to make quick work of the pursuers. Willa and Wren tended to the woman's injuries.

"Sir," the young Half-Elven soldier reported, "The market is overrun. We got off the road and into Tenement Alley behind the Merchant's Court. We ran north just as something hit the buildings from behind us, exploding them into flames. Those undead found us just as we heard your fight, so we diverted here."

"Good work," the captain was looking frantically in every direction trying to decide what to do next.

"Is there a more defensible position nearby?" Jonah grabbed the captain by his shoulders to get him to focus.

"Uhhh, yes, yes," Remme shook his head and made eye contact with the taller paladin. "The Tenement Alley Jalen just mentioned. There are only two ways in or out, but one is connected to the market, which he says is overrun."

"Which way?" Jonah was ready to move.

Remme pointed at an alley heading southwest.

"Ok everyone," Jonah commanded, "we're moving southwest. Circle around the healers and civilians. When we get in there, we find a defensible corner. Civilian fighters form a protective line around the non-fighters. Soldiers clear the alley and push toward the two entrances until we clear any undead. Once it's clear, we fortify and defend."

The civilians nodded, getting to their feet. The guards looked at Captain Remme unsure of whether to listen to this stranger.

Remme didn't hesitate, moving to the front line beside Jonah, "You heard the man. Let's move!"

The Tenement Alley was larger than Jonah imagined. The businesses had entrances facing into the alley allowing shoppers access from both sides of their shops. There were several abandoned carts and kiosks around the perimeter, likely used by mobile or temporary vendors. The noise of the group moving into the area must have attracted a couple of undead, as a shambling orc and a goblin appeared from the market side alley. Jonah, Remme, Leo and two guards made quick work of them, while the other guards fortified and guarded the northern access. The armed civilians and Willa set up a defense in the south corner away from both alleys. A half-dozen people from the surrounding buildings saw the group and joined them in setting up a defense.

Jonah and Remme pushed carts into the market alley as a few more zombies headed their way. "Wren, can you close this down like you did in those caves?"

"Yes," she responded confidently, "I definitely can, but I need a minute." The two men nodded understanding her need for cover to make it happen. She began to pray to God for strength and guidance. The earth began to rise from the ground leaving no space to crawl under the bottoms of the carts. Wren took a few deep breaths and repeated the prayer. This time the earth formed in and on top of the carts to a height of about six feet. She caught her breath, hands on knees while the people of Magdala looked on in wonder.

"Are you ok?" Jonah asked, concerned.

"Yeah," she replied between deep breaths. "I just need a second to finish up." She took a few more deep breaths, steadying herself, then began to pray again. Roots, vines and plants began to sprout throughout the mass of earth she had created. Normally meant for a flat 100' radius these plants grew on the sides of the buildings and around the barrier they had created. The carts creaked in protest as vines constricted around the wood. The mass of vines twisted together at the top making the structure almost as tall as the adjacent single-story buildings. "There, that should keep them out."

The guards at the north alley fended off a few more undead. One of the men took a vicious claw strike, but Willa was quick to heal him.

As Jonah, Wren and Remme surveyed her handiwork on the barricade they saw a fireball fly high above the market. It flew from south to north at a high enough arc for them to see it briefly as it passed over the alley. From the sound, it had hit a target somewhere on the north side of the market breaking glass and splintering wood.

"That came from due south," Wren's sense of direction was impeccable in her cat-like form.

"Remme, protect this area," Jonah was speaking quickly but confidently. "We're going to try to stop this. We will send survivors here to aid in the defense."

"Do you want a few men?" Remme offered though he hoped it would be refused.

"No, we're going to try to stay quiet for as long as possible," Jonah explained. "Thank you though."

Within seconds the trio and the wolf were outside the north barricade and heading south down the adjacent alley. They hugged the western buildings as two of the structures on the east side were ablaze. The bright light of the fire eradicated any shadows that they could use to hide.

Suddenly a voice rang out above them and to the southwest. It was a familiar voice, "There you are breathers. Go, my children, stop them." Then she started speaking in words of magic. When she finished, another fireball soared over their heads hitting the building at the end of the alley.

Jonah knew instantly this was the voice of Zelitra, the woman who had escaped them in Gilgal. He couldn't help but think that this attack and any deaths were their fault for letting her get away the first time. He put those feelings aside for now as they came to an asymmetrical four-way intersection. He could see zombies shambling toward them from each of the other three directions. "Stay close," he instructed before running across the intersection and into the west alley. He stopped halfway down and checked the doorknob of the building that the voice had come from. It was locked so he kicked it open, splintering the door jam, "Get inside!"

The paladin guarded his family's movement, spearing an undead orc through the head with his sword. It slumped to the ground as he followed them inside.

Willa ordered, "Get large furniture to reinforce the broken door." She and Wren began pushing a cabinet, then a sofa and chairs into the entryway.

For a moment everything went silent except for the scratching and pounding at the door. Their pursuers wouldn't be held off for long.

"Was that Zelitra's voice out there or am I hearing things?" asked Wren, though she was sure she was right.

"That was her," Willa agreed. "Is all of this our fault?"

Jonah didn't hesitate, "Not now, no distractions." Just as the words left his mouth, they heard a creak above them. Someone was moving upstairs.

Wren reacted first, hitting the third step before anyone else, except Leo, had even moved. She never saw the rune, carved into the wall about waist high, as it lit up. The stairway exploded with magical force slamming her into the other wall and sending her tumbling back down the stairs into Leo. They were both dazed but still moving.

Jonah lost control at this show of gross recklessness. He grabbed his daughter by the shoulders, "Don't ever do that again! You could have been killed." Seeing her beautiful face frightened, his own softened as he pulled her into a hug.

The tabaxi girl nodded at her father, "Focus, I know," and shifted forms. A large, densely muscled wolverine stood where the girl had been. She growled loudly then scrambled back up the broken stairs, Leo in close pursuit.

Willa put a hand on Jonah's shoulder knowing he was feeling guilty for snapping at his daughter. "It had to be said," his wife encouraged him, knowing the heart behind the outburst. "Let's stay with her."

The animals were out of sight by the time Jonah and Willa hit the stairs. Wolver-Wren got to the top first, slamming into the wall, unable to negotiate the sharp corner. In her rage she barely saw the two ghostly creatures melding into the walls on either side, but she did catch a glimpse of someone running around the next corner ahead. She gave chase, her wolf companion pacing with her. As she turned the next corner she saw a doorway. She heard a voice yelling inside. The door exploded into the room as the wolverine and the wolf scrambled to slow their charge on the wooden floor. They arrived just in time to see the elder woman turn into a gas and rise upward. Wren lunged for her, getting only a piece of cloth from her blue dress before she disappeared into the ceiling.

Unable to keep pace with the animals Jonah and Willa reached the top of the stairs. Seeing no one there they cautiously moved down the hallway. Suddenly they heard screaming. Zelitra was ordering her 'children' to regroup here and kill the intruders. A loud crash rang out from downstairs stopping them in their tracks. The timing was fortuitous as the two wraiths reached out from the walls on either side to touch them.

Jonah had looked back toward the noise downstairs, but Willa saw this new threat, "Jonah, we have company."

Seeing the frightening creatures, he grabbed his wife's upper arm and nudged her back toward the stairs. Just then the wolverine and the wolf rounded the corner ahead and leapt toward the attackers. Before Jonah could warn them, they passed through the wraiths, both animals yelping in pain before landing awkwardly. They both rolled back to their feet but were clearly hurt deeply just by the touch of these ghostly things.

Willa grabbed her holy symbol holding it forward, "Should I…"

Jonah put his hand on her forearm, "Not yet." He kept moving them back until they were on the middle landing of the stairs looking left, he could see at least a dozen zombies coming.

Willa prayed, eyes closed, desperately asking for deliverance from this situation.

Jonah watched both the zombies and the wraiths advancing. As both groups of enemies reached the stairs, he said, "NOW!"

Willa released the brightly glowing radiant energy from her Holy Symbol. To Jonah, Wren, and Leo it felt like little more than a warm breeze, but to the undead the wave was devastating.

The front four zombies instantly disintegrated. It reminded Jonah of the old movies depicting nuclear blasts. At least six more of the creatures shambled away and out the broken front door. One of the wraiths took off down the hallway and right through the closed door at the end. The other receded into the wall.

Seeing an opening, Wolver-Wren dove down the stairs tearing into the few zombies still heading toward the stairs. Leo followed suit.

Jonah saw guards appear at the door led by Remme. They quickly surveyed the chaos then jumped into the fray. Jonah yelled, "The animals are with us," prompting nods from a couple of the nearby soldiers.

Seeing things were in hand downstairs, Willa said, "Should we go after Zelitra?"

Jonah was already in motion, "We must stop this. It can't happen again."

Willa followed but stopped abruptly halfway down the hall when one of the wraiths appeared, reaching for Jonah. "Look out," she warned, but too late as the incorporeal hand brushed her husband's shoulder.

The pain Jonah felt was like nothing he had ever experienced before. It felt as if his life force itself was being pulled from him. His left arm went numb, but his sword arm was unaffected. He thrust the sword upward into the ghostlike creature. The screech it emitted hurt their ears. It seemed unable to free itself from the sword.

Willa used its immobility to fire a guiding bolt into it at point blank range. The radiant energy caused the creature to recoil. As it pulled away from the pain it ripped itself nearly in half on Jonah's still embedded sword. It screeched once more in protest and then dispersed into the air.

"You ok up there?" Remme's voice rang out from below.

"We're good," Jonah replied. "We're going to the attic."

There was a door around the corner concealing the stairs to the attic. They took the stairs two at a time, arriving in the storage room to the sight of Zelitra standing in a dormer window as if she was about to jump.

"Zelitra, please stop this." Willa's tone was kind but forceful. "We know you were wronged but this isn't the way to fix it."

"You know nothing," she rasped. Her voice sounded as if she spoke while inhaling.

"Not true," Willa explained. "We found the evidence you gathered. We proved your case to the townspeople. Justice was done."

Jonah tried to move slyly into a flanking position, but there was little room in the space to do it without notice.

"Stay where you are breather," the elder human warned Jonah. Looking back at Willa, "Justice for all but me and my children."

"Is it justice to kill innocent people and destroy their homes?" Willa hoped to keep the woman engaged until an opportunity presented itself to subdue her.

"My children killed no one who didn't try to hurt them," her voice was forceful now. "All they had to do was leave."

Willa paused for a moment, "Don't you see? You have become like the people who wronged you."

The woman seemed struck by this statement. Her features softened a bit as if finally understanding her mistake.

The sounds of footsteps and voices nearing the attic brought Zelitra back to focus. "I didn't make the rules," she claimed defiantly. "You tried to help me so I will repay you with your lives. Get in my way again and I make no such promises." With that she fell backward out the window.

Jonah ran to look out, but she was gone as if she had never been there. Willa spotted a satchel near the window that wasn't as dusty as everything else in the room. She examined the contents just as Wren, back in her normal form, and Remme entered the attic. "She's gone…again."

Willa looked to the captain, "Is anyone hurt?"

"Yes, several downstairs." Remme answered. "We left a few behind to protect the civilians in the alley and followed when all the dead turned tail and headed here."

Jonah shook the man's hand, "Thank you. Your arrival made all the difference."

"Can you get your men and rally back at Tenement Alley?" Jonah asked, clearly still struggling with this less than adequate resolution. "We will care for the injured and follow after making sure she's not still nearby."

Remme turned to leave then hesitated, "Don't be too hard on yourself, your incredible family saved this entire town."

Jonah shook his head, "She eluded us once before in Gilgal. If we had done better, she'd have never gotten here. Now we have to live with this and whatever she does next."

"I get the feeling of responsibility Jonah," Remme offered. "Her actions are not your fault. Somehow you were here to stop her again. I can't even imagine the set of circumstances that made that possible."

Willa answered, "God sent us."

Remme's brow furrowed in skepticism.

"She's right," Jonah explained. "We were up north on a mission from Adonai. We completed that part of his plan and were on the way south to the next. He put us right here exactly when we were needed."

Remme's face blanched, losing all color as he stammered wordlessly.

Wren slapped him on the back, "Yeah that's the same reaction we all had when the evidence started to outweigh our doubt. Welcome to the path less traveled."

Remme couldn't get out of that room fast enough, "I'll meet you at the alley." His footsteps on the stairs were hurried.

The pack Willa had found was clearly Zelitra's, forgotten in the chaos of her escape. Inside were spell scrolls of animate dead, fireball, explosive runes, gaseous form, some blank parchment, a quill, a container of spell ink and a stack of papers that upon cursory glance may have been a diary. She stuffed them all back in the satchel and followed Jonah and Wren downstairs. They tended to the wounded in the main room, some with basic first aid and a couple with healing prayers. When everyone could move, they headed back to the rally point. The guards and able civilians there were taking care of the few remaining undead. Others were putting out fires and assessing the damage to their homes and businesses. The wounded guards were welcomed back by their friends and families. All conversations stopped as Willa led her family into the now packed merchant's court. Every eye was on them, some filled with tears. The awkward silence lasted for what seemed like minutes before Remme began clapping. His mishtala guardsmen joined him, then the others they had helped did as well. Soon everyone was clapping and cheering for the people who had run into danger when their own friends and neighbors were running away. These three helped them despite having nothing to gain.

An elven man stepped forward, "I am Shandraél, the mayor of Magdala. I am told you credit your God, Adonai, with sending you here to help us."

Willa didn't hesitate, "Yes, that is true. We were here following his will for us, and we ended up right here tonight."

Shandraél nodded, "I don't know much about your God. Perhaps you will share a meal with us and tell us more about Adonai.

They agreed, spending the rest of the night helping put out fires and clear bodies. They found it curious that only a single civilian and two mishtala guards died in the assault. The trio were killed on the south side of town trying to retake the market area. Zelitra's actions were indefensible, but she was truthful when she said that killing these people was not her goal. As morning came in the town the family was given rooms in the inn to rest. When they awoke, they were invited to lunch in the market. Jonah led in prayer for the meal and all God had provided to protect them, especially last night. They took turns explaining the basics of who God was and why Adonai was the only true God. Though many seeds were planted that day in Magdala, Jonah, Willa and Wren knew that it was up to the Holy Spirit to bring the harvest.

The duergar and the yuan-ti from the Blue Recluse Inn watched from the shadows of a nearby alley. They had mistakenly followed the caravan for half the night before realizing their error. The fight, cleanup and Jonah's desire to travel mainly at night allowed the pursuers time to backtrack. Their quarry back in sight, the mercenaries waited patiently for the family's next move.

Chapter 7

S.O.S.

When the frantic trio arrived in Haven, they sent messengers to retrieve the rest of their group from wherever they might be in the compound. Lia, the sea-elf paladin, was training with seneschal Saphic. Shay, the earth genasi warlock, and Elowen, the eladrin druid, were having a meal and serving in the tent city. The trio that saw the kidnapping went straight to Barnabas. Azure, the eladrin cleric, was with Barnabas and others studying in the library when her friend's arrived in a panic. Draco relayed the entire story of the scrolls even faster than he usually spoke. Filipina chimed in with the story of the kidnapping and chase through Ramah.

Barnabas was clearly concerned by this news and struggled to remain calm. Rake, though he continued to resist surrendering to Adonai, had become a close friend and confidant to the elder cleric. He had sworn to help his friend see the truth of Adonai one way or the other and was now concerned that he may not get the chance. Through his concern and fear he remembered something he had heard, "Did you say you found his backpack?"

Draco threw it up on the large table they had gathered around, "Right here."

Shay and Elowen burst into the room followed closely by Lia. "We're here," they exclaimed almost in unison.

Shay exclaimed, "They told us what happened. Where are we on a rescue mission?"

"I have an idea," Barnabas assured them as he examined the pack. "The scrolls you mentioned, are they in here?"

"Last I saw them," Draco tore into the pack, finding them quickly and handing them to Barnabas.

"I think our best option is to try to scry on Rake," Barnabas explained. "We will see things around him and may get a clue about his location from his surroundings."

Draco handed Barnabas the three scrolls. The human cleric began to pray, waving the objects over a small font of holy water. The water began to ripple then bubble, then suddenly it calmed.

In the calm liquid they could see Rake walking, surrounded by at least six of the black-garbed ravens. Beyond them was the open wilderness common to Israel and Judah. In the distance was a large mountain. To the right of the mountain was a lush forest.

Elowen gasped, prompting everyone to look in her direction. "That is Mt. Tabor!" Her voice held a mix of urgency and surprise. Her memory had been sketchy at best since her return to her home world from Earth mere weeks ago. Her dreams were haunted with disjointed memories of her life here giving her little clue about who she had been and where she had come from. Despite her struggles she was never more certain of anything. This was Mt. Tabor and the neighboring Ever Grove.

"Are you sure," Draco asked, feeling hope for the first time in a while.

"Yes, I've never been more certain of anything," she replied, unable to look away from the scene. "The wood beside the mountains is the Ever Grove, my home."

Azure touched her friend's arm, "Does this mean your memory has returned?"

"Just flashes, faces, sounds, locations, nothing deeper yet," she sighed, a tear in her eye. She pushed away the emotion. "From the look of it they are less than a day away, we need to move."

Azure and Gadget comforted her while they all continued to watch hoping to hear something helpful. The only words spoken were by one of the raven men, but they were in a language none of them completely understood.

Azure stepped forward and translated from elvish, "I think he thanked Rake for not continuing to fight them."

Rake responded, in common, "What will happen when we get to Mount Tabor?"

"Your destiny, of course," a beak faced woman responded this time, matter-of-factly.

Barnabus looked back to Elowen, "any other details jump out at you?"

Elowen studied the pool, "They are taking a southern approach from the placement of the Ever Grove. There appears to be a path there," she pointed far ahead of Rake. "I see movement up there. I'd say that is their destination."

"Ok. It seems we have a location then," Barnabas noted. "Go gear up for travel. I may be able to provide you with some support, but I need to find Moonbow first. Meet back in the war room in thirty minutes."

Chapter 8
Showdown in Aijalon

The family's pace was even quicker than usual. The towns between Magdala and Aijalon were deserted or destroyed so there was no one to speak to or help in any way. Judging by the path of destruction the Assyrians had marched southwest destroying only the towns in their direct path. Nearby towns in the area had either evacuated or the people were in hiding, though Jonah didn't dare take his family close enough to investigate. Memories of small villages in Kandahar rushed back to him, but he pushed the thoughts deep, refusing to be distracted. The brief flashbacks of his military days reassured him that avoiding these unknown, seemingly vacant towns was the best choice. By midday they had reached their destination. Aijalon was not abandoned or destroyed. There were many people out in the streets in this small town. It was the first place they had seen in the north that seemed unaffected by the chaos of war.

As the family entered the town, they garnered little more than mistrustful looks. Most of the people, more concerned with their daily routines, ignored them completely.

A small child approached, "Do you have any coin to spare? My family is so hungry." The girl was filthy and seemed to be suffering from malnutrition.

Willa dug through her pack, giving the girl all the food the people of Magdala had sent with them when they left.

The girl was about to scamper off toward the town center when a shrill voice rang out, jarring amid the dull murmur of the other voices in the area. "Who are you and what do you think you are doing?"

Jonah stepped in front of Willa to stop the middle-aged human woman's advance. "I think the words you are searching for are 'thank' and 'you'."

"Thank you?" the shrieking woman asked. "For what? Assuming we can't take care of our own?"

"The girl asked for our help, and we provided it," Willa insisted, stepping up next to her husband.

"Typical believers," she spit out the word as if it was poison in her mouth as she eyed the insignias on their clothes. "No one else can possibly take care of their own. What is your business here?"

"We come seeking a tomb or memorial to Elon, one of the judges of Adonai," Willa's voice remained calm despite the crowd starting to encircle them, preventing any further movement toward the center of town.

"There is certainly nothing of that sort here," the woman huffed indignantly. "You should keep moving south, back to the safety of your God.

Willa could see that this woman was lying in the faces of a few of the people gathering. The rest had twisted anger masks like their spokesperson. "We apologize for any inconvenience or slight. We will be on our way."

Jonah and Wren were surprised by the move but trusted Willa implicitly. They walked briskly back to the edge of town, followed closely by about twenty residents led by the shrill woman. As they exited the town limits the townspeople disengaged, watching them for a short time before returning to their day.

A short way out of town, Willa stopped.

Wren was first to speak, "You know she was lying, right?"

"Of course, sweetheart," Willa responded, pulling her daughter close. "I noticed a good number of her followers knew too. If I'm right, someone may follow us."

They ate a leisurely picnic lunch in a clearing just off the road, discussing what to do next if an opportunity didn't come. Wren and Leo scavenged nearby for edible berries and mushrooms, another benefit of her newfound abilities. As she was crouching down inspecting some roots Leo alerted. There were three women walking toward their clearing. Wren held Leo back as the trio didn't seem to notice them. After the women passed by, the druid and her wolf fell in behind them. Soon they all walked into the clearing near the family's picnic spot. Jonah saw them coming but didn't react, waiting to see what they would do.

They continued to move toward Jonah and Willa cautiously, "Hello?" they called out when they were within twenty feet, showing their hands. "We mean you no harm."

"Good to know," Wren replied, startling them from behind.

The three women circled up back-to-back, showing genuine fear at being surrounded. "We only came to talk, we swear."

Willa was on her feet now, she and Jonah approached the strangers, "We're listening."

"Luella, the woman who yelled at you in town, wasn't completely honest with you," the shorter woman, probably half-elven, admitted. "We found a box in a nearby temple that we cleared out to use as a shelter. It had strange markings on it. No one knew what it said until Brinn moved here," she replied.

"The people speak Hebrew where I am from," the stout woman explained. "The word on the box is 'Elon', the name of the judge you mentioned."

"Are you from Mt. Nebo?" Willa was genuinely curious.

"Yes, how did you know?" Brinn replied, unable to withhold her surprise at the question.

"We have met a few of your people and call them friends," Willa responded. "How does a woman from a clan that knows Adonai, come to be here following Ashtoreth?" The three women reacted visibly at this statement. Willa noticed their discomfort, "The Asherah poles were in plain sight."

"That is a long story that I didn't come here to tell," the dwarf replied, effectively ending this line of questioning. "We think you should have the box, but we aren't sure how to make that happen."

Jonah finally spoke up, "Can you get us back into town and in front of the leadership?"

"Yes, take our cloaks," the first woman was speaking again. "Wait here until dusk. Go to the center of town, everyone will be there for our evening ritual. Be prepared though, I don't know how they will react when you reveal yourselves. We are not the only ones skeptical of Luella, but the majority are loyal to her."

"Thank you for coming here," Willa said with all sincerity. "We know you took a great risk. We won't mention your involvement."

The three women seemed pleased by the assurance. "We appreciate that." They turned and walked back into the forest along the same path they had come.

When the family arrived at the town center the ritual was already in progress. Luella was leading it with help from some young members who were dancing in circles around a fountain. The statue that was once there had been removed and replaced with an Asherah pole. The elder woman chanted about all that Ashtoreth had provided for her faithful followers. Willa could see dissent, among some of the gathered townspeople, at that statement. Many of the townspeople looked malnourished and dirty, while those involved in the ritual itself were clean, well fed, and dressed finely.

At one point Luella, as a routine of the ritual, asked, "If any have reason to challenge the chosen priestesses of the queen-mother, speak now."

Willa, still hooded, stepped forward, "I do." There was an audible gasp among the gathered people.

The crowd parted allowing Willa to approach Luella. She lowered her hood as she moved forward. "The one true God challenges your pretender," Willa had never sounded more forceful. "You are done misleading these people."

Some of the assembled were incensed by this statement, drawing weapons and encircling the fountain. Jonah, Wren and Leo had followed Willa but were now cut off from her.

Jonah spoke out, "Your god is so weak that she needs her adversaries to be outnumbered to win?"

Luella's face reddened as she waved off her allies. The disgruntled crowd allowed Willa's family through, then pushed forward to see this play out.

"Show us what Ashtoreth can do," Willa encouraged with a wave of her hand.

Luella began to chant then tapped her staff on the ground. It softened and changed to a greenish color, wrapping around her shoulders as it became a serpent, its head inches from Willa's face hissing and flicking its tongue.

Willa didn't flinch, "The magicians of the pharaoh could do such parlor tricks centuries ago." She began to pray, "Lord God rid us of this serpent as you promised in the garden, vowing that one day you would send a Messiah to crush its head once and for all." The serpent stiffened and fell from her shoulders, the staff dancing to a rest on the ground beside her.

Luella called for her dancers to gather the food all the followers had brought as tribute. She chanted over it, and it began to ripen, then over-ripen, then rot. She stared daggers into Willa, who just smiled.

"Interesting choice," she said calmly. "I wonder where all this food would have gone had we not come here today. Would it have gone to them?" She said pointing toward the gathered people. "Or would it have all gone to you?" She again prayed, "Father God, you are our provider, and you are generous. Your adversaries, these false gods, feed their chosen few, but you provide for all who seek you." As Willa prayed this prayer the food recovered and multiplied falling out of the baskets onto the ground around Luella's feet.

The priestess was livid. She began chanting in a screeching voice, lowering her hands to the ground and then high in the air. The ground began to crack and crumble at her touch. Suddenly a hand appeared from the dirt, then a second as an undead creature rose from below. It stood there as if waiting for orders. The crowd gasped. Jonah and Wren readied themselves. "This is what your Adonai has in store for all of us, death."

"You understand nothing Luella. Death is real, but it only exists because of the rebellion of man, not the design of God." Willa turned to the crowd, "Death in this world is inevitable for us all, but those who choose Adonai will live with him eternally in Heaven."

"Liar!" Luella snapped both in voice and mind. "Kill her, my pet."

The undead humanoid lurched forward but Willa was ready. She spun to her right causing the clumsy creature to lumber past into the now terrified crowd. It stopped directly in front of a young dark-haired girl. It shrieked in her face as she was immobilized with fear.

Suddenly a thorny whip appeared wrapping itself around the creature pinning its arms to its sides. Wren pulled hard on her conjured weapon, yanking the emaciated zombie to within five feet of Jonah.

Jonah swung his shield in a wide arc, bashing the creature to the ground next to Luella.

The elder witch shrieked in anger.

Willa was already praying. A sphere of radiant light formed around the creature just as it turned back toward Willa. It lashed out at her with a claw, but it was harmlessly deflected by the sphere. "This is what your god is capable of? This creature that would have killed even your own innocent?" The elven cleric walked to the fountain where the ritual pole had been placed. "Your god is nothing more than a story created to sow chaos and excuse disobedience. Your leaders are wolves taking from you to give to themselves."

Willa fell to her knees prompting Jonah, Wren and Leo to take up places at her back. She began to call out to Adonai while the gathered Ashtoreth followers stood transfixed. Jonah wondered if the people gathered were hoping for her failure or somewhere down deep yearning for her success. Either way Jonah knew that God was about to do something big, he could feel His spirit moving. As her prayer continued a calm settled over the cleric despite the tenuousness of the situation.

Suddenly, her body stiffened as if no longer in her control. She rose to her feet then, off the ground entirely, her arms reaching toward Heaven. Suddenly, though the sky was cloudless, a few drops of rain hit Willa's face. It quickly became a deluge. The warm caress of the water washed all the blood, dirt and sweat from her equipment and clothing. The pouring rain then moved toward the Asherah pole. The gathered people gasped, and Luella finally fell silent, unsure what was going to happen next. The downpour doused the torches near the pole, drenching everything. Within seconds even the fountain was overflowing with fresh, warm water.

Luella regained her composure and began to yell again, "Anyone can cause rain. I will…"

"SILENCE!" The voice came from Willa as she floated before the gathering, but it was not hers. Willa looked down at the witch, her eyes now fully ablaze. The voice came from her mouth again, **"The Lord of Lords is not done yet."**

Willa's entire body, still hovering, turned to face the waterlogged Asherah pole and fountain. The flames in her eyes flared so brightly that the gathered people had to shield their own eyes. The flames leapt from her glowing eyes hitting the water, instantly causing a thick cloud of steam. The heat from it caused everyone to step back but Willa and her protectors, who didn't seem to feel it. When the steam cleared everything was gone. The wet wood of the Asherah pole, the torches, and even the stone fountain were incinerated, leaving only a charred crater in the ground where they once were. Willa floated softly to the ground completely dry, her eyes back to their normal green. A murmur began among the gathering. As Jonah and Wren looked around more than half of the remaining townspeople were on their knees or faces worshiping Adonai.

Willa never took her eyes off Luella, who was still livid but could see this was not the time to act rashly. She and her assistants were surrounded by angry men and women demanding answers and threatening action.

The three women who had come to them in the clearing approached. Brinn, the dwarf, was carrying a box. She handed it to Willa, "This is what you came for, please take it with our gratitude."

"What will you do now?" Willa was genuinely concerned.

"I have been such a fool. I hope they will try to rebuild the town in a different way, with new leadership," she answered for the other two women. "As for me, I think it is time I go home to Mt. Nebo for a while. I have some amends to make."

Jonah spoke up, "I'm not sure that it's safe to stay here with armies on the move. We have been sending refugees toward Gilgal. All are welcome who are willing to serve the rest of the community there."

"A good option for those who want a fresh start," Brinn agreed. "Where will you go?"

"South," Willa answered. "We still have work to do."

From the cover of a darkened alley a gray-skinned dwarf and a yuan-ti woman watched and waited unmoved by what they had seen. As the family left the town they followed, at a distance. At the edge of town, they were joined by two blue-skinned tieflings and at least a half-dozen Assyrian-garbed soldiers.

Chapter 9
"Gods" and Monsters

Jonah didn't feel safe staying anywhere near Aijalon for the night. He had also become concerned when he noticed a small group about half a mile behind them, keeping pace. He asked Wren to find them a plateau higher up in the foothills that was safe to traverse and wouldn't slow them down much. He wanted high ground in case of trouble. Neither Willa nor Wren thought anything of it, Jonah was always overly cautious. Wren easily climbed the wooded foothills and found a traversable way through. Jonah was relieved knowing his family had an extra level of protection, just in case. He continued to watch for signs that it was an actual pursuit and not a simple coincidence as they traveled this way until nightfall.

Wren found a cave with open sight lines in all directions including down, so they made camp there for the night. Jonah asked his daughter to call Moonbow. He wanted her to tell the ranger about the refugees heading to Gilgal, and to ask him to arrange for some help from the town to head north along the Jordan to meet them and make sure the civilians made it there safely. He also wanted to inform him that Kalin was carrying the maps and tactical information from the war camp.

Moonbow agreed to all of Jonah's requests without question but had a request for them as well.

Jonah's mind raced at the possibilities, "Did you find the traitor? Is it something about the necropolis mission?"

"No," Moonbow replied. "Wait, what about the necropolis mission? It's in two days did you hear something?"

Jonah was disappointed that the loops were continuing, but he was certain this wasn't the time to delve into it, "Just grasping at straws. What happened?"

Moonbow accepted the shift back to the topic at hand, "Rake has been kidnapped."

"The old druid, sorcerer guy?" Jonah had seen the Shadar-kai and his group around Haven, but they hadn't really talked.

"Yes," the ranger inhaled and continued, "apparently the halfling rifled through his stuff opening some scrolls that started something in motion. Later in the day they were in Ramah getting supplies when some black-cloaked people with bird masks grabbed him in broad daylight. His friends gave chase, but the abductors eluded them in the alleys. Barnabas scryed on him and saw them heading toward Mount Tabor. They asked me to connect with you for help."

"Well, clearly God wants us to help them." Jonah replied chuckling under his breath.

"I would hope so," Moonbow agreed. "How fast can you get to the southeastern range, near the Ever Grove?"

"We just set camp on the southwestern corner of Mt. Tabor," Jonah answered checking his map. "We can be there by midday tomorrow."

"Paise Adonai for his plan!"

"Yes, only God could continually have us right where we are needed." Jonah agreed.

"Amazing," Moonbow continued. "Lia is leading a team heading to the cave complex about half a day from your location on the south face of the mountain near where the Ever Grove begins. Coincidentally, Elowen remembered she is from that grove."

"There are no coincidences," Wren interjected, "if there is anything this adventure has shown us it's that."

Jonah took the first watch. He walked to the edge of the wood and spotted a campfire about a half mile north of their camp. This other camp was tucked between the foothills of the mountain. If they had camped at ground level, they would never have seen the small fire. His concern was growing that this was not coincidence, someone was following them again. He knew there was no chance of him sneaking up on them to get a better look. Wren could do it easily but then he would have to tell her they were being pursued. Jonah returned to camp and prayed about it as he kept guard through an uneventful shift. By the end of his watch, he had decided to keep an eye on the group from a distance and not to worry everyone just yet.

Willa awoke from her trance without prompting as usual. He was amazed by how that simple four-hour meditation was all she needed to stay at peak health and condition. He took off his armor and rolled out his bedroll. He lay there watching his wife for a while as she sat cross-legged in the cave mouth, silhouetted by the bright yellow moon, praying. He was so impressed and proud of the strong fierce protector she had become. Her anxiety and moments of indecision stemming from cratering confidence had been almost non-existent in this strange world. She used to have near panic-attacks over grocery day and now she was facing monsters and death daily, like a hardened soldier. He couldn't help but think of the old saying that 'God doesn't call the prepared, he prepares the called.' His small family had all grown so much in the midst of these challenges. He prayed once more in gratitude then drifted off to sleep with a smile.

Jonah awoke in the morning to Willa cooking, Leo staring at her and Wren fidgeting near the cave mouth. He was on his feet strapping on his armor, "I'll do a quick recon, then we can head out." They had learned to only unpack what they used so there was less to do to break camp. Jonah circled back down to where he could see the other camp the night before. He could see the remnants of a dead fire between the hills, but no people were visible. He wasn't sure if he was relieved or more worried at finding them gone.

About a hundred feet north, above and behind Jonah a metal crossbow bolt tip glinted in the morning shadows on Mount Tabor. A blue tiefling had the paladin in his sights, his finger caressing the trigger as a hand appeared on his forearm.

The duergar man said nothing. He simply shook his head causing the rogue to lower his weapon and nod. He pointed two fingers at his eyes then at Jonah to signify that he was just watching the man.

Travel was quick and uneventful as the family and their pursuers headed east along the south face of Mount Tabor. By midday the family had arrived at the designated meeting point as planned. Leo tensed and sniffed the air, sensing people concealed nearby. Seeing it was their reinforcements, the larger group stepped out from their concealment. Filipina the centaur fighter, introduced Gadget the gnomish artificer, Shay the earth genasi warlock, Azure the eladrin cleric, and Liathana the sea-elf paladin.

Jonah returned the courtesy, "Looks like you brought an army."

"Draco is checking out the cave approach by ground and Elowen is doing the same by air," Fili explained. "Are you all good to go when they return, or do you need some rest?"

Jonah replied, "We're good. I assume this is time sensitive."

Just then Draco burst from the underbrush, "I don't think they are expecting visitors. There are only a few guards at the cave entrance, and they are not acting worried or even vigilant." He looked at the three newcomers and the wolf, "Oh good, the cavalry is here."

An owl swooped down landing on a stump near the group. It began to shift and stretch quickly becoming the flame-haired eladrin elf they had met at Haven. "There are a few Ravens hidden in the trees, but they don't seem too attentive." Elowen looked over at Jonah, "You know you have a tail about half a mile back?"

Jonah looked at Willa and Wren. They were both staring daggers at him, realizing from his face that he already knew. He looked at the ground then up at the clouds, "Yes, I noticed them last night. They were gone this morning, so I wasn't sure they were following until just now. How many did you see from above?"

"Eight," Elowen replied. "Four well-geared mercenaries and four in Assyrian uniforms."

"Great," Jonah sighed, "reinforcements."

"Do you need us to help deal with them?" Filipina asked, her spear in hand.

"No," Jonah replied, unsheathing his own sword. "Rake is priority one. We will deal with them later."

Using the information provided by Draco and Elowen, Fili and Jonah planned the assault. They would take out the outer guards quietly, even those in the woods. Using stealth and non-deadly force they would subdue them so they couldn't provide reinforcement later. Once in the cave they would stay dark until they had no other choice. Once they were noticed they would go into immediate shock-and awe tactics to keep the defenders off-balance. Everyone agreed to the plan, anxious to get moving. As soon as the sun was down, they went to work.

Fifteen minutes later they were at the mouth of the cave, the plan had worked almost perfectly. Two of the Ravens resisted subdual efforts and fought fiercely, forcing the group to put them down. The rest were incapacitated and restrained in a nearby cave. When they arrived at the cave mouth, they could hear echoing raised voices.

Fili whispered, "We need to move!"

Everyone ran down the cave tunnel fearing that they were already too late. Fili, with Gadget on her back, and Jonah arrived first. The others formed up behind the two tanks, leaving Lia to cover their backs. Fili investigated the massive cavern, spotting the narrow winding path down to the platform.

"Fliers, recon," she said looking over her shoulder at the druids, "Go!"

Wren and Elowen instantly changed into an eagle and an owl and were gone. The rest of the group began the treacherous walk down the dizzying path, trying not to look down into the seemingly endless abyss below. As they traversed the path, they couldn't help but look to the main platform below. The scene there was terrifying, their worst-case scenario was playing out. There were six cultists in black with bird masks, and one leader wearing a much more ornate version. He was speaking words of power. The ritual had already begun. The three 'chosen ones', including Rake, were tied up on stone tables near the edge of the abyss on the far side of the platform. They were not moving, causing the worried onlookers to wonder if they were already dead. The six cultists were chanting and dancing between the stone tables and the cavernous pit. One by one a pair of the cultists threw a sacrifice into the pit.

Draco screamed, "No!" He watched in horror as Rake was the last to be thrown over the side.

The two druids in bird form flew into the pit near where their friend was dropped. The rest of the party reached the platform and began running across to the ritual site. They were not even halfway across when they heard the screeches of the two birds, followed by their terrified flight out of the pit. Seconds later a bright light of shifting white and gold erupted from the pit and lit the surrounding area. The party members shielded their eyes as they could barely look at the radiant explosion. Four silhouetted shapes with huge wings flew out of the pit. When they appeared from the light, those daring to peek through loose fingers could see that they were angels. Three of them, two males and a female, were carrying bodies. They landed on the platform and softly set down their burdens near the party as the light receded in the pit. Seeing that one of them was Rake, his friends rushed to his side. Tears welled up in their eyes as they reached his battered and broken body.

Jonah, Willa, Wren and Leo formed a defensive line between them and the cultists.

The three angels took flight, hovering about twenty feet in the air above them. The fourth angel leaned down and touched Rake, "He is gone, the ritual was completed." His facial expression changed to curiosity as he rose into the air between his companions. The four angels looked around intently trying to find the source of their sudden concern.

Two of the shadar-kai cultists ran up the path, giving in to their fear, and running for the exit.

The ornately robed leader of the ritual screamed, "This cannot be. Centuries of planning and effort. So many have toiled and died for this day. For nothing?" The man hidden behind the feathered Raven headdress suddenly turned, looking at his remaining followers, who had gathered by the edge to watch for the Raven Queen's arrival. If the party members could see his face, they would have seen the inspiration cross it just before he shoved several of them into the pit. The ones he pushed grabbed others to try to save themselves but only doomed them too.

Only one of the four managed to stay on the platform. She screamed at her leader, "What have you done? They are not the chosen ones!"

"It was them or nothing," the leader replied. Before he could say more there was a sound like thunder from the abyss. As the thunder faded another flying figure burst out of the deep, barely visible against the dark cave walls.

The cultist leader and his sole remaining follower fell to their knees shrieking, "The Raven Queen has come," almost in unison. The figure flew forward toward them, hovering at the edge of the platform. As it neared the pair of worshippers, the party could see that the creature was not the Raven Queen. It was a hideous bird-like thing with blacks and grays and reds in its plumage. Its face was a twisted beak full of sharp teeth. Its eyes held the dead stare of a killer shark.

"Finally, I am free!" Its speech was more like a cackle than a voice. "Thank you, human meat, for your poor judgment!" The cultists looked up from the ground, confused by this comment, but said nothing. The bird-creature continued, "I need only one more thing from you, then your service will be complete."

The cultist leader rose. "Anything m-my R-raven Queen," he stammered no longer exuding the confidence or leadership he had until now.

The creature replied, "You weak minded fool, clinging to your delusions to the bitter end. I am not your Raven Queen. That was a ruse to get you to free me. I am Blackwing and I am not pleased that you took so long. It is a good thing I have no further use for you," he paused for a moment, "well, I do have one more use for you." At that, Blackwing tore into the two cultists still alive, eating their flesh ravenously, as they screamed. When he was sated, he threw aside their carcasses, finally taking notice of the others nearby.

Jonah fought the urge to vomit and yelled back at the other group, "Uhh, we have company, and it still looks hungry."

Blackwing looked at the party then up at the angels hovering above them. He licked his lips, and said, "Ahhh, more food and celestials even. I haven't feasted on divine blood in centuries."

The creature was instantly airborne and streaking toward the angel positioned in the center. "I have not forgotten you, celestial. You were there when I was imprisoned." As it flew its jaw widened, almost disconnecting.

Only the wings of the angel moved at all. They flapped once and the celestial was instantly ten feet away from the demon's path.

"This is not our fight vrock." The angel spoke softly but could be heard clearly throughout the cavern. "You have stolen something from them. Their demands must be answered."

The other three angels each brandished a golden whip. They lashed them at the vrock-demon, two wrapping his legs and the third pinning his wings. With a flick of their wrists the creature was flung toward the platform.

It flipped in the air and spread its wings wide. It flapped furiously several times, halting its descent mere feet from the ground.

Jonah and Willa were just ten feet from the beast with their weapons and shields ready. They were close enough to see the vocal cords of the creature begin to vibrate.

"Incoming!" Jonah's warning was cut off by an ear-piercing screech that was amplified by the acoustics in the cavern.

Lia, Azure, Gadget and Elowen fell to the ground holding their now-bleeding ears. The others just barely resisted the effect of the scream.

The creature landed on the raised shields of Jonah and Willa and began to speak words of magic gesticulating with its taloned claws.

A portal opened near the downed allies and three hideous ape-like creatures appeared. They had thick white hides and heavily muscled bodies. Their faces were fright masks with a wrinkled snout, snaggle teeth and long flat ears pointing straight out from their heads. As if commanded silently their heads snapped around to the four stunned people and they began scrambling toward the easy prey.

Fili, who had resisted the effect of the scream, was at full speed instantly. She ran at two of the beasts that had stayed close together. She rammed the one going for Gadget, slamming it back with her chest plate then using the distance to rear up kicking it with both forehooves. The beast howled in defiant pain, a foul green gas exploding from it, possibly involuntarily. The centaur then stabbed to her right at the second creature, but the overwhelming odor and now cloudy air caused her to miss.

That creature leaped onto the back of the still stunned Lia. It slammed its meaty fists down on her back repeatedly, like a gorilla, knocking the wind out of the prone elf.

Draco was outside of the noxious cloud. He moved to cut off the third beast before it reached Elowen and Azure who were down and close together. Translucent blue daggers appeared in each of the halfling's hands. He instantly threw both aiming one at the creature's head and one at its heart. The first hit square in the beast's face just above its snout. The second flew harmlessly through the remains of the creature as it turned to dust before it even hit the ground. Draco didn't waste any time, his body began to convulse as he shifted into the form of the Aetherian symbiote that now shared his body. The smoky black form, wielding a black, great axe, entered the green cloud unaffected by the odor.

They had formed a defensive circle around the fallen Rake out of habit or maybe it was reverence for the dead.

Elowen, back in her eladrin form, rolled up to a knee and began to pray. An ice knife formed in her hand. She launched it at the flying demon. The agile creature flapped causing the projectile to miss, but as the knife flew by it exploded into a dozen shards like shrapnel. Half of them embedded in the creature's side. It screamed again this time in pain, not for effect.

Using the distraction Azure crawled to Rake's still body, she prayed over him asking Adonai for mercy. She pleaded for one last chance to speak the truth to her friend so that he would not have died without surrendering to God. Even in this tragic moment she was less concerned with his temporal flesh and more concerned with his eternal soul.

The dretch that had pummeled Lia felt her stop resisting. It scanned the field for the next easy target as lesser demons tended to do. It saw Azure praying over Rake with her back exposed and it leaped.

Unseen in the melee yet another fiend exited the portal the dretches had used. This one was a humanoid female with red skin, horns and bat-like wings. She walked straight to Gadget and began to whisper in her ear.

The already stunned gnome's eyes began to glaze over.

Just then a spear shaft swung wide above the gnome's head catching the fiend square in the mouth sending broken teeth clattering to the ground. Fili grabbed Gadget with her left hand, tossing her onto her broad back. The gnome shook her head to clear both mind and vision and fired her clockwork crossbow at the creature hitting it squarely in the shoulder.

It stepped back in surprise, pulling the bolt from the wound. The cambion smiled as it regained its composure, crouching to attack.

Fili smiled back as she saw a familiar shadow rise behind the demon.

Elowen's bear-form was at full height on hind legs as it swung a huge paw at the fiend. The claw raked into its armored back and wings sending it to the ground. The bear then landed on her foe with both front paws, her weight pinning the creature. She sunk her teeth deeply into its neck, shaking it violently several times until the fiend went still and as if it was never there it fell to dust.

Wren and Shay stepped up to aid Jonah and Willa. Wren lashed out with a thorny whip that took purchase on one of the beast's arms while Shay assaulted the now restrained creature with purple bolts of arcane energy.

Blackwing flapped furiously, pulling Wren into the air with him. It dove toward the chasm, slashing the whip free with its free claw.

Willa screamed, "Wren, no!" She ran toward the edge as her daughter disappeared from her sight in the depths of the abyss.

Completely oblivious to the danger, the frantic mother didn't even see Blackwing swoop around to ram her in the back. The vrock hit her squarely, sending her tumbling into the abyss after her daughter.

Jonah didn't hesitate. His eyes went black, spectral wings opened on his back and he too dove into the pit.

Shadolok appeared from the noxious cloud near the vrock. He had not seen any of what had just happened but saw his foe distracted, so he struck. He slashed at the creature with his great axe, catching its right wing near where it connected to its shoulder. This unexpected strike threw Blackwing off balance.

Azure took advantage of the opening with a quick prayer. She then made eye contact with the beast and said, "STOP!"

Blackwing turned and stood, pausing for a second, then rasped, "Do you think I am as weak willed as you mortals?" Without warning it flapped its wings again, blasting spores into her face. Half of them went wide as his injured right wing couldn't move completely. But the ones that hit her were enough to incapacitate the cleric in a fit of coughing.

Leo, who had just seen his whole family disappear into the abyss, charged at the demon. The full weight of the muscular wolf hit the creature in the side throwing them both into the cloud of spores with Azure.

The smell overwhelmed Leo's heightened senses, stopping him in his tracks. The wolf and the elf coughed and dry-heaved as they tried to blindly find their way to clean air.

Fili and Gadget were twenty feet away as Blackwing appeared from the spore cloud unaffected, but clearly showing signs of damage. The gnome fired a bolt at the creature as the centaur charged.

Blackwing tried to use his wings to dodge again but this time the damaged one failed him. The bolt hit his abdomen seconds before Fili struck him in the chest with both front hooves, throwing him to the ground.

Shay ran toward the downed foe, launching purple bolts at the now prone creature, who had landed just feet from the edge of the abyss. Azriel, the weapon granted to her by Adonai to do his will, appeared in her right hand. She dragged the weapon along the ground as she moved causing it to attract jagged rocks from the ground. She thanked God for this gift of power as she saw a welcome sight behind her foe. Jonah rose up from the abyss, his spectral wings flapping slowly. In his arms was Willa, tears in her eyes from the ordeal but no worse for wear physically.

Jonah landed away from the edge, setting his wife down gently. Behind them a giant eagle rose up from the chasm. It flew up twenty feet almost to where the angels still hovered, then it dove straight at Blackwing. Its massive talons shredded the creature's remaining functional wing causing yet another scream from the demon.

Lia, now recovered, and Shadolok joined their friends, completing a defensive circle. The companions had now surrounded and pinned their foe against the edge of the chasm. They looked at each other questioningly, no one sure what to do next.

Suddenly, there was a sound like white noise. Everyone looked in the direction of the sound as a small hole appeared in the air near the body of the half-eaten female cultist. A beak protruded from the hole, pulling left then right causing the small hole to rip. When the tear was about a foot long a raven flew out, landing on the nearby corpse. The raven settled on the woman's chest, then began to melt leaving a viscous black puddle. The inky substance quickly absorbed into the body causing the eyes of the dead woman to open wide.

She sat up causing many of the companions to step back and take ready stances. The new arrival silently surveyed the battlefield with jet-black eyes as she rose to her feet. Jonah and Wren were ready to move but unsure of this creature's intentions. Shadolok dispatched the last remaining dretch who had tried to use the distraction to strike. Shay checked on Lia, who still looked unsteady, both had their weapons in hand. Everyone else was transfixed by what was playing out in front of them. The now animated corpse began to float effortlessly toward Blackwing, its feet not even touching the ground.

The vrock demon seemed to recognize the entity, turning to face the only creature in the cavern that it truly feared.

As the corpse neared Blackwing a translucent vision began to form over the hijacked body. The ghostly visage was that of a black-haired woman, lithe with elven features and stature.

She wore a long black dress adorned with feathers throughout. Her large black wings were folded on her back. They pulsed softly, opening and closing as she floated across the room. "You never learn, do you demon?" Her voice was soft but supremely confident and came from the apparition not the body it controlled.

Coram Deo and their companions were frozen in place, still unsure what to do, if anything.

Blackwing, defiant to the last, replied, "You should talk, goddess. Pretending to be divine for these meat-sacks."

She looked up at the angels. Her answer clearly directed to them, not the demon, "I never claimed any such thing. I am simply a woman who fought evil creatures like you for a lifetime, until I lost my reason to fight."

"Oh, the tortured hero," Blackwing chided.

Her eyes returned to the demon, causing him to stop talking as if the words were choking him, "I returned once to help imprison you. Now I live a solitary life far from the needs and cares of mortals. I do not understand why so many would elevate other mortals to godhood rather than accept the clear evidence of the true living God." She turned her head toward each of the group, in turn. The black pools of her eyes made them feel as if she could see into their souls, "But I see little of that doubt and rebelliousness in these men and women. You will not be their demise, demon. Their purpose is greater than either of us."

Blackwing knew that this might be his only opportunity to act, He once again flapped his battered wings blasting spores straight at this hovering corpse wrapped in the visage of the Raven Queen, before him.

She simply spread the arms and wings of her ghostly form wide, taking in the full blast. As the spores covered her borrowed body, she closed her spectral arms and wings around the mass. She glowed for a second or two and then opened them again to reveal a single remaining mote of spores. She lifted it to the face of the corpse she was inhabiting on her flat palm, then blew, sending the remains into the air like dust. The witnesses stared at the display in amazement. The Raven Queen then disappeared, reappearing directly behind the now desperate demon, "We should have known imprisonment would not be sufficient." She grabbed him gently by his shoulders, enveloping him with her wings. He let out one last ear-piercing scream and when she opened her wings again Blackwing was gone.

The threat ended, this powerful being turned her attention to the companions, most of whom were still in defensive postures. "I will do you no harm." She floated toward Rake, "You have already suffered greatly due to my inaction. Adonai has looked out for each of you though, surrounding you with these others. I was once much like you. I gained great ability, but I have never claimed to be a goddess as the demon accused. I am just a woman who traded her humanity for power. There is one true God amid all the fraudulent ones. Do His will. My mistake cost you so much. I would like to correct that error." She looked up at the lead angel who descended in front of her. "May I correct my mistake?"

The angel looked up, closing his eyes. He hovered there for seconds that felt like minutes, then a light from nowhere cascaded across his face. He opened his eyes as he lowered his gaze to the visage of the Raven Queen, and simply nodded.

"Thank you," she paused for a second, looked upward, "I mean, thank you, Adonai."

The angel nodded once more.

She knelt by Rake's shattered body and placed both hands on his chest. His friends began to weep as the wounds and bruises faded in the bluish light. When the last wound closed there was a bright pulse that made all of them shield their eyes. When the light subsided, and they looked back, Rake was sitting there returned to life.

Rake stood, unable to take his eyes off the Raven Queen, and began to drop to a knee.

"No." She stopped him with an outstretched hand. "Enough harm has come from false worship. Your life was taken because I allowed your people to revere me. I thought it was harmless, but I was wrong. I have returned your life and half of your misspent years. Use them to do the right thing."

Rake looked down at his hands, now free of the spots and wrinkles of age, "Th-thank you," he stammered. He felt different inside as well. This ordeal had changed more than his age. He knew he would need to pray about it, and the truth of it all would be revealed in time.

The Raven Queen bowed slightly and turned to the rest of the companions, "My mistake cost you all as well. Forced to see your brother die for a lie. Most of you have chosen the right path and I can see that for the rest it is inevitable. In payment for your suffering, I offer you a boon. I can be found in the shadow realm if you ever want to claim it." She looked at Shadolok, "You should know the way, Aetherian." She turned back to the group and nodded one last time before the raven flew out of the body and back through the rip in the air. It was closed and gone before the now empty husk fell back to the ground.

No one had even noticed that the lead angel was once again among them on the platform. He whispered into Rake's ear, "Isn't it time you got off the fence? You have work to do for the Lord of Lords."

Rake nodded as the angel continued, asking him, "Do you finally accept your mission?"

"Yes," Rake said without hesitation, "I do accept my mission."

The angel smiled broadly and replied, "Then go fight for it, you have been equipped to be victorious in His name." The angel then rose into the air with his companions, and they all left through a swirling white and gold portal in the ceiling of the cavern, which closed behind them.

Fili broke the silence, "I don't know about you all, but this place is creeping me out. Let's get out of here."

A short time later the two groups were back outside. Shadolok yielded their shared body back to the halfling rogue, who timidly walked over to Rake and handed him his backpack. "You died and it's my fault. I let my curiosity get the better of me and read your scrolls setting all of this in motion."

Rake looked down at his friend accepting back his belongings. "Yeah, maybe you should work on your impulse control issues." He then looked over at Jonah and his family, who were preparing to leave. "Thank you for coming here to help."

Jonah responded, "God made sure we were nearby. We need to get back on our way to Shamir."

Elowen was checking Leo for lingering effects of the spores, "Do you need help with your pursuers before we split up?"

"I've been thinking about that," Jonah unrolled his map on the ground. "I think we will head south across the Jezreel Valley then continue south in the foothills of Mount Gilboa. We should be fine."

"That sounds like a good plan," The eladrin druid agreed. "I'm hoping we will head north into the Ever Grove to see if it jogs more of my memory."

"Ever Grove?" Rake seemed surprised at the mention. "You're from the Ever Grove?"

"I think so, it has been in my dreams lately. When we scryed on you, to find out where you had been taken, I recognized it," Elowen responded. "Do you know the place?"

"I trained there with Valmoira for a time," Rake explained.

"Well, it sounds like we have our next mission," Fili announced. "Let's go!"

A short distance away in the tree line, a young woman watched from the shadows. She was heartened by finally catching up to the group. She watched silently as the family headed south. She thought it odd that soldiers and mercenaries were following them from the shadows. She wanted no part in trying to evade more soldiers, so she continued to follow the main group. She stayed far behind them concealed by the thick growth of Ever Grove. She could be patient. She would follow, verify they were the right group and once certain she would find an opportunity to repay them for what they had done. Then she would start heading south again to find her sister.

Chapter 10

Out of the Frying Pan

They had barely entered the Jezreel Valley when they noticed their pursuers once again. This time Jonah told his family right away. The small group, now twelve strong, watched from the foothills of Mt. Tabor as the small family passed into the valley. They were hidden enough to conceal details but still easily noticed by Jonah who was expecting them to be there.

When they reached a point where they were obstructed from their stalkers sight lines, Wren wild-shaped into her namesake and circled back to get a closer look at them. She stayed low in the hills until she passed them then approached from behind. She flew within sight of the group, but stayed well back, moving from tree to tree to avoid drawing attention to herself. She confirmed that the four mercenaries Jonah had seen in the Blue Recluse were present. The rugged duergar with the hide armor and great axe was clearly the leader. He walked beside the cloaked female, but they didn't interact much. Judging by her gear she was probably a mage of some sort. Wren could swear she saw scales on her right hand and face and thought she saw the flick of a long thin tongue at one point. Her left hand never left the folds of her cloak. A few paces behind them were two blue-skinned tieflings. The female wore the chain mail, shield and holy symbol of a cleric, though Wren did not recognize the symbol. The male wore dark leather armor. He had a dagger and short sword on his belt and a crossbow on his back. He had to be a rogue or ranger, she guessed.

Walking about twenty feet behind them were two squads of four soldiers in Assyrian uniforms. The first group were all green-skinned humanoids. The large male orc appeared to be in charge. The female orc and male half-orc walked behind him, with the goblin bringing up the rear. The final group, dressed similarly, lagged further behind them and were all human. The soldiers stayed together in their squads and well back from the four mercenaries.

Wren watched them as the flatlands of the valley gave way, once again, to the foothills of a mountain range. Whenever their view of her family became obscured the duergar would give instructions. Several members of the unit would dash off to high ground or around a hill to keep in contact with their prey. When the huddle broke the twelve pursuers had spread wide continuing on parallel trajectories but now ten feet apart. They were not taking any chances with losing her family and based on the instructions Jonah had found in the Aramean war camp they had no need to be subtle.

Wren began to wonder if they had noticed her missing from their group.

She decided to take an even more convoluted route to return to her family. The thought that their pursuers might have noticed her recon mission nagged at her. Once she was sure she was again out of their sight line, she transformed back. As the day waned, they moved up higher into the side of Mount

Gilboa to find a spot to camp for the night. As they set up camp, Wren filled her parents in on what she had seen.

Jonah found a spot high enough in the low mountain that it wasn't visible from the ground. They ate cold rations again so they wouldn't need a fire. Even here in the mountains it stayed warm enough to sleep comfortably. Jonah took the first watch as usual. Leo stayed with him for a while but then settled in between Willa in her trance and Wren snoring away under the stars. Jonah walked to the edge of the rise and looked down on the plain below. He could see their pursuers' campfire, right out in the open as they had been directed. He knew the tactic. They were simply trying to keep the family fearful and looking over their shoulders. Jonah was certainly cautious with enemies so close, but fear was another thing. To allow their fears to pull them off their course would put their faith into question. They either trusted God with everything, or they didn't. He always believed that fear and faith were opposite forces like light and darkness.

He remembered the story of Simon Peter walking on water in Matthew 14. When his faith was strong, he walked on the water toward Jesus, but when, 'he saw the wind and became afraid' he began to sink. Jonah knew that he was chosen by God to lead this family and he was not going to allow any fear to overwhelm his faith or theirs.

Willa relieved him from his watch. He filled her in on the whereabouts of the others. He gave her a kiss goodnight and held her close for a moment.

Jonah pushed back from the embrace to look into her eyes and whispered to her, "I love you. We've got this."

"I love you too, always," she responded. "I don't know if we've got this, but I do know God has us."

Jonah smiled as he went to his sleeping spot and prayed before falling asleep.

The next two watches were uneventful. Willa stayed up with Wren since she only needed a four-hour trance to feel fully rested. They didn't talk much, they simply sat there together enjoying the moment despite the circumstances.

The sun rose into view earlier than usual as they had camped on the east face of the mountain. Wren reached out to Moonbow who was very thankful for their help with Rake's situation. He updated them on the investigation which had some close calls. A couple of newer recruits were shirking protocols but when questioned were found to be simply lazy, not treacherous. Wren told her mentor about the group following them. The ranger was certain he had crossed paths with the duergar before. He suggested a little-known pass between Mount Gilboa and Mount Ebal that, if followed all the way through, should leave them close to Shamir. He cut the conversation short telling them that he had to meet with Xof to make final preparations for his mission today. Wren still wasn't sure what to say about that situation, so she told him she was praying for them and cut short the call.

She passed on Moonbow's detour suggestion, which Jonah confirmed on his map. That route would save them at least a day of travel as their original plan went around the southern face of Gilboa and backtracked north to Shamir. By taking the pass they could avoid the city of Samaria entirely. Jonah could only imagine that the once capital of Israel would not be hospitable to them, if it was even still standing after that army had passed. They decided to start moving, packing quickly. They would eat and share from the 'Monday Mug' as they continued south. They didn't even need to send Wren to recon their pursuers as they had closed the gap and were now following a mere two hundred yards behind them, down in the foothills.

Near midday they found the pass. Wren had devised a plan to at least slow down their pursuers. They crossed the pass as if continuing south then went back up into the mountain as before. As soon as they were out of sight Wren prayed asking for God to allow them to pass without trace. Then she summoned a large warthog from the area. She told it to continue walking south at a moderate pace, which it did. They doubled back as stealthily as they could, turning southwest into the pass. The plan worked well but was never meant to do more than give them some distance.

After about an hour they began to hear their pursuer's armor echoing faintly behind them. As the pass continued southwest Wren noticed an unnatural floral growth on an outcropping of rock. Leo seemed baffled as to what she was looking at, sniffing around, the wolf was confused by his keen senses. The flora was an illusion, behind it another pass through the mountain going due west. Jonah quickly herded the family into the pass and asked Wren to help them be stealthy again. They didn't wait to see if the plan worked.

They doubled their pace and continued west for another hour until they came upon a twenty-foot-tall wall made of wood. There was a gate in the center with four guards.

A human female stepped forward, "State your business in New Vitala, please."

"We are on our way to Shamir. Soldiers from the north began to follow us," Jonah explained, "I seek only temporary asylum for my family."

The woman, dressed in red and black with a chain shirt over the top, as were the other guards replied, "We don't have any interest in the fights of Israel."

"I understand," Jonah implored. "The soldiers don't care who believes in what. We have seen the destruction the army wrought as they came from the north. They went west around this mountain, so they likely missed you, but there is another army approaching from the east, they may find you as we did,"

The woman turned as the gate opened behind her. Standing in the entrance, flanked by a squad of soldiers in variations of the gate guard attire, was a tall man with pale skin and gaunt features. He wore full plate armor covered by a black tabard with red striping. The symbol on the tabard was a black arrowhead design with a fancy 'V' in the middle.

"I am Petarku, Protectorate Captain of New Vitala. You may enter the city temporarily." The captain's accent sounded almost eastern European. "Do not leave the market square. Make no trouble or you will be removed at once."

"Thank you, we won't cause any trouble," Jonah replied shepherding his family through the gate.

Petarku held up a hand, "Hold!" He looked down at Leo, "Is that thing trained?"

Leo whined a bit at this man's glare. None of them had ever seen him react this way to anyone even before he was a wolf.

"Yes," Wren answered. "He is smart and obedient and would never hurt anyone unless they tried to hurt us."

"Fair enough," the man replied. "Proceed but see that he is as well behaved as the rest of you."

The streets of New Vitala were bustling. They hadn't seen anything close to this kind of activity since they walked through Jericho weeks ago. But there you felt as if all eyes were on you, unsafe at every turn. The cares of the world had certainly not found their way to this place and from the look of it, that was by design. The road to get to here was magically obscured, the entrance was well guarded, even the streets were patrolled at regular intervals by pairs of guards, dressed like the gate guards. The guards did not seem imposing or feared by the citizens either. They greeted townspeople and were cordial and well-liked. As they walked west the streets to the south were open, accessible and heavily trafficked at this time of day. The streets to the north were guarded by soldiers dressed like Petarku and there was no activity in those directions.

Willa noticed an inn nearby that had rooms facing the street and the main gate. "Let's get a room and see if they try to follow us in here."

Wren waited outside in the alley with Leo while her parents arranged the room. She was impressed by the sheer number of different races in this city. There had been many different races in Jericho, but they tended to stay together in communities with certain races enjoying much better conditions than others. In Haven many races were represented, living in harmony, but they were tied together by faith. There were races here she had never seen before. She wondered what was unifying these people.

Jonah and Willa approached the innkeeper. She seemed half-elven until they spotted her legs. They were fawn-like and furry with cloven hooves.

"Welcome to Riela's Respite," she almost sang the words. "I'm Riela. I don't believe I have seen you before, first time in New Vitala?"

"Yes, it is." he replied. "I am Jonah, and this is my wife, Willa. We would like a room facing the gate and the street if possible, and food would be amazing."

"Interesting request," she replied. "Don't worry I won't ask."

Willa started to feel more comfortable due to the woman's demeanor, "Our daughter is outside with our wolf companion, do you have a kennel."

"We are animal friendly here," she looked down at her legs, shrugging. "Is he trained?"

"Yes, very well trained," Willa assured the woman.

"Well, bring him in and have a seat," she said still in the singsong manner. "I'll bring you some food while we prepare your room."

The family sat and ate. Leo was on his best behavior as promised. The food was very tasty and so welcome after having only cold rations for days during their harrowing trek south. They kept the conversation light, careful not to air anything that they might not want overheard. After a short time Riela returned to escort them to their room. The third-floor room was on the northeast corner of the building and had a great view of the main street and a decent view of the gate from the balcony. Wren occupied herself with Leo in the room, picking any locks she could find for practice. Jonah and Willa sat on the balcony waiting for any sign of their pursuers. As the sun was nestling in the western mountain peaks there was an uproar at the gate. They couldn't hear anything, but they could see town guards gathering there. Seconds later Petarku arrived with two squads of heavily armored soldiers. After a short exchange the two squads surrounded the intruders and began escorting them west along the main street.

Jonah was concerned that only the four soldiers led by the orc were present. They were being led somewhere by the New Vitalan Protectorate, but the four mercenaries and the human soldiers were not with them. As they passed the inn, the orc that Wren had identified as the leader of the soldiers looked up at them. He held his glare long enough to make sure Jonah knew he saw them.

Petarku, who was following behind the escort, noticed the exchange. He also looked up at Jonah and gave a single nod before returning his attention to his duty. They lost sight of the odd parade as the main road turned south further down the street.

Jonah noticed that Wren had joined them at the railing. Her eyes were glassy, as if she were holding back tears. "Are you ok?" He put his arm around his daughter for comfort.

She blinked a few times then looked up at the much taller Aasimar frame of her father, "What is going to happen now? Will they turn us over to them?"

"I don't know," Jonah admitted. "I would hope not, but they owe us nothing and said they had no interest in getting involved."

"You could have lied to make me feel better," Wren retorted a small grin creeping onto her face.

"We're in this together," he said as he put his arm around her. "Are you up for a reconnaissance mission? It might get your mind off speculating."

"Always," she replied, no sign of tears left in her eyes.

Moments later the young druid, once again in the form of a wren, took flight over New Vitala. She flew east until she was out of the city then north until the front gate was in sight. She then followed the road until it connected with the pass at the illusory blockade. Wren had seen no sign of anyone at this point so she continued southwest for a few miles knowing that was the direction they would have gone had they missed the secret pass. Still, she saw no one so she circled back to the northeast. Just past the illusory flora, along the east wall, she spotted the flare of a campfire in the waning light of dusk. She moved in closer and found the mercenary camp concealed behind a large boulder. As soon as she noticed it, she banked hard, remembering her concern that they may be aware of her the last time she spied on them from the air. As she banked, she heard a low whistling sound. An arrow passed her just above and to the right of her head. She flapped her wings as hard as she could heading back toward the city.

Her heart and mind were racing after the close call, so she decided to explore a bit and collect her thoughts before returning. She wanted to calm her racing heartbeat, so she circled the city a few times, focusing on the perimeter. She looked for an alternate way out of the mountain-locked city. The north side was a solid mountain, but on the south side she found what she had hoped for. There was a secondary exit near a fenced area full of tents and walled mansion. She soared high above the pass that went east and west through a couple switchbacks before finally settling on a due west heading. Pleased with finding an escape route and having her heart rate back to normal, the little bird fluttered back toward the inn.

Wren relayed the findings of her mission, leaving out the part about the arrow to spare her parents some worry. Leo somehow knew that something had frightened his friend and wouldn't leave her side. He hovered even closer to her than normal.

Jonah unfurled the map and tried to plot a tentative course through southern Mount Gilboa and into the northern part of Mount Ebal. He guessed that by the starting direction of the pass that they would come out south of Shamir and have to back-track north a bit to get to their destination. Suddenly, there was a knock at the door, startling all of them and causing Leo to stand at attention in front of Wren.

Not expecting visitors in a strange town, Jonah rolled up their maps, notes and journals while Willa readied herself to answer the door. When Jonah signaled that everything was secure, she opened it. She barely held her surprise as she saw a strange man and four guards standing in the hallway.

The man was even taller than Jonah, close to seven feet tall. But this man had pale skin, bony facial features and was rail thin. His robes were jet black with thin red accents around the cuffs, collar and down the centerline. The collar was tight to his thin neck and came up under his chin. His long ears pointed straight back, and his shoulder length gray hair was drawn back into a ponytail. His voice was monotone, but his demeanor demanded attention. "I am Voq, Chancellor of New Vitala. I have been sent to escort you to a meeting with Castellan Astryd." With that he stepped aside, inviting the family to come with him. "The wolf must stay here. My men will ensure his safety. Shall we go?"

Jonah's mind raced through fight and flight options. He forced himself to focus, "May we have just a moment to prepare?"

"Of course," Voq seemed a bit put off by the request but acquiesced. "Please do not tarry, the Castellan is very busy tonight."

Jonah closed the door softly and whispered as he gathered his pack, "I don't think we have a choice. Take your packs with you or they will likely be searched."

Wren looked up from assuring Leo that he would be fine, "You both noticed his canine teeth, right?"

Willa answered, "Hard not to. Please tell me they aren't vampires."

Jonah had regained his composure and wasn't having any of this. "Alright, here's the plan. We go peacefully. If they wanted us dead, we probably would be already. Let's see what they want and go from there, but first we pray."

Voq ordered two of the guards to stay at the inn room door. The other pair brought up the rear, as Voq led them out the back into an alley where they were met by another pair of guards. Jonah had surmised that the uniformed guards at the gate were more like police, while Petarku and his soldiers, including these four, were the military. He wasn't sure if this deduction made him feel better or worse.

The elder man stopped momentarily, turning to the trio, "Please put your hoods up if you have them. The fewer people who see you the better for now. I assure you that you are guests, not prisoners. The guards are for your protection, and mine."

He turned and walked to the end of the alley where a horse drawn carriage awaited. Voq beckoned them in. Two of the guards sat in front with the driver and the other two stood on a platform at the back. The carriage moved slowly west then southwest. Voq gave what amounted to a riding tour, describing the parts of the city. Jonah felt relief at this, knowing that their host wouldn't give this information to people they intended to kill or imprison. Voq told them that New Vitala was a dhampir colony. Only Willa had even heard the term before, but none of them interrupted to ask what it meant. He described how they moved here at the behest of their Patron Vudra. Over the decades they had become more trusting of the people of the region, eventually allowing some of them with particular skills to live here in the Red Quarter. They had two main rules for immigrants, earn your keep and keep secret the location of the community. He told them that people who sought refuge in the city were happy to follow both rules as they were brutally oppressed and even enslaved in the outside world.

They passed through the fenced area with the tents and a small barracks that Wren had seen earlier from above. Jonah recognized it as what his military might call a forward operating base. The fact that they have one in the middle of their city told him that they took readiness seriously. Further to the southwest and up a hill, tucked protectively into the mountainside, was a torchlit, gated stone mansion. The carriage came to a stop just outside the main entrance. The soldiers dismounted, opened the front door for them, reforming into their protective formation to lead them inside.

Willa noticed that Voq's lower body showed no movement under his robes. She wondered silently if he was floating or flying but couldn't tell as his robes were touching the ground. The words 'dhampir' and 'vampire' battled for her attention.

They entered the mansion and were quickly led up a wide stairway and through large double doors at the top. There were guards inside and outside the open doors in the same heavy black and red armor as their escorts. The room was impeccably appointed but not ostentatious. To their left was a desk and bookshelves. To the right were curio cabinets with keepsakes and tchotchkes. Straight ahead was a woman standing by a fireplace. There was a fine almost throne-like chair on the right with a smaller ornate chair on either side. On the left were three smaller but still fine-looking chairs. When they entered the woman seemed to be enraptured by the fire, the flames dancing in her eyes. She was tall and thin with pale, but soft looking skin. Her hair was long and bleach-white, the sides were pulled together and braided into an ornate golden headpiece that wrapped around the back of her skull and came to a point on her forehead.

Voq spoke first, bowing slightly, "Lady Astryd, these are the people you requested an audience with."

The woman seemed uncomfortable with his bow but nodded in acknowledgement. "Welcome, please have a seat," she said, pointing toward the chairs on the left.

Jonah sat in the middle but wasn't sure if he should speak or wait to be addressed. This woman seemed to be like royalty to her people and he was not accustomed to such protocols. As the others took their seats, he extended his divine sense across the room finding no one in range to be of evil thought or intent.

Voq sat quietly to Astryd's right, closest to the fireplace.

Astryd looked each of her guests over carefully before speaking again, "I am Astryd, acting Castellan of New Vitala. While we wait for Captain Petarku we should get to know each other a bit." She paused before continuing, "I am uncomfortable with the rigors of my position so I would prefer that we speak plainly and of course honestly."

Voq audibly huffed at this statement.

"My chancellor here," indicating Voq, "is a traditionalist. He prefers all the protocol and pomp, as you might have surmised. Please, introduce yourselves."

Jonah cleared his throat, "I am Jonah." He then looked to his wife.

"I am his wife Willa," she said softly.

Wren sat up straight when both of her parents looked her way. "I'm Wren, their daughter."

"I am pleased to meet you," Astryd replied, nodding her head cordially to each of them. "Tell me, what do you know of the dhampir race and how did you find us here?"

"We found this place accidentally while we were trying to elude our pursuers." Jonah felt that honesty was the best play here. "I'm sorry though, I have never heard the term dhampir before today."

"I have," Willa interjected, piquing Astryd's curiosity, "but only in legends from some old books I was studying."

"What did these books tell you of our people?" The woman seemed genuinely interested.

"According to the books, dhampir are the product of procreation between actual vampires and other races. The child of a vampire and a non-vampire is born a dhampir."

Astryd interrupted, "This is only partially right. The difference between vampires and dhampir is simple. They are bitten, infected and changed. We are born this way." Her point made, she nodded for Willa to continue.

"Thank you for the clarification. The books state that most of your kind are born with vampiric abilities and features, some are not. The book said that those born fully human were abandoned. I pray that is not true."

Without warning the doors burst open and Petarku entered in full armor, he handed his helm and weapons to the door guards and joined the group sitting to Astryd's left.

"You have met Captain Petarku," Astryd nodded to the man. "Let's ask him your question. Willa asked if it is true that we dispose of any dhampir children who are born with recessive vampiric traits."

"If that were true, I wouldn't be sitting here," Petarku admitted, "let alone be trusted to lead the Protectorate of our lineage."

Astryd returned her attention to her guests, "I do appreciate your thorough research, but you can't always believe what you read. Every author interjects their personal beliefs into their work." She made eye contact with Willa again, "You mentioned prayer. Was that a figure of speech or are you religious?"

Willa looked at Jonah for support. He squeezed her hand gently to grant it. "Where we come from, being religious is not necessarily considered a good thing. We are followers of Adonai; we look only to do his will as he calls us to do it."

"That is a bold statement," Astryd seemed surprised by the admission. "Claiming that publicly brings great persecution in these lands." She looked at both of her advisors. Petarku nodded slightly. Voq made eye contact, his eyes going wide for a second before reluctantly nodding himself. "We are mostly convinced that you are trustworthy. So, I am going to tell you the truth of our lineage, then we will discuss your dilemma. Is that acceptable?"

Jonah looked at his family, still holding their hands, "Yes, that is most gracious of you."

Astryd looked to Voq, "Would you please tell our guests a little about our history. I must get an update from the captain, on our other recent guests."

Jonah wondered if she meant the Assyrian soldiers as he watched the Captain and the Castellan step into a side room.

Voq cleared his throat, "In general those of dhampir descent are, shall we say, cautious. Like any race there have been those over the centuries who believe we are the next step in evolution and seek power to advance that thought. The Nas'Veratus Lineage, who currently live in the Empire of Thrace, believe this. Other lineages look to blend into society and still others choose racial segregation."

He paused to allow questions or comments, but none were offered. "This caused rifts within the race of the dhampir which over time resulted in the formation of the lineages in the first place. Leaders arose with specific belief structures and people followed them by choice. There are currently five recognized lineages Zorae and Nas'Veratus are power hungry. They seek wealth, recognition and glory. They are far to the west on another continent where their advances are held in check by the other civilized races of the land. The Xingzhě and Straega are far to the north and west on this continent but are fiercely xenophobic. Our lineage is called Vudra after our matron. She chose the way of cooperating with other races as you saw in the city. We keep to our neighborhoods more as a show of respect than out of necessity. You may be too polite to ask but I will answer anyway, we choose not to feed on sentient beings except to defend ourselves. Our scholars have developed weapons made of a mystical material, spell craft, and other abilities best called 'blood magic' for use in defense of our city and lineage."

"I'm not even sure what to say about all of this," Jonah admitted.

"Understandable," Astryd replied, returning to her seat with the captain in tow. "We have chosen a different way, but that would mean little to people who didn't even know we existed mere hours ago. We don't know each other but I would suggest mutual trust, until we get to know each other."

Jonah looked at his family and both nodded, squeezing his hand a little tighter in the hope that this was the right decision. "We agree, Lady Astryd. We certainly didn't come here to disrupt your city or people."

"Good!" Astryd's reaction was genuine. "Captain Petarku, please catch them up with what you told me about our other visitors."

Petarku sat forward in his chair, his armor squeaking as he did, "The Assyrians have been a handful. They said you were fugitives, but we could tell they weren't entirely truthful about why. That and the fact that the story you told us at the gate proved true led us to hold them, for now. That leaves us in a conundrum. They know where we are now and probably think of us as enemies."

Wren fidgeted in her chair, "There are eight more of their group outside the illusory blockade."

Petarku grinned wryly, "We are aware of them. Our reconnaissance is much more subtle than yours 'little bird'."

If a tabaxi could blush, Wren did so at that moment. She raised her hands as if feigning speechless surrender.

Jonah looked puzzled, but spoke, "So the ones you are holding and the ones outside know of your location. Only the ones inside know anything of your defenses. We are not well versed in magical things. Can they be made to forget?"

"Yes, but that option is not foolproof," Willa offered.

"Correct," Astryd agreed. "We haven't determined the best course of action yet, but that is more our problem than yours at this point. You have another problem that I think will be news to you. Captain?"

"Three days ago, we captured a changeling posing as one of us." Voq audibly coughed at this claim by Petarku. "Perhaps captured is not the right term. She walked into this room posing as a guard then changed to her true self within arm's reach of Castellan Astryd."

Jonah resisted the urge to question such a move, certain that the captain would fill in the blanks.

"She said her name was Crae and assured me and my guards, who instantly surrounded her, that her intention was not to harm the Castellan. She claimed she had come to warn us about a threat and to prove our lack of readiness. She warned us that a faction of followers of a rogue God called Adonai were in the area sowing chaos and dissension. She claimed these dissidents were assassinating leaders and brainwashing the people to their cause."

"Did she name this faction?" Jonah asked, but he already knew the answer.

"She called them Coram Deo," Petarku said flatly.

"She was talking about you, wasn't she?" Astryd's demeanor didn't change despite the gravity of the question.

"Yes," the door guards tensed up at Jonah's response, but Petarku held up a hand instructing them to stand down. "We are Coram Deo, but we have done none of what she accused. We and others like us are simply missionaries following a calling and telling people about God."

Voq suddenly seemed anxious, shifting forward in his chair, "Is it true that your God changed part of this world for his purposes?"

Jonah deferred to Willa as she had studied this extensively with Barnabas. "Yes, we have been told by people who were here when it happened, that he did."

"Why?" his tone was now short and terse.

Willa didn't hesitate, "We believe that he is giving the people of this world the same choice that he gave the people of ours. He transformed part of this world into a replica of what we refer to as 'The Promised Land' on Earth. It was where his chosen people were given the choice to follow him and live eternally in his presence or deny him and live eternally outside of his presence."

Jonah could see confusion in their faces, so he decided to tell them the story from the beginning. He started with Xof and Barnabas arriving on Aeramor, continued through the transformation of Gadaron into the Fertile Crescent to mimic the promised land, and finished with their arrival in this world and Coram Deo's adventures to date. The looks on the faces of their hosts went from confusion to concern.

After an awkward silence Astryd spoke first, "I am going to grant you the dimensional travel aspect for now. I have seen the impossible happen in my lifetime so I will accept this is possible. I must know, do you believe this Adonai to be benevolent?"

"Yes!" Again, Willa was emphatic and didn't hesitate.

Voq seemed less than convinced. "How did all of this work out on your world, Earth?"

"May I?" Wren perked up at the chance to use years of Christian school theology. Willa nodded. "The believers in our world were persecuted for centuries. Many were killed for their faith, but their willingness to die for the truth only emboldened others to believe. Followers of Adonai eventually became one of a few dominant religions in the whole world supplanting many false gods that were nothing more than heroic people who were elevated by myth and legend."

"Your world is at peace then?" Hope could be heard in Astryd's voice.

Jonah answered, "No, unfortunately not. As time passed and science and technology grew in capability many saw themselves as supremely intelligent and beyond the need for any god. Some began to worship created things instead of the creator. Others used their knowledge to denigrate the faithful, deny the one true God and give in to their basest desires. The followers of the way of Adonai found peace where they could in a world of rebellion and turmoil."

"So, your God failed and decided to try again?" Voq was escalating, his anger plain. "We are his second attempt?"

Willa shifted forward in her chair, "He did not fail. Millions of people believe, and live lives dedicated to his glory. More millions died with their hearts surrendered to him and now live in Heaven for eternity. While the world debases itself in sin, Adonai's people feed those in need, care for the widow and orphan, and even love the sinner despite their choices. While God wants all his children to choose him, he doesn't force anyone to do so. He allows our free-will choice because if he didn't, we would be nothing more than programmed automatons doing the will of the programmer. There is no glory to be found in that."

Voq nodded at that. He was surprised by this woman's passion and eloquence and was unprepared to respond without further thought.

"We know this is a lot to accept and we wouldn't blame you if you threw us out into the street," Jonah was tired and still worried about how this was all going to end. "We have a teacher, a rabbi called Barnabas. Perhaps we can arrange a meeting to go into much greater detail about who Adonai is and why he has chosen to reveal himself to Aeramor. We simply want to continue our mission to Shamir and beyond without the danger posed by our pursuers. We ask nothing of you except safe passage through the south pass."

Astryd rose at this request, "Will you give us a moment to discuss this?"

"Of course," Jonah agreed.

Astryd led Voq and Petarku to the side chamber that she and the captain had spoken in earlier. Jonah, Willa and Wren were left alone aside from the two guards at the door and potentially more outside it.

"Are you both as scared as I am right now?" Wren had tears welling up in her cat-like eyes.

Willa went to her and knelt in front of her chair embracing her daughter. "Of course we are, none of what has been asked of us has been easy."

"True," Jonah added, "but God has not asked us to do any of it alone. He has clearly been with us the whole way." Jonah put a hand on each of their shoulders and prayed. "Father God there is nothing you are unaware of, no situation you are unprepared for, no challenge too big for you. We love you, trust you and are surrendered to your will for us. Give us the strength to endure whatever comes next and the wisdom to do it while always showing your glory to the world. In your name we pray, amen."

The guards at the door fidgeted and looked around as if expecting Adonai to appear and smite them. A few moments later the trio of dhampir hosts returned. Their faces were still stoic and concerned, giving the family no sign of their fate.

Astryd paused to gather herself before speaking, "This whole story of yours is, well, unbelievable, yet somehow we all feel your sincerity." Petarku and Voq nodded in agreement. "We have decided to help you."

The trio all sighed in relief. Willa responded, "Thank you so much."

Astryd nodded, "There are some stipulations to this agreement."

"We will do everything in our power to meet them," Jonah assured.

"Good," Astryd continued. "First, you will stay here tonight. We want plausible deniability that you were ever in the city, so we need as few witnesses as possible. We have already sent people to speak with the innkeeper and retrieve your wolf and any belongings still in the room." She paused to allow questions, but again, none came. "Next, we would like further explanation of this Adonai. We ask that your people send a missionary team here to live among us and teach us if even for a short time. A protective force may come with the missionaries to ensure their safety, but no more than six warriors may remain in New Vitala once the missionaries are settled. Captain Petarku will guarantee the protection of your people once they are here."

"We will relay your request." Jonah hesitated before posing a question, "Might there be a possibility of you sending a similar group to Haven to see what has been accomplished there and learn our ways?"

Astryd looked at both Voq and Petarku, who each nodded, "With the same stipulations, I suppose that is fair."

"They can travel back there with the escort after they leave the missionaries here," Jonah's heart swelled with this opportunity to share the gospel with an entire city.

Willa cleared her throat, "I may be overstepping, but what will happen to the soldiers you are holding and the mercenaries outside the city?"

Petarku responded, "We cannot allow them to return to their masters, with knowledge of our home. We also will not just murder them. I think the best course of action is to pursue arcane means of altering their memories, then teleport them far away."

"You could send them to Ramilon," Jonah interjected. "That's where we first ran across them. If they believe they never saw us they may simply wait there assuming we haven't passed through yet."

The three dhampir nodded at each other in agreement.

When all was decided, planting the seed of the budding friendship between the people of New Vitala and the followers of Adonai, the family was escorted to their room in the keep. As promised Leo and their belongings were already there. Jonah worked on mapping the next couple legs of their journey, first to Shamir, then to Pirathon to investigate the Tola and Abdon dreams. They will be within a day of the Deborah dream and Haven by then. Willa and Wren contacted Moonbow, relaying everything they could about their pursuers, the assassin, Crae, and the potential arrangement with the people of New Vitala. The ranger seemed distracted as he updated them on the traitor investigation which continued to progress. He got quiet for a moment before informing them that the mission to the necropolis had failed and that Xof's team was lost. Jonah joined them as they prayed together before signing off. They knew something had to be done about this mystery soon.

Chapter 11
You Can Go Home Again

Elowen looked like a child seeing a beautiful place for the first time. Her eyes were filled with wonder as she and her friends entered the southern Ever Grove. She was completely enraptured by its beauty but also felt a nagging recognition deep inside her. Rake led them to the home of his former mentor Valmoira. The elder Firbolg druid greeted him with a hug that enveloped the much smaller elven man. She welcomed each of them into her home as Rake introduced them. Elowen had fallen behind, not ready to give up the feeling of connection to this glorious place just yet.

Valmoira excused herself and stepped outside. "It's beautiful, isn't it?"

"It is like no place I have ever seen before," Elowen responded, looking up into the canopy of the trees at the tiny spires of sunlight finding their way through, "but, somehow it feels familiar." She turned to face their host.

Valmoira's face changed to one of shock at the sight of the younger druid's face. "Elowen? Is it really you?"

"You know me?" Elowen's face beamed with hope.

"Of course I do," her hands now cradling Elowen's face, "you are the warden of this grove, as your parents and grandparents were before you. At least you were until you left your sister in charge and disappeared more than ten years ago. We all thought you were dead."

The rest of the group was now back outside with them, gathering around for support. Their faces showed concern, hope and happiness for their friend but also horror at the mention of ten lost years.

"Ten years?" Elowen had tears running down her face. "Can you take me to my sister...?" More tears flowed as she still couldn't remember her own sister's name.

Seeing her struggle Valmoira interjected, "Althaea, dear. Her name is Althaea. Let's go to her right now."

They walked for about fifteen minutes continuing north into the grove. They all noticed that the beauty of the forest waned as they progressed deeper into the wood. The trees were dry and dying. The ground seemed corrupted and overcome by a moldy black and gray substance and the few animals they saw were emaciated. Fortunately, for Elowen, she hardly noticed. She was lost in the anticipation of going home, even though she felt only a vague familiarity with any of this. Valmoira seemed unmoved by the condition of the wood, as if she had grown accustomed to seeing her home this way. Soon, they entered a small village. There were few people about and the ones that were visible seemed lethargic and ill. Valmoira greeted them warmly and they returned her greeting. They eyed the strangers suspiciously until their eyes found Elowen. Each person reacted in a cascading wave of recognition at the sight of their former Grove Warden. In turn they fell to their knees in respect. Whispers of her name and title traveled through the village until they were broken by a woman's voice.

"Elowen? Sister, you're alive! We had all but lost hope." Althaea ran to her older sister embracing her tightly.

Everything came flooding back to Elowen in an instant when she saw the face of her sister. While they embraced, her mind raced through returning memories that filled the gaps in the fragmented dreams she had been having. She remembered the growing corruption in the grove and leaving her sister Althaea to care for the clan so she could investigate the cause. She flashed on a river in the mountains to the north. There she saw orcs, goblins, hobgoblins and the like. She wasn't surprised at the involvement of her people's ancestral enemies but knew they couldn't be the masterminds behind this kind of corruption of nature.

She stiffened in Althaea's grasp as she was taken back to that place and time. She used skill and stealth to infiltrate the cave complex, finding stores of gems, materials that looked like spell components, and other supplies. Further in, she found prisoners in cages who she freed in the hope that they could escape the fate that was intended for them.

She continued deeper into the complex maze, finding odd demonic and infernal looking creatures. She evaded their sight and eventually found a huge cavern with a narrow path leading across a deep chasm.

Elowen's heart raced as she relived the dream that had plagued her since her arrival on Aeramor with Azure and Gadget. Her sister knew better than to interrupt her trance. She and Valmoira carried her inside and made her comfortable as her friends watched in helpless concern.

Despite the dim light Elowen could see across to the far side of the chasm where a creepy black castle with tall, crooked spires seemed to have appeared from the rock itself. The portcullis was open and many of its inhabitants were in front of the building. There were seven humanoids in the center of a huge circle of demonic creatures. The circle parted near the castle gate as an eight-foot tall, winged man with dark red skin, curled ram-like horns and black hair approached the gathering from the castle. Beside him was a human looking woman with deep purple robes and a menacing staff.

Following closely behind them were seven more powerful looking people of various races. The seven in the circle were joined by two hunched and hooded creatures. Little could be seen of their faces, only gnarled claw-like hands were left uncovered by their cloaks. One, holding a large gem, moved to the left of the humanoids. The other, holding a gemmed staff in one hand and a strange, black-barbed symbol in the other, moved to the right.

The tall man looked down at the woman and said, "Noxia, begin."

The woman walked to each of the seven in the line, looked them in the eye and asked, "Are you doing this of your own free will?"

Each of the seven responded in turn, "I am."

She looked back at the seven people gathered behind the winged man and nodded. A tall dark-skinned woman with yellow eyes and fangs, wearing all black leather, came forward and stood before the first of the humanoids, a dragonborn male. "You will be my avatar of wrath." The oracle with the gem began chanting. Light flowed through the gem bathing the dragonborn. He screamed in pain, falling to his knees, as boils formed across his skin. The oracle with the symbol and staff then began chanting, mercifully causing the boils to recede. The dragonborn stood, his eyes now a frightening red for a few moments before returning to their normal serpentine gold.

Elowen watched from her hiding place as the process was repeated six more times. Each of the tall man's allies imbued a humanoid with power declaring the avatars of pride, greed, envy, lust, sloth and gluttony.

While the ceremony continued Elowen's attention drifted to her left where she saw and heard flowing water. Moving closer to the flow she found the smell overwhelmingly noxious. She touched the water, finding it viscous and dark. Within seconds she could feel her skin begin to tingle and harden. She wiped it off quickly, knowing that the cause of the corruption in her grove was coming from below this mountain! She returned her attention to the ceremony, seeing the final humanoid, a Half-Orc, rise to his feet, eyes flashing red like the others, before reverting to their normal brown.

The tall, winged man stepped forward, arms in the air and huge wings wide open. As the cheering waned, he announced, "It is done, but this is just the beginning of our effort to depose the so-called One True God. We have much to prepare for, during the next decade. Fortunately, time is no longer our adversary." He tilted his head as if sensing something out of place, "But, first, we must deal with our uninvited guest."

All who had gathered for this rite turned and looked directly at Elowen simultaneously. She tried to run but found herself unable to move. Her body was lifted from the ground and drawn toward the tall man unwillingly. His power moved her around in the air before him as he inspected the spy. "You were not invited, small one, why are you here?"

Elowen said nothing in response, continuing to strain against the invisible force holding her.

"So be it druid, take your secrets to your death," he said as he urged the invisible force holding her to throw her into the chasm.

She plummeted for what seemed endless moments before she began to see something at the bottom. As the floor of the dark chasm rushed up to meet her, she accepted this as her fated end, but it was not to be. A bright light erupted around her. She felt a gentle but powerful hand grab her belt causing her descent to slow. She landed softly on the floor of the vast cavern turning to see her savior. Her eyes adjusted to the bright light slowly, but not completely. It was her savior himself who was emitting the glow, preventing her from getting a good look at him.

He spoke directly into her mind, "It is not your time yet, Elowen. You must be kept safe until His time. Go through the portal behind you. You will be safe there. Do not be anxious, though you will not remember any of this, He will send you helpers. You will return with them at the appointed time. Go, now!"

Somehow the young druid knew that what her rescuer had said was true, so Elowen turned and stepped into the portal, and everything went black.

Elowen heard her name echoing in her ears. She felt hands on her shoulders gently shaking her. She felt her eyelids flutter allowing in some light. As she continued to blink, her vision returned though still unfocused. "Claire?" She called out remembering her time in the hospital on Earth with the volunteer who read to her and kept her company.

"Yes, Elowen, it's me," Azure replied, acknowledging her former name. "We are all here for you. Are you alright?"

As her vision cleared, she saw the rest of her team, Valmoira and her sister Althaea looking on with love and concern. She sat up and looked directly into her sister's eyes. Through tears she uttered, "I remember everything. I know how to save the grove."

Chapter 12
The Scenic Route

Jonah and his family were well on their way by first light. They were eager to get back on their appointed mission. Petarku and his men escorted them through the pass and bid them farewell before turning back. Jonah knew that the journey to Shamir would take most of the day, so he set them on a healthy pace. As they left the beauty of the mountains that hid New Vitala they realized that this was the furthest west they had been. The landscape to the south was mostly dry desert wilderness. The only breaks in the flat terrain were occasional craggy hills.

As they left the mountain pass behind, they turned north and hugged the mountain giving Samaria, former capital of the fallen Israel, a wide berth. The low mountains provided hills and trees for cover, making the small group feel much safer. By midafternoon they arrived in Shamir to find yet another town in disarray. Some of the buildings and farms along the northern and western outskirts were burned and destroyed. Many of the townspeople were packing and leaving. A smaller group huddled near the center of town was arguing over resources, property and power. Some of the people they passed looked at them with suspicion, most paid no attention to them at all.

Some whispered to each other in Hebrew, as the family of strangers, entered their town. Willa could tell they were speaking Hebrew, though it sounded just like common to her now. They were saying unkind things about her family, questioning why they were in Shamir, why they were heading north instead of south to safety. The people of Shamir were clearly inhospitable, but Willa had dealt with people like this before.

Jonah approached a group talking in the town center. He waited for them to finish what they were saying before addressing them.

None of them reacted to his presence for an uncomfortable amount of time. Eventually, a few of them began to look at him oddly, then more joined in on the activity. The one who had been talking looked at him, with a perturbed look on his face.

"Shalom," Jonah bowed slightly. "I am here with my family on a pilgrimage…"

"You do not belong here," an older man interrupted then turned away from Jonah.

"We do not plan to stay or cause disruption," Jonah assured the few still looking at him. "We simply seek information about the Judge Tola who was once here."

"Followers of Adonai," a younger man spat. "Your God is not welcome here, nor are his liars and manipulators." This man and several others turned away after this comment.

Jonah was clearly frustrated by the claims of these men. His focus on them caused him to miss that some of the other townspeople had been moving closer to the conversation, methodically surrounding his family.

Willa did notice. She touched Jonah gently on the arm, "We don't want any trouble, we should go." She jerked her head toward the forming crowd.

Jonah quickly got her hint and rushed his family back down the south road. Some of the men from the town followed them all the way out of town and watched them until they were out of sight.

Once they felt safe again, Willa realized that they hadn't eaten in their rush to get to Shamir, so she suggested they stop and eat while they discussed what to do next. They prayed to God for revelation and guidance, then sat in the dirt about fifteen feet off the road and ate while discussing the fact that they had no other leads to this resolution of the dream.

A short time later two carts approached them, heading south out of the town. A man called both carts to a stop just past where the family was eating. He adjusted the load in the rear cart then began looking at one of the wheels.

Willa nudged Jonah, who was watching the man work, "God provides."

He leapt up, instantly getting her meaning, and approached the man to offer help. "Did something break? Can I be of service?"

At Jonah's approach the man motioned to his children in the cart. Instantly they disappeared from Jonah's sight. Only then did the man acknowledge Jonah, "Yes, I think this may have come loose." He pointed at a bracket near the axle.

Jonah leaned in close and saw nothing wrong with the bracket.

The half-elven man, now right by Jonah's ear, whispered, "I am Kenath, we are of the Unseen, have you heard of us."

Jonah shook his head.

Kenath seemed surprised, he quickly explained, "The unseen are people of faith in Adonai who have decided to use fellowship and community to spread his word. We move into communities, mix in at work and in family gatherings looking to grow belief in Adonai through acts of service and fellowship."

After the man's explanation Jonah did recall the leadership in Haven mentioning them in passing.

Kenath continued, "There is a tomb and memorial to Tola near the base of the mountains to the east." He gave detailed directions to get there. He apologized for the behavior of his former townspeople and explained that Shamir is governed by prideful people who believe there is no objective truth. They assert that the only truth is the one decided by those who ascend to power. Many are using the rumors of war as an excuse to leave, but it is more about getting away from these arrogant and misguided leaders.

Jonah pretended to be fixing something under the wagon, "There is a refuge to the south, in Gilgal. Go east through the pass then head southeast to the Jordan. Follow the river south and you will find the town just west along the north bank of the El Qelt River." Jonah then acted as if he had resolved the problem and told the man that they would be praying for his family. The family watched them continue south for a few moments before packing up their camp and heading east.

Wren took the lead and easily found the path the man had told them about. They continued east back into Mount Gilboa before turning south. They found a cedar forest and about a half a mile in they spotted a cave that would have been nearly impossible to see through the trees without the directions they were given. They climbed the low hill that led to the entrance to the cave.

What they found inside was completely unexpected. A few feet in the rough dirt and stone changed to polished marble showing no sign of wear or even dust despite the remote location. The ten-foot-wide hallway opened into a vast hundred-foot chamber. The outer twenty feet were made of the same marble as the hallway. The inner part was tiled in a gold and beige checkerboard pattern. Each tile had a word or number carved in it in Hebrew, which they all could recognize by now though only Willa could read them. Willa inspected all the words thoroughly.

"There are words on the wall back here too," Wren offered from the back of the chamber. "I think this is another puzzle."

Jonah stayed near the entrance with Leo, not wanting a repeat of the ambush in Kamon.

Willa joined her daughter by the wall and read the inscriptions. They were indeed clues. The first was the Hebrew word for lineage. Willa found the tiles labeled Dod, Puah, and Tola which she had remembered were Tola's father and grandfather from the dream and scripture. She tested the tiles with her foot. They recessed easily, when she put weight on them. Willa asked Jonah and Wren for their backpacks, setting one on each of the large tiles with the names on them. As she stepped off the other tiles, they could hear an audible click and the sound of gears moving behind the walls. The second clue on the back wall was the Hebrew word for 'duty'. Wren answered but Willa already knew the answer was 'judge'. She found the word on the floor and asked Jonah to stand on that tile. Again, the sound of gears could be heard under their feet and behind the walls. She returned to read the final clue which simply said 'service'.

Wren seemed puzzled at this, "Aren't duty and service the same thing?"

Jonah spoke up, still standing on his tile and watching the entrance, "It probably means how long he served, twenty-three years, wasn't it?"

Willa was already moving. She found the symbol for twenty and asked Wren to stand on it. While her daughter complied, Willa found the symbol for three and stood on it herself. All the gears seemed to activate at once this time, culminating in three loud thumps that shook the entire room. As the echo of the sounds died down a small door in the back wall released and opened slightly. Willa approached cautiously, pushing the door open with the handle of her mace. Wren joined her helping her to remove the long narrow box inside. They opened it together revealing an ornate golden rod.

"Stow that thing, we have company outside." Jonah's voice was measured but the seriousness of the situation was clear. Leo was at full alert and only stayed back at Jonah's command.

The trio left their backpacks in the corner of the puzzle room and drew their weapons. Willa touched Jonah and Wren on the shoulder and prayed for God's blessing over them. They could feel the power enter their bodies. Together they moved slowly out of the cave, into the afternoon sun.

Jonah shielded his eyes against the jarring brightness as they adjusted to the light. He clocked three armed men in the open, straight in front of them. He also saw two more figures hiding in the trees with crossbows trained on them.

"Kind of you to check on our safety up here," Jonah began calmly, but his words dripped with sarcasm. "We are fine."

"Just give us your money and valuables," the dirty man replied. "No one will get hurt." Jonah didn't need his divine sense to tell these were evil men. The expressions of the three in front of him clearly showed that he was lying. They had no intention of refraining from violence.

Jonah looked down at the ground, his arms extended to his sides as if in surrender, but when he looked back up at his attackers his eyes were pools of black. Spectral wings appeared again from his back as he readied sword and shield.

"That is not going to work for me," he replied. He flapped his wings twice, gaining speed instantly, "Leo, Go!"

The wolf instinctively dashed to the woods throwing his full weight into one of the crossbow-wielding bandits. Wolven growls and human cries of pain were heard from the low brush.

Jonah hit the leftmost assailant square in the face with his shield crumpling them to the ground instantly. His sword drove deeply into the shoulder of the one in the middle.

The other hidden archer fired at Jonah as the middle bandit stabbed at him with a dagger, seeing that he was vulnerable. The dagger found the flesh of his forearm, but the bolt flew over the top of his shield.

Jonah, lost in battle, barely heard Wren shriek, "MOM!" as he brought his shield up under the central man's chin crushing both jaw and teeth. He turned in time to see his wife hit the ground, a bolt protruding from just below her ribs.

Wren was standing next to her, tears welling in her cat eyes as she lashed a vine-like whip at the woman who fired the bolt. It hit her on the left shoulder wrapping around and under her right armpit. With the lash secured Wren pulled with all the strength her fear and rage provided. The archer flew forward out of the brush and onto her back, landing at Jonah's left, her crossbow left behind in the bushes.

The Paladin kicked the man on the right off his blade and placed the point under the chin of the woman. "Yield or die!" There was not a hint of softness in Jonah's voice and the assailants knew it. One by one they dropped their weapons and kicked them away at his order.

The injured crossbowman threw out his weapons, "Call off the wolf."

"Leo, come here," the wolf complied, never taking an eye off his adversary.

Wren had already begun tending to Willa while Jonah dealt with their attackers. The wound might have been devastating if not for the incredible abilities God had granted them in this world. Willa was going into shock from the impact, and blood loss, having never been hit like that before. Wren prayed for healing and watched as the wound closed almost entirely.

While Wren continued to tend to her mother, Jonah ordered the bandits to remove their armor and remaining weapons. They sat on the ground wondering if their lives would be lost for their crime.

"You can thank Adonai for your lives today," Jonah began. He paced between them and the pile of their equipment for a few moments, praying under his breath for the right words. "You have a decision to make today. You can change your lives and look to serve others, or you can continue to victimize people. One of those paths leads to death. I think it is easy to tell which."

"You're not going to kill us?" The woman who had fired the crossbow bolt asked incredulously. She couldn't take her eyes off Wren and Willa. "W-will she be alright?"

Jonah glanced over his shoulder, "Praise Adonai, yes she will." He moved closer to the group and dropped to one knee. Leo sidled up next to him to discourage any aggressive moves. "Lord, these people are ignorant of your truth. They have been taught nothing but hate. In their minds the world is theirs for the taking. Open their eyes, show them the glorious riches that you provide to the servants in your Kingdom. In your mighty name we pray for their salvation. Amen." Jonah stood again to his full height. "Your equipment is lost instead of your lives. It will replace what was given to us in this tomb. If you want it back, you will need to study the life of Tola in scripture and solve the puzzle inside. Go home and tell the others there that we are leaving in the morning. If anyone else comes here to do us harm this will be their tomb as well as Tola's. Do you understand what I am saying?"

They nodded in unison, some with tears in their eyes.

"Go, then." Jonah made no move, his sword still scabbarded and his shield on his back.

The five rose slowly, turned and walked away at a brisk pace. The less injured helped the few that were more injured. Within a minute they were out of sight.

Jonah helped Wren get Willa into the tomb then gathered all the bandit's gear. He placed it in the compartment that the puzzle had revealed. When he closed the door, he could hear the gears resetting in the walls.

The light of day was waning in the valley by the time they set up a quick camp. Jonah suggested they rest there in the relative safety of the memorial, but still worried that a larger force may come. Wren and Leo went hunting in the wooded mountainside, while Willa rested. When they returned, Jonah took Leo and went to look in on the town. He watched them go about their lives for an hour and saw no evidence that they were planning an assault. Jonah returned in time to enjoy a rare hot meal of rabbit stew with wild roots and mushrooms.

After eating they checked in with Moonbow who updated them on current events in Haven. Barnabas was leaving in two days to meet with Astryd in New Vitala. He was bringing two of his acolytes, the twin half-elves Taran and Tarai to lead the missionary team. Rhesa the Firbolg druid, who had created and led the farming community in the mountain above Haven, offered to send two of her apprentices, a young married couple named Abiud and Elia, to teach the New Vitalans some farming techniques for mountainous regions.

The ranger updated them on Elmore's investigation which had yielded a few more suspects, but all were easily cleared upon deeper investigation. They had started to look at traders and associates outside of Haven as well. His thinking was that someone inside was oversharing and the person outside was selling the information. It was unlikely but worth a look. They considered asking about Xof but decided against it. A conversation so complicated should be held in person. Wren let him know that they would be heading to Pirathon next to investigate the Abdon dream, then on to Ramah where the Deborah vision seemed to be leading them. After that they would finally head home to Haven for a rest. They signed off fondly, set up a watch schedule and got some sleep.

Jonah took the first watch as usual. He put out the cooking fire as it was no longer needed. Wren and Willa rested inside the memorial which stayed warm enough for their comfort. His innate dark-vision worked much better without the interference of nearby light sources anyway. He saw and heard only small nocturnal animals throughout most of his shift.

Toward the end he had wandered about fifty feet from the memorial to relieve himself. Leo was lying in the entrance to the tomb. Nothing was getting past that wolf.

As Jonah made his way back to his post, he heard a familiar growl followed by a warning yip from Leo. Jonah knew that his high-pitched yip had replaced the incessant barking that served as Leo's warning system before he had transformed from a shih tzu into a wolf. Jonah thought that their attackers had returned but resisted the urge to run back to his post. Instead, using the cover of the trees to assess the intrusion, he crept back as stealthily as he could. As the memorial entrance came into view Jonah could see three humanoid figures being held at bay by his loyal wolf. The trio had long handled weapons leveled at Leo. Jonah could swear one of them looked like a hoe, but he wasn't taking chances. He crept up behind them while they whispered forcefully trying to get Leo to calm down.

Once six feet behind them Jonah whispered, "Who are you and why are you here?"

The trio spun in surprise. One of their weapons, which turned out to be a rake, glanced off Jonah's shield. The three intruders were now panicked, looking back and forth at the man and wolf now flanking them.

"Don't hurt us," one of them said.

"I told you we shouldn't have come here," another offered.

The third, much shorter than the others, and still holding a hoe near Leo's face, said nothing.

"Put down the weapons, step away from the entrance. Go sit by that tree," Jonah motioned to his left with his sword.

They followed his commands without taking their eyes off the wolf.

Once they were unarmed and seated Jonah asked, "Why are you here?"

The tallest one answered, "We heard you asking about Tola in town. Our parents raised us as followers of Adonai, but they died of a sickness two years ago. Some townspeople took us on as servants, caring for us and feeding us in exchange for work."

Jonah's adrenaline waned as he realized that these children were not a threat to his family. He sheathed his sword and sat on a nearby log. "What are your names?"

"I am Azor," the tall one answered. Jonah could see the children had Elven features.

"My name is Zadok," the other boy answered.

Jonah looked at the smallest one, a girl of about nine, but she said nothing. She sat still staring at the ground with tear-filled eyes.

The eldest spoke up again, "She is Mari. She doesn't talk much and never to strangers."

Jonah nodded in understanding, "I am Jonah." He looked at Leo, now at his side sitting calmly, "This is Leo. He doesn't trust strangers either, but he is fiercely loyal to his friends, even new ones."

The sounds of movement came from the memorial causing everyone except Leo to look in that direction. Leo could smell that it was Willa.

As the cleric appeared from their shelter Mari gripped her brother's arm tightly. Willa noticed and said, "You are safe here little one."

Jonah made the introductions and caught his wife up on the story so far.

"So, what was the plan in coming here?" She posed the question to Azor, as the eldest.

"Truthfully," he paused after that single word, "we were hoping to steal supplies and run away from this awful town and these nasty people."

"To where?" Willa's questions were genuine and not judgmental. "Do you have someplace to go?" She knelt in front of Mari and reached for her hand. The girl cautiously accepted the offering then leapt into the cleric's arms, hugging her tightly while shaking with sobs.

Azor's facial expression softened at the sight, "Our father told us that his family came from a community of elves in Galilee, near the Sea. He always spoke of it fondly."

"That sounds beautiful Azor, but It is not safe to go north just now," Jonah interjected. "There are armies marching from the far north and east. Many of the cities in their path have been abandoned or destroyed."

"Oh", was all the boy managed. He couldn't hide his disappointment.

Willa held Mari's tear-streaked face, but looked to each of them in turn, "I know we just met, but would you trust us enough to come with us to a safe place?"

Azor looked at his siblings, who both nodded back at him. "We would like that, thank you."

"Good," Willa was thrilled by the answer. "Go inside with Jonah and get some sleep. Leo and I will stand guard. We leave in the morning after a good meal."

The young ones did as they were told. Jonah set them up on his and Willa's bedrolls. They were asleep before he could rest his head on his backpack.

Willa spent some time during her watch examining the rod further. On closer inspection she noticed that the long golden cylinder had a seam about six inches from a crystal at the top.

She assumed that twisting these two sections in opposite directions would activate the rod but decided it was better not to try it until someone could tell her what would happen. This was a mystery for another day.

Chapter 13
The Depths of Corruption

Elowen easily navigated back to the woods leading to the cavern complex and the caves themselves. Having experienced her first trip to this place repeatedly in her dreams so many times, there were no surprises. When they neared the cave, she was surprised that there was almost no orc or goblin activity. The rangers and druids of the Grove easily handled these few enemies. Inside the cave, there were some of the demons she had seen before, but they were far fewer in number than her first time there and were easily evaded.

A wave of fear came over her when she arrived in the main cavern and saw the black castle and the chasm again. The memory of the winged man throwing her to her death flashed in her mind, but she resisted it. Adonai had a purpose for her, so she was spared that day ten years ago, to return today and save her people and their land. The Lord had also given her these companions who had been steadfast in serving both the Lord and each other. Shaking herself free of the memories, she led her friends deeper into the cavern. She remembered finding the corrupted stream just before she got caught last time. She could examine it more thoroughly this time. She quickly found a path that curved west following the stream, but on a steeper angle cutting through the chasm. As the group moved down the narrow path single file, it began to split from the stream, forming a sheer rock wall on their right as it led them downward to an open area under the castle. Filipina struggled a bit to keep her balance on the narrow path, but it soon widened as it curved back under the keep.

Elowen stopped at the mouth of the huge cavern that appeared to match the entire length and depth of the castle above. It was twenty to twenty-five feet high. The ceiling of the cavern and the castle above seemed to be held up by dozens of stalagmites that had connected with stalactites forming massive pillars. These huge formations ranged in size from five to twenty feet in diameter and were randomly placed around the enormous space.

As Elowen crept in past the first two columns she began to see a purple glow from the central area. She waved Filipina and Draco forward. The others, having traveled together for so long, knew that this meant she sensed danger, so they took defensive positions. They edged cautiously closer until they could see the source of the eerie light.

A weird purple, red, and brown crystal was glowing in some sort of stand. The crystal was like nothing any of them had ever seen before. Surrounding the object were a dozen or more humanoids casting magic at it in a rainbow of colors and forms. Though clearly powerful, their magic seemed to have little effect. Every so often the crystal pulsated with a strange force, a type of energy that the party could feel even from their supposedly safe distance. The apparatus holding the crystal sat in a pool of water that seemed to be fed by a spring from below. The water was lifted from the pool, through the crystal, and up in what could only be described as a reverse waterfall. They could see the water changing, being corrupted, as it flowed through the crystal and up. Elowen knew instantly that this crystal must be the cause of the corruption of the stream above them and her grove as well.

The stealthier team members moved from column to column surveying the area. To the north of the gem Draco spotted more humanoids sitting or lying against the stalagmites in various states of injury and exhaustion. Circling between the humanoids currently casting at the gem and the humanoids along the sides were three huge creatures. Draco had seen one before when they broke Elmore out of prison.

They were powerful demons called barlgura. The three gorilla-like demons had thick blue hide and shaggy brown fur in patches. Their arms were densely muscled and ended in hammer-like fists. They seemed to be guarding the crystal and 'encouraging' the exhausted humanoids to continue whatever they were doing to it. Draco pointed at his eyes then toward the creatures. When Fili nodded in reply, he held up three fingers, then held his hands wide to show size.

Fili tapped Shay on the shoulder and pointed to a column next to Draco's. The young earth genasi warlock crept forward as instructed. She peered out from her position, not far from the resting humanoids. From there she could see that these people all looked somewhat like her. She looked closer at each face, lit by torches mounted on some of the columns of rock, and saw some that she recognized from her clan warren in the Veridian Mountains on the Sundered Isle off the east coast of Ebreyon. Shocked and dismayed she turned away from the scene, her back pressed against the column, her breathing ragged and fast, as fear gripped her mind.

Draco appeared at her side. He reached up and grabbed her shoulder, pulling her down to face him, "Focus," he whispered.

With the halfling's encouragement, the young earth genasi nodded, fending off the panic attack.

Fili had taken up Draco's earlier spot, while the others behind her moved up to keep her in sight. They all watched for her to call them to action. Having made sure everyone was in position she motioned for them to go.

Shay began to pray, a translucent black chain wrapped around the nearest Barlgura. Draco fired a crossbow bolt, hitting the same beast, then shifted into his Aetherian form. Shadolok charged at the beast, his smoky battle ax at the ready.

Fili charged at the second demon, with Gadget on her back. She hit it full force with her front hooves, then speared it viciously. Gadget had become good at holding onto her centaur friend while firing her clockwork repeater crossbow. Her aim was true, hitting the creature in its wide muscled chest.

Elowen sprinted across the far side of the cavern assuming the form of a black bear as she ran. The third barlgura had turned to see what was attacking the first so Elowen barreled into it from behind knocking it to the ground, slashing and biting its back with vicious animal rage. Lia had followed the bear for support. She sang a quick psalm as she ran, inspiring the druid, before swinging at the demon with her maul.

Rake, transformed into the lizard-like creature he was fond of using as his wild shape. In this form he was about seven feet tall with short front arms, densely muscled back legs and a long thick tail. Jagged blue plates ran down its back from neck to tail. He skidded to a stop five feet from Filipina's barlgura, lashing his wide tail at its feet knocking it to the ground.

Azure remained back by the columns preparing prayers to support the various teams.

Fili stabbed at her adversary again just as Rake-zilla took it down. From what she could see, the first assault had gone as planned she yelled, "Shay, go!"

Shay sprinted from cover toward the gem. She prayed and sent two bolts of purple light at the demon she had marked with the chains. They hit and melted away a chunk of its flesh, revealing muscle and bone beneath. As she neared the gem, she summoned her pact weapon. It was called Azriel, which translated to 'God is my help'. She dragged it along the ground as she ran. The weapon, gifted to her by Adonai, gathered stones from the ground, affixing them to the handle and head.

Shadolok saw the barlgura react to Shay's blasts and turn its attention to her. He roared in rage and recklessly gave up any defense for offense, swinging repeatedly to get the monster's attention back.

Staying with the plan and trusting her allies, Shay rushed forward toward the gem. She began to feel nauseated and weak as she got closer. She could feel some sort of sickening waves of force emanating from the object. When she got to within ten feet of it the nausea became overwhelming, driving her to her knees. She could barely hear Fili and Shadolok calling out to her in concern.

Suddenly a voice rang out in her mind. She knew instantly that it was the voice of an angel. She was there when an angel spoke to Rake just a day or two ago.

"This is not of our Lord's creation. Your clan mates are being forced to undo what Adonai has done for this world. They must stop defying God's will by empowering this crystal. Instead, they must attune to this new world that He has made. Only then will they unlock their destiny as you have done."

Shay looked toward her earth genasi people on the ground recovering. Then to those casting magic into the crystal. Finally, she glanced at her team fighting demons to give her time to strike. She gathered her strength, rose from the ground and yelled, "Stop what you are doing brother and sister genasi. Fight with us against this abomination!"

The genasi heard her words. Most turned their magic on the Barlgura, some just stopped what they were doing and watched as their sister began to move toward the crystal again.

Shayera had fully succumbed to the will of her Lord, swinging her blessed weapon with all her might. As it hit the object it fractured but didn't shatter. The chunks of rock that had adhered to the head of her hammer released, flying past with the momentum of the swing. Onlookers sighed thinking she had failed, but suddenly the dislodged rocks circled around and flew back at the weakened gem. One by one they struck it pummeling the already weakened crystal. The last rock smashed through it entirely. Shay barely had time to exhale before the devastated gem pulsated with an unnatural glow. Her eyes widened as she turned and yelled, "Run!"

Seconds later the broken object exploded sending shards of jagged shrapnel flying in every direction devastating friend, foe, and structure alike. The concussion from the release of so much magical energy threw Shay and the genasi casters fifteen to twenty feet. Some landed hard on the ground, some hit other creatures. The most unfortunate hit the rocky columns or outcroppings with deadly effect. The devastation was not limited to the captives or their rescuers. The barlgura were also thrown from their feet by the powerful blast. The two fighting

Shadolok, Rake and Fili were most injured and turned to dust as their bodies, peppered with shrapnel, skidded to a stop on the jagged floor of the cavern. The third demon limped away but didn't get far before a large broken stalagmite fell on it, crushing the beast.

Azure was far enough away and had enough cover that she felt little effect of the blast. From her position she could see that many of the columns had been damaged causing them to fracture and fall, bringing down large portions of the ceiling above with them. The elven cleric yelled, "This way!" Genasi captives and team members alike grabbed the fallen and ran toward the side path that the group had used to enter this place.

Lia and Elowen, still in bear form, were furthest away from the exit but moved quickly. About halfway to Azure the bear sniffed the air and roared. Lia followed, as the bear veered to the right, deflecting rocks with her shield as they ran. After about fifteen feet the bear stopped at the dust covered and unmoving form of Shay. Lia threw her friend over her shoulder then continued to shield the trio as they ran for the exit.

Seeing Rake appear from the dust, back in his elven form, Azure told him, "I'll shield them, can you heal Shay from here?" Rake nodded as the cleric began praying.

Lia, Elowen and Shay took a hit or two from small debris, but the pelting stopped suddenly as a shimmering field appeared above them. The bear and the sea elf pushed hard, sprinting toward the help up ahead. Shay's body began to glow, and she started to move on Lia's back.

"Stay still, little one," the paladin managed through gasping breaths. "We can't stop now."

The pair reached their teammates as large chunks of ceiling shook loose and fell behind them. Shay, with her backward view saw the black bear take a vicious hit from a medium sized rock knocking her to the ground and forcing her back to her natural form. "Elowen!" She yelled but no one heard her in all the noise. Shay saw the druid get to her feet for just a second before the orange of her hair and green of her clothing was obscured by debris and dust.

Shadolok, Fili and Gadget had made it to the edge of the ramp and were directing people onto the narrow walkway up to the main cavern. The genasi people thrived in this environment and moved easily on the cliffside, even while carrying their wounded.

Azure and Rake arrived next.

"The others?" Fili asked, looking past them into the chaos.

"They were right behind us," Rake answered, hands on knees gasping for breath as he and Azure joined the line on the path.

Lia came running out of the dust. Shay didn't wait for her to stop before leaping from her back.

"Elowen got hit and fell," she exclaimed through ragged breaths, moving back toward the cavern.

Fili and Shadolok grabbed the girl, preventing her from returning to the cavern now completely obscured by dust. "Did she get up?"

"Yes, but…"

"We have to trust that she will get herself out or we are all dead," Fili hoped the young soldier would see reason.

The young genasi looked up the path at her friends and clan-mates scrambling for their lives, then back into the now completely obscured tunnel. Tears ran down her filthy face as she joined the line on the path helping the injured make it safely to the top.

The remaining party members took to the trail. They weren't at the top for more than a minute before the ground beneath their feet cracked and gave a final heave. They could see the black castle lean to the left then sink what seemed like ten or fifteen feet. Its spires and walls crumbled and collapsed. The sound was deafening, and then suddenly it just stopped.

Shay watched as the cliffside path crumbled and fell away with no sign of Elowen. "She saved me," tears were flowing freely now creating streams of gray skin between the caked-on mud and dust.

The others joined her looking down at the sheer cliff where the path used to be. Lia put her arm around Shay pulling her head into her shoulder.

"Do you hear that?" Rake's head tilted to hear better as everyone else fell silent.

A faint fluttering sound could be heard, though with the echo it was impossible to find its origin.

"I hear it," Azure and Lia said almost in unison. "It sounds like flapping wings."

Suddenly a dense cloud of movement lifted out of the chasm. Hundreds of bats had been evicted from their habitat by the catastrophic collapse. The colony shifted left, then right almost like a wave in the air, before heading over the onlookers' heads and toward the caves beyond them. As they passed over one of the creatures broke free of the colony. That one adventurous bat landed on a rock near the group. It began to shake and then stretch. Seconds later Elowen was standing in its place. She was covered in dust but alive. She fell to her knees, blood flowing freely from her head and left shoulder blade. Before she could even speak her friends ran to her aid.

"Elowen! I thought we had lost you," Shay knelt before her looking into her eyes as Azure prayed for healing over her.

"Not gonna lie," she stammered, "I'm not entirely sure how I made it through that."

"Thank Adonai that you did," Lia exclaimed.

"Yes," Elowen replied, "only God. That's the only explanation that makes any sense. I was injured and dazed, and a mountain was falling on me, but through it all I heard bats. I wild shaped into a bat and followed the sound. My sonar guided me through the chaos until I found the colony. I followed them until I saw light and then all of you."

"Amazing," replied Azure.

Gadget agreed, "another miracle."

The group tended to each other's wounds and to those of the now freed earth genasi. Shay went to speak with the few that she knew. Rake and Lia followed for support as the only others in the group to have even seen an earth genasi. The exhausted but grateful people explained how they were duped into helping with this debacle. They were told that a usurper god had come, and he had remade the world to his whims. They were asked to help put it right and stop this mad god's destruction of Aeramor. They knew, as soon as they connected with the planet through the gem, that they were lied to, but they were forced to continue, many were killed who tried to escape or fought back in any way.

After the explanation one of the three genasi Shay knew, a druid named Strata, stepped forward. "Thank you for helping us, Shayera Spinel. We would not be free without your help."

Shay looked around at the dozen or so remaining Genasi, "So many were lost. I'm so sorry."

Strata looked around at those who survived, "True, many have gone back to the earth, but all these were saved."

Shay wiped the tears from her face, "Yes that is true. I just wish they would have known Adonai before they died."

If an earth genasi's face could go white, Strata's face did in that moment, "Adonai? That is the name of the God our captors said was destroying the world." She seemed terrified.

Shay put her hand around the older woman, "Let us tell you the truth about Adonai."

Chapter 14
Wedding Day Woes

Jonah awakened in the morning alone in the memorial. He could hear muffled voices and the crackle of a fire coming from outside. As he appeared from the tomb the smell of freshly cooked game tantalized his nostrils. Wren, Leo and the boys were sitting around the fire talking while Willa cooked with the aid of Mari. Jonah's heart leaped at the sight. This was the image he had of his family with Willa when they planned their future as newlyweds. Though they tried everything they were never able to have biological children. Willa struggled with it mightily, even blaming God in moments of private despair. Jonah tried to encourage her, but he was fighting difficulties of his own. He struggled with God's seeming denial of their prayers for children. More than ten years later, when Wren had come into their lives, they finally began to understand that God was never ignoring them. He didn't say no to their prayers. He simply asked them to trust Him and wait for His time.

Seeing Willa surrounded with children today filled Jonah's heart with joy. This was who she was meant to be. He walked wordlessly to her, hugging her from behind. She melted into his embrace as he kissed her gently on the cheek, "Good morning, beautiful."

She smiled widely, "Good morning handsome." Looking down she noticed Mari watching the exchange, smiling up at them. As soon as she realized Willa was looking at her, she returned her attention to cooking. The smile remained on her face while she poked at the food.

After eating their fill, they packed up the camp. Wren created water to fill all their containers and douse the campfire. She contacted Moonbow again, this time asking for Madisyn to lead a small group to meet them in Pirathon to escort the kids back to Gilgal or Haven. He agreed.

Soon they were on the way west out of the mountain then south. They crossed the pass that led back to New Vitala and continued south. Now Mount Ebal was on their left. They traveled in its shadow until well past noon when the sun finally crested its tallest peaks, bathing them in the glorious sunlight that Wren and Willa loved so much. The kids traveled well, though Mari had trouble keeping up with adult strides. When they stopped for lunch, the boys chided her for lagging. Mari began to cling to Willa for respite, showing her growing trust for the elven woman.

A few uneventful hours later they spotted Pirathon nestled into the northwest face of Mount Gerizim. As they walked down the south road into town they passed several small farms. There were many people working and walking about. The family of six drew less attention than the wolf that seemed to be following them. There was no wall around Pirathon and the northern entrance to the city held a large market area. There were vendors with crates, carts and tables hawking their wares. Some tried to entice them to buy as they walked near their goods. The younger kids seemed a bit wary of all the activity and noise, so Willa and Wren kept them close. Azor stayed at Jonah's side, almost mimicking his actions as they traversed the chaotic scene.

Suddenly a voice rang out, "Wren, you made it!"

Wren turned to see her friend Madisyn in all her fire genasi glory. "Madisyn! You made great time getting here."

"You said you had followers of Adonai in need, so we came running." She said extending a hand to the young man and woman with her. The brass skinned woman with scaly black patches, pointy ears and small horns on her forehead looked over at the children, "You must be Azor, Zadok and Mari."

They all nodded, seemingly entranced by her yellow-orange hair that seemed to flicker like a fire even in the daylight.

"Excellent!" The garishly dressed woman continued, "Your new friends here asked us to bring you to their home, a safe place we call Haven. I brought my friends Madran and Anneth with me." She turned to give the kids a look at the lute slung across her back, "Madran is squire to a knight named Chapel and Anneth is a student of our Rabbi Barnabas."

Willa embraced her friend and colleague, Anneth, then introduced her to the kids. The two women hadn't seen each other in weeks and were each thrilled to see the other doing well.

Jonah greeted Madran, "Well met! I don't know your patron personally, but it is good to meet you. This is Azor, he is the eldest of the siblings and may have some interest in your chosen service to the community."

"Good to finally meet you as well, Jonah," the half-elven man of about twenty replied. "Word of your family's exploits gets around Haven. I'm happy to put faces to the names."

Wren looked at Madisyn, "when are you heading back?"

"As soon as our companions are ready to go," she replied. "We want to be back to Haven just after dark."

Wren nodded understanding protocols for entering the underground from the ruined city above. "It might be best for the kids to be spared the worst of that scene anyway."

Madisyn looked down at Mari, who was peeking out from behind Willa, "Do you know how to ride a horse? I like to play travel songs, but I can't while I am holding the reins."

Mari nodded excitedly, stepping out a bit.

"Well, let's go get those horses and be on our way," Madisyn's voice was almost a song as she held out her hand to the girl.

Willa saw that Mari was staring up at her expectantly. She hugged the girl tightly, "We will come find you as soon as we get back. I promise!"

Mari nodded and smiled, then grabbed Madisyn's hand.

The bard pulled the girl close, "When should we expect you all back home?"

Jonah replied, "Tomorrow, we hope."

Wren added, "I'll check in if plans change."

The friends bid each other farewell and went their separate ways, the family heading into Pirathon and the rest heading out of town and back to Haven.

This was the first town they had visited since heading north that seemed unaffected by the threat of war. People went about their days working, buying and selling. They seemed to be living their lives to the fullest. Jonah thought they should get a room at the inn then explore the town for clues about Abdon. The dream about this judge was short and focused only on a wedding and a farmhouse near mountains so they did have at least a couple of leads.

As the family neared the business center of town, Willa noticed a large group of people heading in the same direction. She knew better than to assume a coincidence when God was involved. She urged Jonah and Wren to follow her as she trailed the locals. They cut through an alley then up a street and into another alley before coming to a closed gate. Dusk was beginning to settle over the town as the gate opened and the people began to stream in pushing Willa along with them. Jonah, Wren and Leo followed instinctively.

They were greeted fondly by an older couple and a young woman. The young woman, a strawberry blond haired half-elf of about thirty years, introduced herself as Poppy, the wedding planner. She directed people to the coat room, the stables for pets and gifts of livestock, and the main celebration area. The family went to the stable first. They found Leo a comfortable spot there, stowing their armor, gear and weapons for him to guard. They gave him some food and left him to get some well-deserved rest. Wren scratched him on his neck, under his chin. The wolf closed his eyes, loving every moment of the attention.

Returning to the reception line they first met an older couple at the front who called themselves Felix and Farah, the parents of the bride. They passed the trio off to the parents of the groom, Rymon and Jué. Next, they met the best man Rogeet and the bridesmaids. Willa and Wren, both thought it was odd that the bridesmaids and the bride were dressed exactly the same. Finally, they were introduced to the newlyweds, Canda and Jethro. As they left the reception line Willa realized that no one, including the bride and groom, asked why they were at this wedding or who they knew. They were simply welcomed as if they were old friends or distant relations. Jonah chose a table near the back of the room and sat with his back to the wall for a better view of the space.

He surveyed the rather gaudy estate as was his habit to do when in new public places. He remembered that the other homes they had passed in town were modest, but this one was large, well-appointed and impeccably well-kept. Various servants met every guest's needs. There were fresh flowers at every table in this large, enclosed courtyard. The main table for the wedding party boasted a handmade lattice-work arch that framed the bride and groom's seats. There were ornate lanterns throughout the area providing comforting light as the sun receded and invited in the night. Every detail had been considered. This was clearly an important event in Pirathon. Jonah suddenly felt out of place.

As the last guests trickled in and were seated the gate was closed and Felix walked to the front, "Friends, neighbors, and other guests who saw fit to celebrate with us today, welcome to our home. Please indulge yourselves in food and wine, dance and revel in this moment as our only daughter Canda has found her husband the good man Jethro. Enjoy with us," he pulled his wife closer to him for effect, "this once in a lifetime moment."

There was a smattering of modest applause. The bard and her minstrels began to play softly while food and wine were brought to each table. Jonah, Willa and Wren enjoyed the feast, watching and listening to these strangers as they chatted and gossiped through the meal. They almost felt like they knew some of these people by the end of dinner. They had learned that Jué was all about appearances and had little substance. They learned that Poppy, the wedding planner, had once been courted by the groom, but the engagement ended abruptly. They were surprised she was here working on this, of all, weddings. They were also told that the best man Rogeet was a grifter, and that Dukaril the camel farmer had only come because the groom's family owed him money.

After dinner the tables were cleared, and the guests began to mill about and mingle. Now deeper in their cups they began spreading all the gossip they had heard from their table mates at dinner. Despite all the gossip, Willa and Wren seemed to be in their glory at this event. They didn't even show signs of embarrassment at not being dressed for the occasion. They mingled around introducing themselves as Ambassadors of the Temple of Adonai, sharing his word with any who would listen. Some showed interest, while many politely excused themselves at the mention of God.

Jonah continued to patrol the place. He took in the atmosphere, the guests and the staff as if he had been hired on as security. Jonah had just found the back door and was heading back to the party in the courtyard when he noticed Felix coming his way.

"Excuse me, Jonah, was it?" The man's face looked strained.

"Yes, Felix, that's right," Jonah replied. "Are you ill? You look a little green."

"Oh, I'll be fine," he assured the stranger in armor. "I just need some air. Family can be difficult and all of them at once is nothing I would wish on an enemy."

Jonah chuckled at that. He fully understood the comment coming from a family that could be a bit much at times. As Jonah returned to the party, he heard the back door open, then close.

The revelry continued as the minstrels stepped up the pace of their songs and people began to dance. Some dancers looked intimate, others looked like they were doing it for show, and still others talked the whole time, probably making deals.

Jonah spotted his wife in the crowd holding court with some other women. He approached and tapped her on the shoulder, "Would the lady care to dance?"

Willa turned to respond, "What? You want to dance? Who are you and what have you done with my husband?"

"Only with you, milady," Jonah answered. "Only with you."

Wren watched from their table. Seeing her parents enjoying each other's company instead of always in protective mode brought a smile to her face. She wondered if anyone would ask her to dance. Tabaxi were apparently rare around here as she had seen many diverse guests but no others of her kind. Her question was soon answered as a young human boy asked for a dance. He was clearly dared to do it by his older sister, but Wren didn't care a bit. She smiled broadly and they twirled around the dance floor as if they were Cinderella and the prince.

Jonah noticed that Poppy had come running in from outside looking distraught. She went straight to the thirty-something human bartender, who promptly went back outside with her. Jonah returned his wife to her group, bowed politely then went to the back door to see what had made the young woman so upset.

The backyard was impressive. To the left were sheep pens. The young shepherd was settling the livestock after a day grazing in the grassy hills nearby. To the right was an elaborate archway decorated professionally with flowers and woven silks. This must have been where the wedding ceremony was held. Just behind the archway was an idyllic pond. It would be hard to imagine a more beautiful backdrop for this wedding. Poppy and the bartender were crouched down by the water's edge. As Jonah approached, they both turned with a start. In the water before them, clearly dead, was Felix, face-down, wisps of blood mingling into the water near his head.

"I found him like this when I came out to get water from the well," Poppy pleaded, through tears.

"Stay calm," Jonah said, placing his hand on her shoulder for comfort. "What is your name?" He asked, looking at the man he recognized as the bartender.

"I am Caviner," The human male replied without taking his eyes off the corpse. "I am part of Poppy's staff for the event."

"We need to call the authorities," Jonah announced.

Poppy regained some composure at the suggestion. "We need to find out who did this first. The authorities around here are likely to just blame the help. They won't even look at the wealthy guests as suspects."

Jonah didn't like this idea much but his lack of understanding of this culture swayed his decision. "If we are going to investigate this, we can't just leave the body here."

"The caretaker is away," Poppy announced, pointing at a small but pretty shack among some trees over by the stables.

"Caviner, help me get the body there," Jonah began, before noticing that the man was distracted by something in the tall grass along the water. Jonah watched as he stepped away then leaned down to pick something up. "Don't touch it, Caviner!"

Caviner stood up straight, startled by the much taller man's forcefulness.

"Sorry," Jonah apologized. "There may be clues from the killer on it." Jonah grabbed a nearby stick working it into the handle of what turned out to be a brass wine decanter. Jonah noticed it had a dent in it with blood and hair caked on it. "See, evidence."

Poppy looked it over as well, "There is blood by the handle too."

"Yes, good catch," Jonah agreed. "Caviner and I will get everything to the caretaker's shack. Can you find my wife and daughter and have them meet us there?"

Poppy nodded and handed him the house keys she was given for the day before scurrying off back inside the main house.

Once inside the shack, Jonah and Caviner laid Felix's body on a blanket and folded it over him. Jonah had noticed blunt force trauma on the back of the man's head, matching the size of the dent in the decanter. A few minutes later there was a knock on the door. Caviner opened it to let Willa, Wren and Poppy in.

Wren looked around the room while Jonah explained the clues so far. After they were all up-to-date Wren asked, "Poppy, when did you say the caretaker left?"

"Two days ago." She replied. "He took advantage of the event to go see family."

Wren picked up a huge leather boot, "Then why do his work boots have fresh mud on them?" She flipped it around a little, "Oh, and some blood too."

Poppy stammered, "But why would the caretaker…"

Before she could finish Willa interjected, "He didn't." She pointed back at the boots, "See, they are still laced. Only someone small could get them on and off while still laced."

"Ok," Jonah got their attention. "Here's the plan." The aasimar outlined all they had found so far, then gave everyone assignments to investigate further. Poppy and Caviner would keep the party going, serve more wine and listen closely without asking any questions. Willa and Wren would continue to mingle with the women without pressing too hard. Jonah would check out the yard thoroughly then head inside to mingle with the men. In thirty minutes, they would regroup in the shack to share information. Jonah resisted the urge to say 'Ready, break' when the huddle split. It wasn't the right time, nor would the locals have understood the earth colloquialism.

Poppy and Caviner went back to the party first. A few minutes later Willa and Wren followed. Jonah went back to the yard scouring it thoroughly. First, he found small footprints in the grass from the shack to the stable. He stopped in, to check on Leo. On his way back out he couldn't find the small prints leaving the stable, only larger ones the size of the muddy boots they found in the shack. He followed them around the house then down to the pond near where they had found the decanter. Looking more closely he saw blood splattered on the mud and tall grass. The large boot prints then led into a bunch of trees ending there in a disturbed area of dirt and grass. It seemed like the person changed back to the small shoes then went back to the shack. Finally, the smaller prints led to the house at the same back door.

As Jonah was entering the back door to return to the party he spotted some vomit in the bushes. He remembered seeing Felix exit there earlier, claiming he didn't feel well. Jonah collected some in a handkerchief that was in his pocket. Finding no other clues in the yard, he went back to the shack to secure the new evidence before rejoining the party.

Jonah saw the others doing what he had assigned to them, so he jumped right into his assignment. He spoke first with Rymon, the father of the groom, finding him to be aloof and completely self-centered. The way he kept looking at his wife Jué, anytime anyone asked him a question, Jonah could tell that she made the decisions in the family. Rabbi Tarik was an insufferable man. The volume of his demands was only exceeded by the sheer number of complaints he issued, to all who would listen. He didn't seem impressed when Jonah mentioned their faith in Adonai and offered no insight when Jonah asked him about the judge Abdon. Men of God, in title only, like Tarik, were common on Earth too, so Jonah was not surprised.

Rogeet had been Jethro's best friend since Torah school. Jonah could see that he was something of a grifter. Jonah overheard him asking for 'investors' for multiple money-making schemes. He only took time away from the grift to give attention to various ladies-in-waiting. Jonah couldn't help but notice that Rogeet gave one particular table a wide berth. This piqued his curiosity. As he watched the elder, heavy-set, turbaned man sitting there, he noticed that everyone gave him space.

Jonah approached the large man and introduced himself. "Hello, I am Jonah. Are you with the bride or the groom?"

Dukaril eyed him for a few moments before answering, "I am Dukaril," the man grunted. "I was invited because both families owe me money." He looked around the room slowly. "I think everyone here owes me money."

"That must be why they all seem to avoid you," Jonah quipped to see the man's reaction.

Dukaril laughed, "Yes, this is true. I like you Jonah, and you owe me nothing. Sit and have a drink."

Jonah sat and the two men talked for a while. He learned more from this man than everyone else combined. The wine was sweet and not potent, which was fine with Jonah who rarely if ever drank alcohol. He assumed it to be what his study Bible referred to as the 'new wine'. After a glass and some great conversation Jonah excused himself. He saw Willa and Wren go out the back, so he went to Caviner's station. He saw the bartender leave through the front door, so Jonah went out the back. He passed Poppy on the way. She was setting up the next wedding tradition before sneaking away. He could tell by the atmosphere that no one was aware of the incident just yet, except for the killer, of course. He scanned the room one last time then headed to the shack.

Poppy was the last to arrive at the caretaker's home. Jonah quickly caught everyone up on his findings. Of all the men he spoke to or heard about, only Dukaril, Rymon, and Jethro had any motive. Thinking it all the way through though, it made no sense for Dukaril to kill someone who owed him money. Rymon was a typical self-absorbed dilettante. If he was getting attention, he was content. Jethro could have held a grudge about the job situation, but to kill the father of his bride on their wedding day would take an extreme level of anger.

Caviner had overheard a lot of gossip from his station. Of the most interesting tidbits was when two town gossips, Clauta and Wistra, were discussing a conversation they had with Jué the previous week. Wistra had congratulated her on Jethro's new job working for Dukaril. She described Jué's reaction as 'a full-on tantrum'. She had expected Felix to hire Jethro after the wedding and was enraged at the thought of her son leaving town. The attentive bartender also saw the bard, Gloril, hovering near Rymon more than seemed normal. Whenever Rymon noticed her encroaching he looked around guiltily and moved away to mingle. He was certain that this little dance was evidence of something more between those two.

Poppy started her recap by freely admitting that she was once engaged to Jethro. A short time into the courtship, rumors began to swirl about everything from her purity to the fact that she was socially climbing through this relationship. All the negative attention became too much for Jethro, who was coddled through life by his overbearing mother and flaky father. He disengaged and the relationship fell apart.

Caviner was visibly angered by this story. Jonah could tell that the young bartender had unexpressed feelings for Poppy, but that was an issue for later.

Poppy gathered her strength with a deep sigh and continued. She told them that Farah, the bride's mother, hired Poppy for the wedding and told her she didn't believe the lies that had been spread about her. Poppy had wondered if her hiring was intended as a passive shot at Jué, rather than for her personal benefit. At the end of the day she didn't care, this would be the event of the season and if handled correctly it could propel her career to untold heights. Willa and Wren comforted Poppy as she paused to see if any accusations would come her way. They didn't, so she moved on to relate what she had seen while inside.

Poppy had been positioned near Wistra while handling event details. The woman was insufferable. She bent the ear of every person who passed her orbit with gossip about someone else out of earshot. She accused Rymon of having an affair, Jué of framing poor Poppy, and even claimed Jethro was leaving town for a job to get away from his parent's drinking and wanton behavior.

Willa and Wren then each took their turns. Willa had heard some of the same rumors as the others. She had also learned that Rymon and Jué were in dire financial straits. Their lavish living was quickly wasting their wealth. Willa overheard Clauta tell Gloril that Rogeet was angry with Felix. She claimed that Rogeet wanted to borrow money from him to pay back Dukaril for one of his schemes that had gone wrong. Rogeet would then work for Felix to pay it off. She claimed that Felix backed out of the arrangement and told Rogeet that employing a grifter wouldn't look good to his clients. While this strengthened the rumor that Felix was trying to clean up his business, it still left Rogeet unemployed and on the hook with Dukaril.

Willa purposely withheld that she had heard a similar version of Poppy's story from Wistra. Poppy had come forward with it honestly, confirming the facts, so there was no reason to bring it up again. She did, however, tell Poppy that the gossipers seemed certain that Jué had started all the rumors to get Poppy out of the picture so Jethro could marry into a wealthy family. Willa could tell that the revelation wasn't news to Poppy, she almost seemed relieved at the confirmation.

Wren had decided to take a different approach. She went full on CSI. First, she retraced Felix's steps to see if any other clues presented themselves. She started at the table where he was seated for dinner. His plate had been cleared but his wine glass was still there and had been refilled. She held it up to the light and could see something gathering at the bottom. She went to the kitchen and carefully emptied the glass revealing some kind of detritus in the bottom. Between her keen sense of smell and her druidic training she knew it was Monkshood, more commonly known as Wolfsbane. She informed the group that it wasn't enough to kill him but explained his nausea.

As she was leaving the kitchen after her experiment, she walked in on a conversation between Rogeet and Gloril. He was hitting on her, but she was clearly distracted, watching Rymon and Jué having one of those public arguments where both parties aggressively whisper through gritted teeth. Canda, the bride, wandered by asking Rogeet if he had seen her father. He responded that he hoped the old man had dropped dead somewhere. Canda responded, "A class act as always." and stormed off.

"Ok," Jonah exhaled, "great job everyone. We seem to have several suspects. Let's each name our prime suspect right now."

Caviner barked, "Jué, nothing is beyond her ability for selfishness." He couldn't take his eyes off Poppy when he said it.

Poppy hesitated, "Rogeet seems to have motive, and he'd go to any lengths to avoid responsibility."

Willa spoke next, "Though none of us found evidence of it, I don't think we can rule out his wife Farah. Drugging and bashing someone's head in, is extremely intimate and personal."

"Always the wife," Jonah agreed with a wry smile, prompting a slap on the shoulder from Willa.

"Focus up, you two," Wren chided, embarrassed by her parents' flirting. "Since we are talking family, don't we have to leave Jethro in the mix? He did get snubbed by Felix for a job. Maybe he decided to take a shortcut to the family fortune."

Jonah nodded in agreement at the choices, "Unfortunately, I think both Poppy and Caviner could be suspected as well."

"What?" Caviner exclaimed forcefully. "How dare you!"

Poppy placed her hand on his forearm, "He's right. We both have our reasons to hate and distrust them."

"Please, understand that we don't suspect you," Jonah explained, while both Willa and Wren nodded. "You are not family and fingers have been pointed at you before. You are both easy targets when word of this crime becomes public."

Caviner had calmed, though his face was still flush, "How do we clear ourselves?"

"Simple," Wren answered. "We figure out who did it. If I know my dad, he has a plan to flush them out."

"As a matter of fact, I do," Jonah went to the caretaker's desk and grabbed some parchment and a writing quill. "I need this written in Hebrew."

Poppy took the quill hesitantly, wondering what the large man had in mind.

Jonah thought for a second, "Just write this, 'I saw what you did, and I have the evidence. Meet me where you left the boots to negotiate for my silence'."

Poppy translated it exactly, "Ok, there you go."

"Great," Jonah replied, "now give me three more just like it."

As Poppy wrote them Jonah sealed them with wax and wrote the names Jué, Rogeet, Farah, and Jethro on them. "Have one of your servers deliver them then get back here. We will wait and see who shows up." Jonah looked as if something dawned on him, "I have one quick thing to do. I'll be right back." He and Poppy left while the others doused the lamps and hid.

A short time later Jonah and Poppy returned from their tasks. They concealed themselves and waited silently with the others. The click of the lock on the front door rang out in the silence like a gunshot. A figure entered and closed the door softly. They stood there quietly for a moment waiting for their eyes to adjust to the darkness. After a moment they hunched by the door where Wren had found the boots. There was an audible inhalation in surprise when they weren't there.

"I'm here," a woman's voice whispered.

"In here," a man's voice softly replied from the bedroom. The door, just slightly ajar, creaked open. The shadowy figure looked over her shoulder one last time out of paranoia before pushing into the pitch-dark room. Leaving the door open, she lit a small lamp. As the light bathed the room it revealed the person holding it to be Jué. The first thing she saw was the bare-fanged face of a large gray wolf. Felix's body and the other evidence was on the floor right behind him. Leo growled at the woman, who stepped back in surprise, bumping into a firm object behind her.

Wren said, "Let there be light," and the pendant she had found in the basement of the Jericho jail lit up the area.

Jué turned to find Jonah, Wren, and Poppy standing in the doorway and hallway. Caviner was in the corner of the room having provided the whispered voice.

"I shouldn't be surprised it was you," Poppy said calmly.

"Surely I don't know what you are talking about," the woman was a well-practiced liar.

Just then Willa arrived with Farah, Jethro and Canda in tow, along with two Mishtala city guards. Farah ran shrieking to her husband's body, uncovering him and sobbing uncontrollably. Jethro tried to comfort his new wife and her mother through his own tears.

Jonah started to speak to the Mishtala but then looked at Poppy, "I think you should explain."

Before Poppy could start Jué started screaming, "She's an unclean woman, you can't seriously believe what she says!"

Caviner stepped forward, very close to the woman's face, "Be quiet, your lies have caused enough pain." The two Mishtala stepped into the room and placed manacles on the woman.

"Please proceed," the taller guard said to Poppy.

"Yes, sir," she looked at her friends who all nodded in solidarity. "She is the mother of the groom. She is a manipulator, a gossip and just not a good person at all. She committed this crime for selfish reasons. She arranged this marriage to get into a wealthy family."

"We are wealthy," Jué spat, straining against her manacles.

"Word around town is that she and her husband have wasted his inheritance," Poppy replied calmly.

"Easy enough to check out," the female guard added. "Go on."

Jué had no response to that statement.

Poppy nodded, "When she found out her son was going to work out of town for a camel breeder instead of joining Felix's business, it was too much for her."

Jethro looked at his mother, "Seriously? You killed him over that? He arranged the job with Dukaril for one year to get me experience and to prove my devotion to his daughter. I was happy to do it and grateful for the opportunity. He had every intention of bringing me into his business after I proved myself and he got it cleaned up."

Jué looked down at her son, shedding no tears at her mistake, "Everything I have ever done was for you…"

"Liar, it was all for you," Farah screeched, leaping to the bound woman and slapping her hard in the face. "If your son saw any benefit, it was merely due to his proximity to you. I have no idea how such a good man came from your dysfunction, but he is our family now. You should die for what you have done."

The tall guard held Farah back, "I understand your grief, but don't hit her again." He looked back at Poppy, "the story is convincing, but do you have any actual evidence?"

Poppy looked to Jonah, "Jonah can you explain that part, please?"

Jonah cleared his throat, "There is a lot, so please bear with me." Both guards nodded. Jonah retraced the investigation starting with finding the body and the decanter. He explained the two sets of boot prints and the vomit outside. He tied that to the poisoned wine and the Monkshood.

Wren stepped forward, "Dad, we can confirm two more pieces of evidence right now." The guards turned their attention to her. "May I touch Jué?"

The taller guard nodded tentatively.

Wren pulled off her white glove to show the cut on her hand, "We found blood on the broken handle of the decanter. She swung it so hard she broke the handle and cut herself."

The guards nodded in agreement and tightened their grip on the prisoner. "And the second thing?"

Wren lifted the hem of the woman's dress the petticoat underneath was caked with dry mud as were her shoes, "These will match the smaller set of footprints in the yard. She used the gardener's boots when she did the actual killing then changed back to confuse the tracks."

The female guard, fully convinced, said, "Well done people. Are you all willing to sign statements about all of this?" They all nodded. "Come to the guard house in the morning."

As they began to haul Jué out of the shack she snapped, screaming, "Jethro help me. I have always helped you. Get your father, he will help me." The guards lifted under her arms and carried her out. Many of the wedding guests had gathered in the yard outside the shack, other guards keeping them away from the footprint evidence and the pond. None of them made eye contact with Jué as she was escorted past them, begging them for help.

When they got to Rymon, he could only manage, "Why?"

"I did what you couldn't, for our family." she screamed, spraying spittle in her rage.

Rymon looked at the ground, a tear on his face, and went into the shack to find his son.

The party guests stayed to comfort the families, or continue their gossip, some did both.

A man approached Jonah and introduced himself. "I am Benaia, the town Rabbi and father to Rogeet."

Willa couldn't resist asking, "If you are the town Rabbi why didn't you perform the ceremony?"

"Let's just say my son's reputation has been a problem for our family in the community," he responded tactfully. "I overheard Jonah asking Rabbi Tarik about Abdon, the judge of Adonai. I thought this day would never come." He handed Jonah a scroll case, "This has been in my family for generations. We were told the faithful of Adonai would come asking after Abdon and would perform a great service to the community. This is clearly meant for you."

"Thank you," Jonah bowed slightly, unsure what to do.

Farah insisted that the family stay in her house for the night. She assigned some staff to see to the needs of the trio then retired to her room to grieve. Jethro and Canda stayed with her there. Jonah and Willa were glad to have a bed to sleep in, and a comfortable one at that. They opened the scroll case and found a map rolled up inside of a spell scroll. Willa unrolled the scroll and found it to be Protection from Energy, which would certainly come in handy. She rolled it back up and replaced it in the scroll case for safe keeping. Jonah examined the map. It showed the way to an old farm on the western outskirts of Pirathon. The map legend said that the farm was rumored to have been built by Abdon himself with the help of his forty sons.

They planned to go there in the morning after stopping at the guardhouse to give them their statements. They called it a night, exhausted from the events. Wren gave her parents some privacy, choosing to sleep in the stable with Leo.

In the morning, they regrouped for breakfast provided by the house staff. Jethro welcomed the family to the table and made apologies for his wife and her mother's absence. Jonah spoke for his wife and daughter, offering sincere condolences and Willa asked if they could pray with him. The young man hesitated but then agreed.

"Father God," Willa began, "Lord of all that was, and is, and is to come. We thank you for this glorious day and the opportunity to do your will. We come to you in lament and supplication for this family in pain. Please give Farah and Canda comfort and peace in their grief. Give Jethro and Rymon strength and wisdom to guide their families through this tragedy. Lord, give Jué the wisdom to understand her crimes and the heart to seek forgiveness. We are just your servants,

Lord, but if there is anything we can do, guide our words and steps and we will see it done. In your glorious and mighty name, we pray. Amen"

"Thank you," Jethro managed, holding back tears. He was quiet for a few moments, but clearly looked like he wanted to say something. They all allowed him time to gather his thoughts. "Can you tell me why your benevolent God would allow this?" His voice was shaky but calm, despite the obvious emotion behind the question.

Jonah turned his chair to look into the man's eyes. "God created a world without sin, evil and death, but he knew his creation couldn't resist them. Adam and Eve chose to defy God to try to be more like him, as any of us would have. This released evil into his world. God wants all of us to choose him and resist the temptation of sin, but he knows many of us won't. This evil act wasn't caused by God, it was the result of Jué rejecting him."

"Can I ask you a question?" Willa's voice was soft, her hand on Jethro's forearm, comforting him. He nodded. "As a child who did you run to for comfort after a fall or a heartbreak?"

"My parents," He replied.

"That's what we should do with God as well." Willa looked into his eyes. "Don't run from him in your time of need, seek his face, his comfort."

"It will take time," Jonah added, "but you must forgive your mother. Until you are ready to do that, serve the rest of your family. They need your strength now, and you need Adonai's."

Jethro nodded as tears now flowed freely. Jonah sent Wren to feed Leo and get him ready to go, while he and Willa comforted Jethro.

Soon they said their goodbyes to their host, thanking him for the hospitality. They made their way to the guard house where they wrote and signed their statements. Caviner walked in as they were leaving. Jonah pulled him aside and recommended that he get over whatever was holding him back from telling Poppy how he felt. He tried to deny his feelings for her, but he couldn't pull it off. He reluctantly agreed as sweat formed on his brow at the thought of it.

Chapter 15
Fierce Princess

The farmhouse was easy to find using the map from Benaia. The property was abandoned and clearly hadn't been kept in years. The fields were overgrown with everything but crops. A sad and lonely scarecrow was the only remnant of a time when life and growth was prominent in this place. Willa suggested they split up to search for clues around the place more quickly. Jonah went to the barn, Willa the stables and Wren the house.

Wren picked the lock on the front door with ease, she was getting pretty good at simple locks. The house was abandoned and empty. She searched thoroughly for secret compartments in various empty, dusty rooms but found nothing.

Willa entered the stables cautiously. The structure was in good condition considering how long ago this farm had fallen into disuse. She found nothing of note until she reached the last two stalls. One had a pile of straw, grass and weeds spread in a five-foot square. The other had a large area of dried blood in the dirt and many tiny bones, probably a bird or rodent. As she examined the remains a shadow loomed over her.

"Jonah," she called out, "I found something."

By the time she realized it wasn't Jonah it was too late, A black gloved hand covered her mouth preventing her scream.

It was dark inside the barn despite the sunny day. Jonah saw nothing of use in this place as his eyes adjusted to the darkness. He turned and looked out the main doors at the fields. Something was different in the unkempt fields. It took him a second to realize that the scarecrow he had seen there before was gone. He shuddered at the thought of that thing being alive, as he instinctively looked over his shoulder. Shaking off his fear he ran to find his family. As he exited the barn, he saw Wren coming around the house.

They made eye contact. She could see concern on his face and looked back inquisitively. He pointed at his eyes, then the stables, then he pushed both hands toward the ground. She knew this signal meant that they were going to check out the stables, but quietly. She almost laughed, remembering all the times she asked her dad why she needed to know these military-like signals. He always said, "Expect the best, but prepare for the worst." As was often the case, he had been right.

Wren commanded Leo to stay outside the stable and wait for her call. Then she and Jonah entered the building, weapons drawn, using swat-like maneuvers. Each clearing a sight line before telling the other to move. They cleared the entrance then moved in further, clearing each row of stalls. As they neared the last set, Wren held up a fist causing Jonah to freeze in place. She could see her mother sitting on the ground tearing off pieces of bread and giving them to someone or something she couldn't see from her angle.

Willa looked over at her and held up a flat hand showing they should wait. "Eat as much as you like," she said. "My family is here, are you ready to meet them?"

They could hear shuffling in the debris on the ground and a soft thump as something hit the back of the stall.

"Don't be afraid," Willa instructed calmly. "We will not hurt you." She gave them the signal to come forward without looking away from her guest.

Jonah and Wren put away their weapons and stepped out into the opening. They saw what appeared to be a girl a little smaller than Wren. In the shadows they could see that she had gray-white skin and an almost featureless face.

Willa held out a hand to the girl, "It's ok, they are safe." She introduced Jonah and Wren then said, "This is…"

"JazSaraénteramin," the girl repeated.

"Can we call you Saraé for short? It means fierce princess in Hebrew." Willa asked.

The girl, who had been staring at Jonah and Wren turned to Willa and shrugged noncommittally. "Alright then Saraé, show them what you can do," she encouraged the girl, who relaxed slightly. "Can you look like Mr. Jonah?"

What they heard made them wince. The shifting of bones and tendons made sounds no one should ever have to hear. When they reopened their eyes, she had stepped forward into the light. She was a nearly exact duplicate of Jonah but about a foot and a half shorter.

"What kind of creature are you, Saraé?" Jonah realized at once how insensitively the question was worded.

Saraé, back in her normal form, looked at him, tilted her head and replied, 'messenger'. She reached into her burlap scarecrow clothing and handed Jonah a scroll.

Jonah unrolled it, finding it to be two separate scrolls. One was a very detailed map of the grounds. It was exact, down to the tree placement. There was a mark by the door to the house.

The other was entirely text, written in Hebrew. He handed that one to Willa for translation.

The cleric read it aloud, "Adonai, we praise you for your providence, all questions are answered in your time whether we understand them or not, now those who camp on the <u>east</u> side toward the sunrise shall be of the standard of the camp of Judah, by their armies, and the leader of the sons of Judah." Under that scripture was written, "Numbers 2:3-25." She continued reading the next part, "Early the next morning Laban kissed his grandchildren and his daughters and blessed them. Then he <u>left</u> and returned home." This scripture was identified as "Genesis 31:55." Finally, she read the last scripture, "For they have gone up to Assyria_like a wild donkey wandering alone. Ephraim has sold herself to lovers." This part was noted as, "Hosea 8:9." Below that was a final instruction, "Dig deep for your faith, only the righteous can accept the gift of life."

Wren almost squealed, causing Leo to come running. The wolf stopped short when he saw Saraé. He tentatively sniffed around the girl then nudged her with his nose.

Saraé looked Leo over then rubbed his ears gently, "Wolf." Leo sat next to his new friend to everyone's amazement.

Momentarily enthralled by this interaction, Wren gathered herself and said, "I think it's a treasure map and the clues are in the scriptures." She looked up and to the left as she tried to recall the details of Abdon's part in the book of Judges. "He had forty sons and thirty grandsons, who rode on seventy donkeys, and he judged Israel 8 years."

Willa noted that the word son was used in the scripture from Numbers as was the direction east.

Jonah walked to the front of the house by the door, the location shown on the map. He turned and faced them, "forty sons and east." He began counting as he paced in that direction. When he reached forty, he turned and faced them again.

"Does the next verse mention grandchildren?" Wren had asked the question, but she was certain she already knew the answer.

Willa replied also not surprised, "Yes, but the only direction mentioned this time is left."

Jonah nodded, "Thirty grandsons and left." He paced back the way he came, stopping this time at thirty paces. He nodded for Willa and Wren to continue, turning again to face them.

Saraé had sat cross-legged by a tree, Leo lay next to her legs. This was very unusual for their companion who was usually unnecessarily wary of strangers.

Willa didn't even wait for Wren to ask this time, "The third scripture mentions donkeys, but no specific direction, though it says they went up to Assyria."

Jonah didn't hesitate. He explained as he paced seventy steps away from the house. "Assyria is north, we were just there." When he reached the seventieth step he stopped. "What's next?" He expected one more clue to correspond to the eight years Abdon served as judge.

Willa read the last clue, "It says, dig deep for your faith."

"I guess it is eight feet down," Jonah replied. "Wren, stand here. I'll check the barn and stables for shovels."

Just then Saraé appeared at his side looking up at him with a shovel in each hand.

"Where did you even get these?"

Saraé shrugged, then sat back down and continued sharing the bread Willa had given to her with the wolf.

Sure enough, eight feet later Jonah and Willa, with the help of Wren's prayer of *shifting earth*, hit something solid. It was another box, this time a wide flat container about three feet long, two feet wide and six inches deep. Jonah pulled it out of the ground and opened it. Inside was a gleaming four-pointed shield, reminiscent of medieval shields on Earth. It was steel, from the weight, but plated with silver and decorated with a gold inlay around the edge. As soon as Jonah placed it on his arm an image began to form on the face. In seconds it was complete depicting the tree of Yahweh symbol they had seen many times in Haven.

Willa and Wren said almost in unison, "Clearly that's meant for you," before returning their attention to Saraé.

"This thing feels great," Jonah exclaimed. "Uhh, there's a scroll inside this box that has Saraé's full name on it." He brought the scroll over and handed it to the girl.

Saraé unrolled it and began to read it aloud. JazSaraénteramin, you are now free. The curse that was so callously put upon you by men who shirked their duty, is now lifted by the faith and perseverance of these people who have selflessly surrendered to the will of the One True God, Adonai. Your life is now your own to do with as you will. The Lord will only say that your past loneliness has left you a prisoner to your whims. The path of righteousness is open to you now if you choose it. You need no longer be alone. He has sent to you His adopted children and they will raise you as their own. The choice is yours. Yesterday you were a doppelganger, today you are a new creation in His image. This is your new primary form. Use your abilities to serve Adonai's people and spread His gospel. As of today, you are a daughter. He is with you always.

Her eyes welled up with tears as she read. She wiped them away twice to be able to continue. As she was reading the words her shape had changed again, as if involuntarily. This time the change was softer and far less painful sounding. Her features became those of a pre-teen girl with dark skin, curly black hair, brown eyes, high cheekbones, slightly pointed ears and a small button-nose. As she finished, she looked up at the three people watching her read.

"It is your choice Saraé," Willa looked at Jonah and Wren, whose eyes were as puffy as hers. "Will you let us be your family?"

"It says I shouldn't be alone anymore," the girl answered, waving the scroll. Her voice was a bit deeper now and her use of their language was improving by the minute.

"He's not wrong." Willa replied in agreement. "Adonai never is."

"Adonai says I am free," she answered. "He said he sent you for me. He said I am a new creation." She grabbed Willa's hand. "JazSaraénteramin the doppelganger is gone, I am Saraé now."

Wren took her other hand, "On our world we have stories of many princesses. I'm going to tell you every one of them."

The girl considered it for a moment then nodded, "Yes, please!"

"Welcome to the family Saraé," Wren announced. "I always wanted a little sister."

Jonah lagged and watched as his wife and now two daughters walked northwest toward the western edge of Mount Gerizim. He muttered quietly under his breath, "It's a girl." He chuckled under his breath at his clever 'dad joke'. He had a sudden craving for a cigar. He looked up into the sky, "Thank you for trusting us with this, and with her." He wiped his eyes as he jogged to catch up with his family.

Chapter 16
Aftermath

Elowen was resting under the care of Valmoira and her sister, Althaea. The grove had suddenly become a refugee camp for the displaced earth genasi. The young druid's body was healing quickly but her fractured mind and memory was another thing entirely. She had all her memories back but now they felt like they conflicted with each other. She remembered her life in this place. Being the Grove Warden was an honor long held in her family line, but it no longer felt like her destiny. She rose from her bed gingerly and walked to the open door. Looking out over the grove she saw the familiar faces of her people healing and helping the visitors in every imaginable way. They were still recovering from the corruption themselves but their desire to serve others was undeterred.

Doing their part among the druids and rangers of the grove were her new friends. Azure cared for those in need of healing and prayer just as she had done for her during her time on Earth. Lia, Filipina, and Draco loaded carts with supplies for the refugees who had decided to head northeast to Tyre to seek passage back to their home in the mountains of the Sundered Isle off the coast of the Regency of Lyon. Elowen watched quietly for a time, so much weighing on her mind.

While inventorying her healing and medicinal supplies, Azure found an object she didn't recognize in her pack. This wasn't unusual considering she too had come from Earth, arriving here in an unfamiliar body with no memories of this new place. The object was a small smooth gray stone. She recognized it as a sending stone, a magically imbued stone that acted like an Earth walkie-talkie. She had no idea why she had one nor did she know who had the others. She stared at it for long minutes, unsure whether it was smart to use it. Eventually her curiosity got the best of her. She walked briskly to the small hut she had been given to share with Lia, Shay and Gadget. She was relieved to see that no one was there. She sat on her bedroll on the floor of the shadowy room holding the stone to her mouth, "Is anyone there?"

Moments passed as the eladrin cleric could hear only her own heartbeat. Then, "Azure?" The voice sounded surprised.

"Yes, it is me," she paused, unsure what to say next. "Who am I speaking to?"

"This isn't Azure," the male voice was now angry. "Who are you and how did you get that stone?"

"I assure you that I am Azure," she wondered if that was true, even as she said it. "I found the stone in my pack. I didn't remember where I got it."

"The stone belongs to a friend who let me down," the voice was now calm and measured. "I suggest you get it back to her."

Azure was suddenly afraid. Who was this person? How did he know Azure? She had tried not to think about the logistics of how and why she and Gadget had gotten these bodies upon arrival here. The name, Azure, which had popped into her head the first time she was asked, clearly belonged to someone else. Did they swap bodies with people from here? Was the Azure from here on Earth now running around in Claire's body? Her mind raced. Suddenly, she realized that the man she just spoke to might be able to track her through this object like they had just done to find Rake when he was taken. She sprinted out of the hut and almost tripped over Draco.

"Whoa," the halfling said as he caught her. "What's the hurry?"

"I did something stupid," Azure admitted. "Maybe you can help me."

"Of course! I'm kinda the go-to guy for impulsive behavior." Seeing her seriousness Draco withheld any further banter. "What do you need?"

"How do I prevent someone from tracking an object?"

"There are spells that prevent location," he unconsciously grasped at the pendant around his neck which provided just such protection, though he still had no idea why his mother had given it to him. "If it is a small object, a lead box might work." You could almost see the light bulb turn on behind his eyes as a thought appeared. "How big is the object?"

Azure opened her palm revealing the sending stone.

"Ok," he was now rifling through his own backpack. "Here it is!" He pulled out a small ornate lead box. It had a simple beauty to it only slightly marred by four clamps holding the lid on securely.

Azure opened it and deposited the stone inside. She quickly latched the clamps, "May I hold on to this until I find a permanent solution?"

"Yes," the rogue agreed hesitantly. "Please return it when you can. Something very valuable came to me in that box, I may need it again someday."

"Please don't put me back in that box," the voice in his head that was Shadolok pleaded.

"Never! We are one now." Draco assured his symbiotic other half. *"I just don't know if you'll need it for protection if something were to happen to me."*

"I understand Draco," Shadolok replied telepathically. *"Let's not let anything happen to you."*

"Deal!" Draco responded as he walked away from Azure completely distracted by this silent conversation.

Azure put the box in her pack, shaking her head at Draco's odd behavior, as she walked back to the triage tent.

Elowen had wandered out of her hut. She couldn't see Gadget nearby but if she knew the gnome, she was in a corner inventing something that would save their lives. Rake was talking with Valmoira. He looked more at peace, and a couple hundred years younger than he did a few days ago. Freedom from his family curse looked good on him. She couldn't help but wonder if the choice she would soon have to make would yield a similar result.

Althaea spotted her wandering by, "You shouldn't be up Elowen. Rest, we have everything under control."

"You really do, don't you little sister?" Elowen's voice wavered with emotion. "Can we talk later?"

"After the feast to send off the genasi," Althaea was distracted by her duties enough that she didn't read too much into the question.

"O-ok," sweat formed on her brow at the thought of making this a public pronouncement. She returned to her bed and prayed to Adonai for the very first time since returning to Aeramor. A warm peace enveloped her and within seconds she was asleep.

Elowen suddenly felt heavy and exhausted. She returned to her hut for a short nap, waking a few hours later. She lit a lamp as the sun was low in the tree line causing deep shadows throughout the grove that was already showing signs of recovery. She found her ceremonial robes, the proper dress for the night's event. Tears welled up in her eyes as she set it aside opting for her traveling clothes, which had been cleaned and returned. She began to hear voices and revelry outside.

The feast was beginning. Her duty called and she would answer, despite breaking the hearts of loved ones to do so. As she arrived at the celebration, she saw her friends sitting together at a table near the front of the gathering. This was a place of honor no doubt granted them by Althaea for their efforts to save the grove. She went to them, greeting each of them fondly, deftly deflecting questions about her health.

When she arrived at the seat they had saved for her, she looked up at a table on a raised platform, "I need to be up there." She nodded to her waiting sister cordially, before returning her attention to her friends. "I love you guys, I truly do!"

The entire table remained silent, feeling the awkwardness of the interaction, as she walked to her place among her people.

"She's staying here," Draco blurted out. He was never one to hold back a thought, he barely edited them before spewing them into the world.

"Draco!" Filipina gasped, smacking the halfling on the back of the head.

"Hey," he responded, rubbing his head.

"He's probably right," Gadget added, barely looking up from an object she had been fidgeting with under the table.

"Some sentiments don't need to be voiced," Azure added, "even if they are true."

Althaea stood and called for attention. "Today is a glorious day for so many reasons. The corruption of the grove has finally ended after these long years thanks to new friends and allies. We thank all of you for your part in freeing us from the threat to our very existence." She paused for a moment as the natives of the grove, the genasi and the party all rose to raucously acknowledge one another with applause and cheers. When the roar finally waned Althaea continued. "The selflessness of every person here cannot be denied. I think you will also agree when I say that none of this would have been possible if not for my sister Elowen."

The gathering erupted once again, this time even louder than before. Elowen covered her face with her hands not wanting anyone to see her sobbing. The gathered admirers must have assumed the tears were due to her boundless humility. They were partly, but the tears also came from the decision she was about to make public.

As the gathering took their seats once more, Althaea pulled her sister to her feet beside her. "Elowen braved the unknown, faced demons and twisted people, was thrown to her death, and spared, to recover in another world until she could return to make things right for all of us gathered here." She paused again for the gathered to applaud and cheer. "Today I got my sister back, but I cannot be selfish. She is so much more than just my sister and my hero. She is your Grove Warden."

The cheering this time dwarfed the earlier examples, but quickly faded as Elowen, her face streaked with tears, raised her hands in the air. "Thank you, sister, and all of you. From the time that I was a youngling, I wanted nothing more than to lead you as my mother did and her father before her. That dream came true, and I did my best for you. All that Althaea said was true about the last ten years of my life, but she left out one key thing…Adonai." This time there were gasps and even a few dour looks from the genasi who had been taught to hate the name. "Only God gets the glory for any of this. Adonai spared me in that cave ten years ago. Adonai sent me to His people on Earth to recuperate. Adonai brought me back here in His time, surrounding me with faithful allies to do His will. Only God could have done all of this… Only God!"

Elowen turned and hugged her sister tightly, whispering in her ear, "I love you, don't be angry, but this is what I have to do."

Althaea nodded, a confused but curious look on her face, "I love you too sister, but…"

Before she could finish her question Elowen continued. "Today I made a decision that will affect many here. I prayed about it, and I know my decision is the right one so please understand. I am abdicating the mantle of Grove Warden and officially passing it to my sister Althaea."

The gasps among the gathering were audible. This had never been done before. Althaea's hands covered her mouth in shock, tears running down her face freely.

Elowen turned, took her sister's hands and spoke to her as if they were alone, "You could have wallowed in grief when I was gone, but you didn't. Instead, you did a job no one expected you to do. You held them all together, you protected them when they had lost hope. So many would have died here if you hadn't done those things. You are their Grove Warden."

"But, by birthright, it is yours," she tried to argue.

"You are every bit our mother's daughter as I am." Elowen looked back to the gathering, one hand still holding her sister's. "What do you say friends? Will you continue to follow Althaea, Grove Warden of the Ever Grove?"

The resounding cheer rang out through the forest hardly dampened by the otherwise oppressive darkness. The will of these people was clear. They would follow Althaea wherever she led.

It took a while for the cheers to die down this time. When they did Althaea asked, "What will you do now, Elowen?"

The druid didn't hesitate, "Adonai has called me. I have surrendered my will to Him. I will serve all His people, including any gathered here who choose him. If they accept me, I will continue to do so, with these heroes, Coram Deo," she said with a nod to her friends at the nearby table. "There is much work to do to prepare the people of the Fertile Crescent for what is certainly coming."

Filipina smacked Draco on the back of the head again, "Leaving us huh?"

"I never thought I'd be glad to be wrong," the rogue said with a grin, "but here we are in uncharted territory." At this food and debris from every direction hit the halfling in the face and chest.

The singing and dancing continued well into the night. Shay spent time with her people, Azure answered questions about Adonai, and the rest just enjoyed a rare happy moment amid their mission. Rake touched base with Moonbow. They each caught the other up with current events. The Ranger told him that Barnabas's escort was making its way back from New Vitala. He gave them the cleric's route and asked them to follow it. That way if anything happened, their leader would have support from both directions. Rake agreed, then asked about the spy investigation and Jonah's family. Elmore was making progress on the investigation. He had decided to step it up by floating false information to different people to see which gets a reaction from the enemy. Jonah and his family were doing well and were scheduled to arrive back in Haven that day or the next. They ended the conversation with customary cordiality. Afterward, Rake, Lia, Shay and Filipina plotted the route back to Haven, and they all got some well-earned sleep.

Her misplaced footstep was nothing more than a slight rustle in the leaves, but to the rangers of the Ever Grove on night watch it may as well have been a scream. Instantly the hunched over silhouette of a woman was surrounded by four watchers each with an arrow trained on her head or heart.

"Who are you, stranger?" One of the rangers asked pointedly.

The young woman could barely stand, her long flaming orange hair creeping out from under her hood. She was dirty as if on the road for a long while. She replied between ragged breaths, "My name is Ember. I am seeking a group called Coram Deo, please tell me they are here." With that her red hued eyes rolled back into her head, and she fell to the ground.

The lead watcher thought for a second then said, "You two, get her to the healer's hut, but restrain her first, just in case." Having missed the celebration due to his duty, he turned to the female ranger, "Go alert Althaea and see if she knows who these 'Coram Deo' people might be."

Chapter 17
Home Stretched

Jonah decided that since they were already this far west, they would continue south along the west side of Mount Gerizim to get to Ramah. Once there they could either continue west to the ruins of Bethel or back north entering Haven through the farming community that they had not yet visited. Leo stayed between Wren and Saraé through most of the journey. He seemed unsure whether to trust the doppelganger turned girl just yet and wasn't taking any chances with his favorite person, Wren. Jonah and Willa discussed feeling like they had been away for months, though it had been just weeks. The feeling was understandable considering the difficulty and danger of those days. They reminisced about their accomplishments, their mistakes, their pursuers and their new allies.

The western face of the mountain was as beautiful as anything they had seen in this world or their own. They saw no other travelers as they continued to stay up into the foothills and away from any roads. Around midday they crossed a river that flowed out of the mountain and continued west as far as they could see, presumably to the coast. Wren noticed signs of an abandoned camp near the river. The camp seemed hastily broken. The small campfire was not completely buried, and at least a half dozen footprints including one small set led south. They continued south uneventfully, seeing only wildlife that Wren was able to help the group avoid. The daylight stayed with them much later as they were on the west face of Mount Gerizim, so they continued traveling later than normal.

A soft cold rain started near dusk, so Wren found them a cave to shelter in for the night, near a second river flowing west. In the morning, she spotted signs of another hastily broken camp, not well concealed. She assumed it to be from the same group as before, but the footprints had been marred by the rain. She wondered if they were a family trying to find safety in this dangerous time. She hoped they would catch up with them to tell them about Gilgal.

At some point along the way Jonah suggested that they come back this way after Ramah and check out the farming community. Willa and Wren agreed, curious to see how farming was done on a mountain. They ate, reviewed the dream about Deborah and spent a lot of time helping Saraé adjust to her new normal. They encouraged her to be in whatever form she felt comfortable with when they were alone together. They didn't want her to think that her doppelganger form was unacceptable to them. She seemed to like the new form that Adonai had given her and understood the need to stay in that form when in public. None of them had any idea how they were going to explain her to the people of Haven. That was a problem for tomorrow.

Wren updated Moonbow on their progress. He informed them that Philistia was under attack by the Assyrian army who was now working with the Babylonians. She realized that they must have cut across Judah between Mount Ebal and Mount Gerizim after they had seen them near the Jordan River. The ranger assured her that Madisyn had delivered the kids safely to Gilgal and had made it back to Haven and that Barnabas's missionary team was returning from a successful visit to New Vitala. He held the news of Xof's passing until the end of the discussion, but Wren knew it was coming. She had decided to try an experiment that may produce information helpful to figuring out the reason behind this repetitive event and everyone else's inability to see it. She told Moonbow to spend some time journaling about the tragedy and how it made him feel, then pray over it. She told him they could discuss it when they arrived the next day. He agreed and they signed off.

They woke later than usual in the morning as this side of the mountains stayed deeply shadowed until close to midday. Still, they were on their way south early after a meal and prayer. They continued south then turned east as Mt. Gerizim led them toward Ramah. Once they were on an eastern heading they began to look intently for the tree in their shared dream. After an hour or so Jonah was certain they had to be near Ramah but didn't see any signs of the town just yet. Willa spotted movement in the near distance. It was a young girl in a simple dress picking berries. Leo seemed confused, not really reacting like he normally would when seeing strangers nearby. He whined and circled seemingly unable to understand what his senses were telling him. The girl continued to pick berries, eating some, and placing others in the basket she carried.

Willa approached cautiously, "Shalom."

The girl's head snapped in her direction instantly, a look of terror on her face, though it softened as she seemed to recognize Willa. The girl then looked at each of the others behind the Elven cleric. Her face continued to soften into a playful smile. When the girl's eyes settled upon Saraé she tilted her head as if unsure of what to make of her. Then suddenly she shrugged and smiled and began skipping to the north.

Willa refused to take her eyes off the girl, "Stay back a bit but follow. No sudden movement or loud noises." She began to follow the skipping girl.

The group followed Willa's instructions and followed, staying ten feet back. As she passed the bushes that the girl had been picking from Wren noticed that they were dried out and long dead. No edible fruit had come from these plants in decades, maybe longer. Now concerned as to who they were following she sped up and kept her mother in sight.

The girl continued to skip through the tall grass humming happily until she spotted some people at the top of a hill near a tree. Seeing them she ran to them joyfully. There was a man, and a boy waiting there to greet her. The man was holding the younger boy in one arm as he waved for the girl to come to him with the other hand. When she got to him, he held her tightly against his hip. They looked at Willa for a moment then as one the three of them looked off to their right where a woman was sitting by a palm tree about twenty feet away.

Willa knew instantly that it was the tree from their dream.

The woman was wearing the breastplate of a warrior over a perfect white dress with gold accents. As she stood to meet her visitor, her garb changed to leather armor and plain clothing covered in blood and damage from many battles. Behind her the idyllic view of God's creation was replaced by the scene of the aftermath of a great battle. The bodies of the slain and injured lay strewn about on the ground as soldiers tended to the latter.

Willa was certain this must be Deborah, the only female Judge of the Bible, who led the Israelites with Barak to victory over Sisera and the Canaanites.

Deborah looked directly into Willa's eyes. The cleric had no desire to look away. As Willa watched, the blood on Deborah's clothing began to fade as if washed away. The battlefield scene behind her wavered and became a hill with three crosses. The blood and damage gone, her robes were again the pristine white from before, but this time adorned by a black cloak and without the breastplate. Her face softened into a smile that seemed awkward as if all too uncommon on her face. She looked at her family on her left and lifted her hand in a wave. Her smiling family waved back and then faded away. Deborah looked at the rest of the group behind Willa before focusing back on the cleric once more. She lifted her hand pointing at Willa as a peaceful look came over her face. She then looked up to the sky, arms spread wide in surrender and eyes closed in total submission.

A beam of sunlight shone down on her face despite the thick clouds overhead and she began to rise into the sky. As she did her black cloak slipped from her shoulders fluttering down to the ground at Willa's feet. The cleric ignored the cloak. She wasn't ready to look away from Deborah as she rose into the sky. Only when both she and the beam of light were gone did Will look down.

Jonah asked, "Are you alright?"

Willa snapped back to reality at the sound of her husband's voice. Her whole family was suddenly at her side, "She was beautiful."

"Who, the girl?" asked Wren.

"No, Deborah," Willa corrected. "She was broken and bloody, but Jesus cleansed her and brought her home."

Jonah was confused, "We saw the little girl rejoin her family and they disappeared. After that you seemed like you were in a trance, staring straight ahead, then up at the sky."

"You didn't see her, then?" Willa was saddened that they didn't get to experience what she had seen. She assumed this lesson was meant only for her. She wondered if she had seen her future in Deborah's past. A portent of personal sacrifice for her family, her fellow believers, and the final reward of Jesus. She kept those thoughts to herself for now. She would happily sacrifice everything for God, faith, and family. She reached down and picked up the cloak. Holding it, she could see it wasn't just black. It was like the night sky, a deep bluish black with pinpricks of yellow representing stars, too many to count.

The family prepared lunch beneath the tree where Willa had seen Deborah sitting as she approached. They hoped it was the palm of Deborah mentioned in Judges 4:5. Willa prayed and meditated and gathered her thoughts. Though she didn't say so, Jonah could tell that she had learned something difficult and gave her some time to process it before they continued home to Haven.

Wren reminded them of their decision to backtrack west and north and go home through the farming community. The abandoned campsites they had seen on their way by were still concerning her, but she knew if they were people in need God would find them wherever they were going. She had always trusted God. Seeing his work so clearly since coming here had only made that belief stronger.

It didn't take them long to get back to the concealed path leading up into Mount Gerizim. It was steep and potentially treacherous but what Jonah lacked in dexterity he more than made up for in strength. He easily pulled himself up to the first plateau and dropped a rope down for the others. Willa went next, struggling a bit with the weight of her armor and imbalance of her gear, but made it without incident.

Wren tied Leo to the rope, and as Jonah pulled him up, she looked at Saraé and said, "Race ya?"

By the time she had nodded in response Wren was five feet up. She looked at her hands as they became clawed and then she scrambled up behind the tabaxi.

Saraé reached the top first but only because Wren had stopped part way up.

"Are you ok?" Jonah called down to her.

"Yeah," she replied. "I'll be right there, I found something." When she got to the top, she showed Jonah some climbing pitons that had been left behind.

Jonah looked them over, "You'd think people would be more careful approaching this way. It's supposed to be a secret, right?" Jonah pocketed the items, determined to say something about this when they got back to Haven.

The group hiked a switchback path up further into the mountain for about an hour before coming to another steep climb. This time Wren and Saraé went up first and dropped down a rope. Jonah removed his armor and pack, tying them to the bottom of the rope. He climbed the steep incline then pulled up his gear. Willa tied the rope around Leo. Once he was up, she repeated Jonah's process.

At the top Saraé found a pulley that had been dropped in the brush. She gave it to Jonah as they moved on again. They were even more methodical now, watching for further evidence left behind.

Less than a quarter mile later they began to be able to see into the valley. The farmland was lush and productive. It was incredible considering the elevation. As they began their winding descent Wren again spotted something odd. The grass to their left had been trampled as if several people had passed that way.

"Dad," she pointed out the tracks. "Why would people who know the way be blazing a new path?"

"Only one way to find out," Jonah replied. "You lead, Mom and I make too much noise. Saraé, stay back with us for now."

The girl tilted her head as if confused but nodded.

Wren entered a small group of trees stopping where they ended at a clearing. She held up her fist to tell the others to stop. She pointed at her eyes and then held up two fingers showing she saw two people. They were armored but not dressed as Haven citizens. These men were on their bellies, using a spyglass to watch something in the valley.

Jonah told Willa to go right, around the trees. He would go left. There was no way they could make it through even this sparse wood without their gear giving them away. He motioned for Saraé to join Wren at the tree line.

Wren waited for her parents to be in position then began to pray. As she did the roots, thorns and grass grew quickly entangling the two interlopers.

Suddenly, realizing they were under attack one fought to get to his feet while the second rolled over and fired a crossbow into the trees. The bolt hit a tree between Wren and Saraé.

Jonah and Leo charged out from their hiding places. The paladin deflected a short sword swung by the standing man and impaled him in the abdomen with his longsword. The man fell to the ground in the fetal position, Leo inches from his face, growling.

Seeing Jonah's assault, the man still entangled struggled to reload his weapon. He suddenly saw a blur coming at him from his left. His eyes focused just in time to see Saraé leap onto his chest placing a dagger under his chin.

Seeing Saraé break cover, Willa ran after her. The woman yelled as the girl leaped for the prone man, "Saraé, stop." She arrived at the girl's side as she held the subdued man down. "Haven will want to question them."

As Wren, Willa and Saraé tied up their captives, Jonah looked through the spyglass. It was focused on a large farmhouse secluded from the main cluster by a couple hundred yards. There was a ten-foot wall around the place providing some protection, but not enough. Jonah could see four figures climb over, the smallest with some help from the others. Someone was infiltrating the farming community.

The small group, followed by two subdued and restrained intruders, arrived at the main gate to the farming community a short time later. The guards were surprised at first as they were not expecting anyone, but they quickly recognized the family and let them in. Lisel, seren of the guard, which translated to captain, listened intently to Jonah's retelling of their discovery. Wren and Willa turned over the prisoners for questioning. In the chaos of the crisis no one even mentioned the new addition to the group, so the family too said nothing about her.

It didn't take long for the Haven interrogators to figure out that they would get no further information from the captives, so they were transferred to the brig in the main compound. Seren Lisel, Jonah and some other key personnel devised a plan. They would use mounted patrols to covertly surround the farm that they had identified as Laban's. Jonah's family would infiltrate it quietly. Their hope was that a quiet entry might allow them to find the family inside before the invaders could harm them further.

As dusk began to fall, segen Audra, lieutenant in charge of the cavalry, sent out regular mounted patrols. This time she sent them in groups of three instead of the customary pairs. When they were obscured from sight of Laban's farm, the third rider peeled off and found cover waiting for the call to converge on the farm. Wren rubbed the segen's horse as Audra waited to lead the final trio.

"Careful, little one," the segen warned calmly, "Nibbles lives up to her name."

As the final patrol trio trotted down the road Jonah's team circled around behind the neighboring farm, approaching Laban's farm through the high crops in the fields. That much of the plan went perfectly as orchestrated. Six cavalry soldiers, including Audra, were dispersed and hidden near the farm. Jonah, his family and three foot-soldiers in light armor, had made it to Laban's barn. Once the structure was cleared, the two infantry soldiers and the medic were left there for close support, if needed. Jonah gathered his family at the rear entrance to the main house. No one had seen or heard anything that would show they had been spotted, but they knew that would change in moments.

Jonah turned the handle on the door, but it was locked. Wren tapped his shoulder and stepped in. She struggled with the lock for a few moments. The nerves of doing this in a crisis were getting to her, but she did succeed in unlocking the door. Jonah pointed at himself, and Wren then held up a single finger, then at Willa and Saraé he held up two fingers. He looked at Leo and pushed his flat open palm toward the ground, his signal for stay. Leo was smart and obedient. He would not move until he was told to come. Wren touched her father's shoulder and asked for a minute. She prayed once again for God to guide their steps and help them to act with stealth and discretion.

Jonah and Wren moved into the house. Jonah went right and Wren left. Wren could see an open kitchen, dining area and a small sitting room near the front door. There were no signs of struggle except for a toppled chair and a half-eaten meal at the dining table. Jonah quietly opened the door to his right, peering into the small bedroom, he saw nothing of note. He pulled the door closed again then moved to the corner and looked up the stairs, nodding for Wren to cross to the other door. Opening it she saw something and stepped inside. Willa moved inside, staying well behind Jonah. Saraé moved to the table training her crossbow on the stairs. Wren looked stricken when she came back out of the room. She stopped on the other side of the stairs and held up one finger then drew it across her throat. She then made a motion like pulling a bow. Jonah and Willa knew this meant one dead and that the invaders had ranged weapons.

Jonah's mind was already spinning up a plan. He held a palm to Wren and motioned Saraé to follow him. Before he took to the stairs he whispered to the girl, stay low and try to take out any bowmen. She nodded and followed as Jonah carefully trod the stairs along the sides hoping to avoid a squeak. As he reached the landing, he looked up the second half of the stairs but couldn't see over the top. Saraé crept up on his right, making the turn and staying low as ordered. Jonah moved again but this step caused an audible creak. Jonah waited a few seconds, but heard nothing from above, so he went ahead. As his eyes rose above the top step he saw a crossbow fire. It missed him, lodging in the wall behind him. Saraé, who had crept along with Jonah, returned fire hitting the attacker who yelped in pain and receded into a room on the left.

Chaos erupted as Saraé reloaded. A man yelled charging from the door on the right side of the hallway at the top of the stairs. Jonah was distracted by a flash behind the man. A small, red creature with a lizard-like face was casting some sort of spell while waving a staff. The mage's lightning bolt hit the charging man just as he reached Jonah. The two men, jolted by electricity, toppled down the stairs hitting the landing hard.

Saraé fired a bolt at the little lizard but missed. Willa ran up behind her, pushing her head down, as a bolt lodged in the wall just above her. She said, "Keep your head down," then prayed for the Lord to grant her spiritual protection. A swirl of light formed in the hallway by the door the shooter was using for cover. It coalesced into a cross of glowing yellow swinging at the man and hitting him square in the jaw. She heard the thud of the man hitting the floor.

The man on top of Jonah had recovered a second faster than the paladin and that was all he needed. He drove a dagger under Jonah's breastplate deeply into his abdomen, then rose up to drive his sword into the still stunned paladin's throat.

An incredible roar caused everyone to turn as a brown bear barreled into the man smashing him into the landing wall then pouncing on him.

Leo arrived, called by Wren before she had become the bear. Jonah pointed up the stairs and said, "Go," just as a familiar face peered over the top of the landing. It was Vixyn and she had him dead to rights. She fired once hitting Jonah squarely in the shoulder then backed away. As she readied another arrow, intended for the charging wolf, she could tell she wouldn't get it off it in time. She dropped the arrow and swung her bow like a bat smacking the wolf through a doorway into a room. A short scream erupted from the room before it seemed to be muffled.

Saraé aimed at the white-haired woman as she backed away toward the room at the end of the hallway.

"They are both down, time to go Kryx!" In all the chaos Vixyn remained calm.

Saraé could see the lizard person behind Vixyn, so she fired at her to prevent their escape. Her bolt was perfectly aimed but Vixyn stepped in front of the shot, taking it in her left ribs.

Wren-bear, her target no longer a threat, joined the wolf and the glowing cross as they raced down the hallway just in time to see the pair of assailants enter a magical doorway and disappear.

Jonah, still lying on the stairs, saw two guards, a medic and Willa coming toward him. They were blurry from the tears in his eyes. He could tell they were yelling at him, but their words were muffled. The last thing Jonah saw was segen Audra pulling out the arrow with one yank as Willa and the medic began to pray. There was a flash of light and then mercifully the wounded paladin's world faded to black.

When Jonah awakened, he was in the Haven infirmary. He recognized the ceiling from his various visits there to get patched up.

Willa was nearby. She leapt to his side when she heard him stirring. "Don't try to get up. We healed you but you were gravely injured, give your body a day or two to recuperate."

"The kids?"

"Untouched," Willa replied, "thanks to you absorbing every hit."

"The farmer's family?" Jonah's voice was barely a whisper.

Willa got him some water. "They are terrified and a bit bruised but all alive. The body Wren found was one of the farmhands. He must have seen the attackers coming and tried to resist."

"Vixyn…" Jonah barely managed.

"Yeah, we saw her," Willa was clearly angry at even hearing the name. "She escaped through a portal with someone she called Kryx. I'm told she was a kobold of some advanced magical skill, judging by the lightning and teleportation."

Jonah tried to get up again, angry at this news, but Willa held him down. "No, stay there. While I have a captive audience, we need to talk about our future."

Chapter 18
Mission Drift

Azure's group had caught up with the caravan heading back to Haven from New Vitala, about a half-day out from their home. They rode along with Barnabas's group the rest of the way home. Azure took the opportunity to tell Barnabas about her 'sending stone' issue as soon as they had a moment alone. He promised that he would investigate it as soon as they arrived in Haven.

That afternoon she waited impatiently in his library while he greeted his family. They were relieved he was safe, ecstatic to have him home, and possibly a bit perturbed to have him hurry off to help Azure right away.

Barnabas took out the stone and studied it for a few minutes. He prayed quietly for God's intervention in this matter. After a few moments he opened his eyes. "I sense no evil or good through this object. Does the city of Borsippa mean anything to you?"

Azure searched her memory, "No not at all. Is it nearby?"

"No, it is many days northeast," Barnabas responded, showing some concern. "It is a small city near Babylon, the massive and deadly capital of the Assyrian Empire."

"None of this makes sense!" Azure was clearly frustrated. "Do you have a secure place to store it so it can't be traced?"

"Are you going to want the stone back at some point?"

"No," she replied without a thought.

He walked over to a bookshelf near the fireplace and removed a book. Azure could tell by how he handled it that it had considerable weight. He set it on the table and opened it. Inside was a hollow, in which he placed the stone. "I'll see if Xof has time before his mission tomorrow. He can teleport the stone across the world and leave it there unprotected. That should redirect any future pursuit."

"Thank you, Barnabas," Azure was clearly relieved. "Please go back to your family, with my apologies."

Wren picked up Saraé at the school set up for children in the tent city. No one knew how old she was due to her species. Her assigned task at the Abdon farm could have been decades if not longer. Despite this advanced age she was educationally even younger than her pre-teen appearance. She was learning quickly though, easily surpassing kids who looked her age. The sisters went by their quarters to check on Leo. They took him out to the exit by the stables and let him run for a while. Wren watched her new sister chasing and playing with Leo, much as she had done with his shih tzu alter ego when she was back on Earth and Saraé's age. Technically she still was, though she was inhabiting an adult tabaxi body now. They settled Leo back into their room and headed to Barnabas's family quarters. It had been weeks since they had shared a meal with their mentor and his family.

Saraé ran off with Jenna. They were becoming the best of friends and were nearly inseparable. Just a month ago it was

Wren running off with Jenna. This mission was changing her. The seriousness of it all was stealing her childhood. More interested in adult things now, Wren helped her mother and Hannah cook. She couldn't help noticing the serious look on her mother's face. She knew that look. It usually meant something big was coming. She wondered for a second if her mother had intuited the big news she was going to share that night but dismissed the thought. She had yet to share her recent dream with anyone. Could something else big be on the horizon? This was shaping up to be an interesting evening.

Jonah and Barnabas were talking at the table when the ladies entered with the food. Both men jumped to their feet, Jonah more gingerly, and helped set the table. Barnabas said the blessing thanking God for protecting their friends and bringing them home safely. Then his prayer shifted into asking for providence for future endeavors and God's direction for our lives. He ended by asking God for the courage to sacrifice to do his will and to do it for his glory.

Wren got the feeling that the prayer was directed at her. She looked around as everyone began to eat in silence. It was awkward but she could tell it wasn't about her. It was clear to her that everyone was struggling internally with something. She felt a small sense of relief that it wasn't just her.

Barnabas mercifully broke the silence, "You were right to connect us with New Vitala." He recounted every moment of his time there. He was so enthusiastic about the progress they had made. Castellan Astryd had shown them every kindness, allowing them unfettered access to the Red Quarter of the city. She gave them a building and a team of craftsmen to help them renovate it as a Temple to Adonai. Captain Petarku's men were always present to protect the missionaries, though they experienced no trouble while there. Rhesa showed the farmers of New Vitala some techniques for high altitude agriculture that they were using in the farming community here. On their last night Astryd invited the entire missionary team to hold a shabbat service in her palace. Taran and Tarai were in high demand that evening, fielding many valid questions about Adonai. They yielded almost a dozen volunteers for the temple that night alone. Barnabas seemed most pleased to relate that some of them were even dhampir, who while welcoming, remained skeptical of the message of Adonai. The families celebrated the glory given to God through this endeavor and prayed that he would send his spirit to empower Taran, Tarai and their group to continue his work there.

After dinner the girls went off to play again and the adults, Wren included, moved to the sitting room to talk. Again, the awkwardness of the silence was palpable.

Barnabas broke it, "Jonah would you like to start?"

"No, but I suppose I should." Jonah hesitated, unsure how to say what he knew he had to say.

Willa seized the opportunity, "Can I go first?"

"Please!" Jonah seemed relieved.

"I think this last leg of our journey brought something to light that I have been ignoring for a while now. Maybe we have all been ignoring it." Willa was thoughtful but didn't hesitate with her words.

Jonah could feel that he wasn't going to like what was coming next, but he held his tongue.

"I don't think God wants me to continue serving him in the way that I have been since we came here." She saw both Jonah and Wren sit up straight, so she held out a hand asking them to wait to comment. "You almost died in that farmhouse," her eyes were now full of tears as she looked at her husband. "I replayed the last few week's events in my head. You purposely and regularly put yourself in danger to protect us."

"You have done the same," Jonah argued.

"Yes, but that's my point." Willa left her seat and knelt at her husband's feet holding both of his hands. "The deeper we get into this the more dangerous it becomes. You need to be with people who know what they are doing. People you don't need to sacrifice yourself to protect."

Jonah couldn't argue, he had no idea what to say.

Willa continued, "Have either of you had any dreams about the Judges lately?"

Jonah and Wren looked at each other, then both shook their heads.

"Well, I had one last night," she stood and paced as she described the vision. "I was on a bridge at the edge of a town. I think it was Gilgal, but so much bigger. Every person there was a child, and they were all crying for their parents. They were weak from malnutrition and sick from various diseases. When they saw me, they came to me and called me 'mother' in unison. I touched a small girl, and she was no longer hungry, then a boy and he was no longer sick. I raced through the crowd, touching each of them, but they were endless. Just as I was about to panic, a voice rang out. It said, '**go to them, love them, train up the children according to my ways.**'"

"Mom?" Wren was up and standing in front of Willa. "I had the exact same dream last night, except the children called me 'sister'. I was going to tell you tonight."

Mother and daughter both turned to Jonah suddenly realizing maybe he shared this new dream too.

He was slack jawed and teary-eyed as he shook his head, "No. I didn't dream any of that." He got up from his seat and hugged them both. "You know I support you in whatever you are called to do. I feel like I'm still on this mission, but I can't do it alone."

Barnabas finally spoke up. He and Hannah had been silently letting this play out. "Oh, you won't be alone. I have that covered."

"I trust you my friend," Jonah nodded to the man. "So how is this going to work?"

Willa spoke instantly, she had already worked out all the logistics in her mind as always. "I want you to bring us to Gilgal. Hannah and I will be working together to organize and create a home for orphans and a school for all the children there. From what we have heard they are already under construction."

Jonah looked over at Hannah, "you're in on this too."

The usually soft-spoken woman replied, "absolutely! His will, not my own."

Jonah nodded, "I will continue to do His will in the mission field and keep looking for our way home."

"Hannah may have found some information linking the Codex of Light to incursions like the one that brought us here," Willa explained.

"The codex?" Jonah exclaimed. "The thing Xof is after?"

"Yes," Barnabas replied. "We are beginning to believe that the Codex can control the incursions and create a stable portal to Earth."

A look of grave concern came over Jonah's face, "But what if the enemy gets this Codex?"

Wren looked at her mother in sudden realization, "Tomorrow is day thirty-nine. Is it time to go try something drastic?"

Hannah replied, "What does that mean? Day thirty-nine?"

"Alright everyone, sit back down," Jonah responded calmly, "this is going to take a minute to explain, and I doubt you're going to believe a word of it." Jonah, Willa and Wren explained their experiences with Xof's repeated suicide mission and their theories about a time loop. To their credit Barnabas and Hannah struggled with the idea but had experienced enough weirdness to refrain from discounting the whole story. Much like they did with Moonbow, they told Barnabas to journal about tonight's conversation. After tomorrow's events the family would remind him to read it back, thereby proving he was being reset by the time loop as well.

The time loop talk had diverted their attention from the heaviness of the earlier revelations. Those thoughts and feelings returned as soon as they returned to their quarters.

Saraé who was incredibly intuitive asked, "Why does everyone seem so sad tonight?"

The family gathered around the girl's bed and told her about everyone's decisions and their new missions.

She thought about the news for a few moments then looked at Jonah, "Do you promise to check on us every day and come back to us?"

"Of course," Jonah assured the girl. "Nothing can keep me from my family."

"If Adonai says to do it, we should," she announced. Seeing the tears in all their eyes, she added, "right?"

"Yes," Willa nodded, hugging her tightly. "Get some sleep, we have a lot of preparations to make tomorrow."

"Goodnight Mom, Dad, Sis and Leo."

Leo huffed at the sound of his name.

Willa snuggled with Wren and Saraé. When both of her daughters were asleep Willa went to Jonah and sat on the side of their bed. He was still awake, just staring at her, his anxiety clear on his face.

"I don't want to leave you," he said softly.

"I don't want to lose you," she replied.

They prayed together and she sat with him rubbing his temples until his breathing finally changed and he was asleep.

☙

This time as sleep took Jonah there was no bird. Instead, the dreamer saw the familiar scene of a newborn but not just any child. This was a child destined to do the work of God. His parents were instructed not to let him drink spirits, eat unclean foods, or cut his hair. He was born in Zorah and Samson grew to be a stubborn and foolhardy man. He violated every mandate when he took a Philistine wife, ate honey from the skull of a lion he had slain, among other things prohibited by his order. He tricked his rivals with a clever riddle that was ruined by his treacherous wife. In his anger he went to Ashkelon and slew thirty men for their clothes. While he was gone his wife was given to another man. Again, his anger burned, prompting Samson to burn their fields in retribution. The cycle of vengeance continued when the farmers killed his wife. Samson's rage continued to grow, making him unable to end the cycle.

He killed all the transgressors and fled to the cleft of the rock at Etam. The Philistines followed Samson into Judah, thinking they were abetting their enemy. The men of Judah gave up

Samson to end the Philistine assault, but during the exchange Samson killed 1000 men with a jawbone from a donkey. After the battle Samson prayed and God quenched his thirst. Samson's need for God waned again as he loved another Philistine woman. The leaders found out and used her to find Samson's weakness. He resisted for a time but eventually gave in to her nagging, telling her his weakness. Once his hair was shorn, he was captured, tortured, and blinded. The dreamer watched as with one last show of faith Samson called to God for strength. God answered, allowing Samson to break the pillars and collapse the building on his enemies, freeing Israel from bondage once more. As the scene faded Jonah could see something new in the landscape. There was a flash of light near Jerusalem, and another far to the north in a mountain near the Mediterranean Sea. The dream faded, again welcoming the sole dreamer to a new day.

Her whole family now asleep, Willa prayed again, this time for clarity. She asked God to assure all of them that this was His will, and that he would be with them in all their endeavors in his name, then she allowed her trance to take her.

Willa dreamed once more. She was on the bridge leading into Gilgal again. This time Wren and Saraé were with her. There was a tent city behind them, and construction was happening all over the town. There were still multitudes of children in the town but this time they were playing, reading by the trees or helping adults with chores around town. She was relieved to see other adults this time, it felt less overwhelming. She looked down at her daughters as they each took one of her hands. Together the three walked into the town and were welcomed with cheers and hugs. Mother and daughters continued toward a large building that Willa and Wren recognized as Jafan's mansion. As they passed them on the street, the children from all around the town followed them. When they entered the mansion, the vision faded, and the dreamers awoke to a new day.

Chapter 19

A New Day Dawning

Morning came with a somber air around the family. Jonah's repeated visit to the dream of Samson coupled with Willa and Wren's shared dream solidified that God was calling them to separate missions. None of them were thrilled by the confirmation, though they all tried to mask it with smiles and pleasantries. They went to the tent city for breakfast. As had become their custom. After eating they served food while the people who had served them got time to eat. When breakfast was finished, they wandered the market gathering supplies. Jonah replenished camping and survival gear, while the girls tried to find someone to help them learn about some of their magical finds.

They found a half-Elven leatherworker named Gaja, of some magical talent, who was able to give them some information on Jephthah's boots and the sling they found in Aijalon. She marveled at the quality and construction of both items, despite their clear age. She confirmed what they had already deduced about the boots, "They allow the wearer to read and understand all languages. Certainly, a useful ability for a missionary!"

"Yes," Willa agreed. "They were very useful in our recent journey."

Gaja focused again, "There's something else. They seem to have a divination on them that can cause a calming effect in situations of heightened emotions."

"Oh, that explains some things." Willa thought back to a few times when the boots may have helped them without them even knowing it. She remembered the tense standoff in Jezreel with the Bael worshippers, their interrogation by the dhampir leadership, and even the confrontation with the witch Luella in Shamir. If this ability of the boots had intervened in those situations, it would have already resulted in their protection from enemies and paved a way for developing new friendships.

Gaja then examined the sling for a few moments. Her expression told them that she had never seen anything like it before. She quietly meditated over it for a few moments. Suddenly her eyes went wide with surprise, "This was once an object of evil, but at some point, Adonai…" she searched for the right word, "repurposed it for good. Anyone hit by this sling becomes frightened and may even run away."

Wren spoke up, "I should have used that more. I had no idea."

"You did fine," Jonah replied. "None of us had any idea."

They thanked Gaja and gave her some gems for her trouble. Next, they looked for a smith or jeweler with similar skills but had no luck. Jonah had a meeting with Barnabas and Saphic in the training area, so he hugged his family and set off in that direction. Willa, Wren and Saraé went back to their rooms to pack before heading to their various studies for the day. They all agreed to gather for dinner and spend the evening together before heading to Gilgal the next day.

Jonah entered the training room to find Barnabas, Saphic and Filipina talking. They were debriefing her group's adventures, close calls and the young wizard they had brought back with them. Azure, Elowen and Gadget had offered to stay with Ember through her interview which was taking place as they spoke.

"Welcome Jonah!" Barnabas always seemed so pleased to see him and his family. He truly treasured the friendship of the family from his home world.

Jonah embraced his two friends and mentors, then turned to the centaur warrior, "I was hoping he meant your group when he said I would have help." They grasped each other's arms at the elbow.

"Good to see you again, Jonah," Fili replied.

The door opened once more. This time Draco, Shay, Lia and Rake entered.

"Heard your group bailed on ya," Draco quipped reaching up to slap the much taller aasimar on the back.

Before Jonah could respond Rake retorted, "Ignore him, he has as little impulse control with his words as he does with his actions."

"Hey!" The halfling feigned being insulted, "I was joking."

"Really?" Shay replied. "Aren't jokes usually funny?"

Lia and Fili chuckled audibly while Draco pouted at being the butt of an actual joke. They each made the rounds greeting and sharing small talk for a few moments before getting down to business.

Saphic spoke up, "You all know the seriousness of our mission and the danger of introducing new people to proven teams." He motioned toward Barnabas, "We thought it would be best to discuss roles and tactics together before sending you out into the wild. Filipina, your team seems to lead by skill set. Each of you takes the lead when faced with challenges in your wheelhouse so to speak."

"Yes," the centaur agreed. "I make many of the strategic decisions with Lia and Shay as we have the most martial training. I would think Jonah would be an excellent addition to that group." She paused for a moment, leading everyone to a table with figures depicting each member on it. "Depending on the situation our team falls into three parts; the melee fighters, ranged support and the healers."

"Makes sense," Jonah agreed.

"Many of us have more than one skill set but generally Lia leads the front-line fighters which include Shadolok, Rake and Elowen. The latter two in their wild shapes. Gadget, Shay, and Draco, when in halfling form, provide ranged support. I prefer to be with this group too as my speed allows me to protect the healers as well."

"That leaves only Azure to heal everyone?" Jonah asked flatly.

"Sometimes," Rake answered, sounding a bit offended. "One of the druids can stay in their elven form and help heal and Shay has some healing capability as well. It has worked for us."

"Oh, sorry," Jonah backtracked. "I wasn't criticizing. I'm just a verbal processor. I meant that with me added to the front line it would afford the group more flexibility in healing capability."

"We were thinking the same thing," Lia agreed. "With two paladins in the front it should lighten the load for the healers to do more to bolster all of us as well."

Saphic seemed pleased. "Impressive, you are already thinking on the same lines."

"How will Jonah fit into the leadership of your group?" Barnabas asked.

"I'm not looking to take the lead," Jonah offered. "I'll make suggestions and do whatever is needed."

"May I?" Rake asked Fili, who yielded the floor with a flourish well practiced in her years in the circus. "Thank you. We discussed this whole 'our group' thing last night after Barnabas asked us to consider this. Everywhere we went people were talking about 'Coram Deo', the group who had helped them in so many ways. Some of them even thought we were you. It was clear that the name was becoming synonymous with hope for the poor and downtrodden. We thought we could continue under that name with you."

"Thank you Rake," Jonah seemed embarrassed by the compliments. "I think you misunderstand what 'Coram Deo' is all about. It was never about us; it was more about choosing a state of mind or a way of life. Coram Deo means living our lives 'before the face of God'. Anyone serving God's people for God's glory is already 'Coram Deo'. You earned that title when you answered His call. I am proud to share the lifestyle with all of you."

"Well said!" Moonbow's voice came from the door behind them. With him was Grand Templar Y'Huda and two of his knights.

The battle-scarred paladin made no grand speech upon entering. He simply approached each of them with a personal greeting. Once the pleasantries were completed, he spoke. "I owe all of you an apology. I let my pride cloud my judgment and I gave many of you a hard time since you arrived here. You have proven me wrong in so many ways. Not only have you met every mission with focus and determination, but you have exceeded all expectations. You have saved lives and done so in a way that has changed hearts." He paused for a moment, showing the first sign of emotion you had ever seen from this battle hardened general. "I am completely on board with this merged group, this new Coram Deo. We have little time to celebrate though, an opportunity to save thousands of lives has presented itself. This mission is of grave importance and will require precision and coordination. Moonbow, please elaborate."

Azure, Gadget and Elowen sat in the interrogation room with Ember. The young wizard didn't seem at all frightened by the questioning. Two guards stood at the door while Elmore questioned the girl. Her companions were as interested in her answers as the firbolg hedge wizard was.

"Tell me again how you came to be in the war camp?" Elmore's tone was kind but direct.

She nodded, understanding the need for repetition to prove her honesty, "I was the youngest of three children in my family. My father had died when I was young and my eldest brother, Ash, joined the military as soon as he was old enough. He wanted to carry on our father's legacy. My sister Cinder, three years my senior, was the family rebel. She pushed back on everything our mother asked of her. She rebuked the only choice for women of the clan; to marry and raise children. Cinder loved music, poetry and art. She wanted to leave and experience life and express those experiences through her art. When she turned sixteen, she ran away leaving me a note. It simply said that she was heading to Jericho to become a bard and that she would someday send for me. Three months ago, I received a letter from Cinder telling me that it wasn't safe in Edrei anymore and that I should come to Bethel. She warned me not to travel alone but I couldn't find anyone willing to go with me. I left Edrei at once, mixing in with caravans going in my direction when I could and traveling alone when I had to. I joined a caravan heading south and west not knowing they were bringing supplies to the war camp. They decided that a fire genasi would fetch a good price, even more so when I tried to use magic to escape. I had been in a cage, bound and gagged for three weeks when someone attacked the camp. My cage was near the animal pens. There was an explosion and suddenly frightened animals and screaming soldiers were running everywhere. The second, bigger explosion rocked my cage. After the blast, I could hear only echoes and muted sounds. I knew that was my chance to escape. I crawled out of my broken cage and slipped away into the night. The soldiers seemed focused to the south and southwest, so I went north to the Yarmuk River then east to Kamon." She paused as if to give Elmore a chance to ask a question.

"Please continue," Elmore replied calmly.

"In Kamon I heard of a group that had helped the town just the day before. The people referred to them as 'Coram Deo' which I thought was odd. I didn't understand how 'before the face of God' would be the name for a band of mercenaries. As I followed their trail through Jabesh-Gilead and Jezreel I began to understand. They weren't mercenaries at all. They were soldiers claiming they acted on the orders of a benevolent God.

I headed north and found the town of Magdala. They were rebuilding there from an attack. They told me that Coram Deo had saved the day again. This time they saved the entire town from the machinations of a mad witch. I had missed them again, but it heartened me that they were heading south again, this time toward Aijalon. By the time I got there the town was in turmoil and it was clear that I wasn't far behind them. I traveled through the night trying to close the gap but instead of finding them, I found the camp of some soldiers and mercenaries. I stayed hidden from the thinking they may be after me and watched them as they ate. It became clear that they were following Coram Deo too, but for nefarious reasons. When the mercenaries slept, I gave them a wide berth and continued to look for my saviors. The next afternoon I found a large group gathering near Mount Tabor, they were planning what sounded like a rescue. I waited outside until they returned but they split up. I followed the larger group heading north and finally caught up with them in Ever Grove. I hadn't slept and had barely eaten in days. I could hardly stand when the rangers there found me."

Elmore considered his next words, "Your story doesn't change, so it is either the truth or a well-practiced lie."

"I don't think she is lying," Azure offered. Gadget and Elowen nodded in agreement.

"I tend to agree," Elmore replied. "Tell me again how you came by your magical abilities."

"In our clans we are tested for various skill sets. When we show capability in an area it is developed, practiced and perfected for the good of the clan." She continued, holding nothing back from her questioner. "I was found to be adept at magic at a young age, so I was apprenticed to our most powerful wizard Tian. She helped me develop my abilities and taught me to research new spells."

Elmore looked at the Ember, then her three companions. "I believe her, she is cleared to stay, though you will be responsible for her."

"Agreed," Gadget replied excitedly as all three ladies put a hand on her in solidarity.

"Good," Elmore seemed thoroughly pleased by the result. "Guards, please inform your superiors to make it known that Ember is one of us now." They nodded and turned to leave.

Before they could even touch the handle, the door burst open. The guards took defensive positions and Elmore spun, reaching into his spell component pouch. Ember and her three new friends leapt to their feet. They were all surprised to see it was Madisyn, the bard who was a member of Moonbow's Duskhunters.

"Ember?" Madisyn asked, not yet ready to believe it.

"Cinder! You are here?" Ember ran to her sister embracing her so hard they almost fell. "This is truly a miracle."

"You don't know the half of it, sister," Madisyn responded looking up in thanks to Adonai. "I go by Madisyn now. Come with us," she said, tilting her head toward the other women, "let us tell you about the God who made this miracle happen."

Moonbow stepped to the table and spread out a map of the region to the east and south of the Jordan River before beginning to speak.

"This is Moab. They were once like brothers to the people of Israel. The current King changed all of that. Bellicose is a half-orc and third in his line. His grandfather, Bellicose I, was a benevolent leader. He didn't want the title, but he did want to help his people. He demanded that the orc and goblins of the region have a seat at the political table and spent his lifetime trying to ease tensions between both the races of the region and beyond. When his father gained the throne things changed. Bellicose II did not follow in his father's footsteps although he did demand unity of purpose among all his people. He used that fear-invoked unity, and some real and manufactured aggression from neighboring lands, to colonize nearby Edom and parts of Southern Israel east of the Jordan. He only stopped his march north when confronted by the dwarves of Mount Nebo. Not wanting a two-front war he focused on Edom to the south. Bellicose III's methods fell even farther from those of his grandfather. He embraced his orcish heritage and denied the human side entirely. He took the throne when his father died under mysterious circumstances. Some believe the son had him assassinated. Others thought he questioned his father's strength enough that radicals assassinated him to effect regime change in favor of the aggressive young prince. The two front war was on and was not going well for Moab. The dwarves remained in a defensive posture. The armies of Moab could get nowhere near their strongholds. The mountain dwarves were adept at guerilla tactics and easily repelled the young King's clumsy assaults."

He continued after a pause, "Recently, that began to change. Bellicose's tactics shifted as he began to receive help from demons. They would appear through portals in the air or ground and turn the tide of battles quickly and decisively. The Moabite army has since pushed the dwarves all the way north to Deepforge, their largest city and greatest stronghold. There the dwarves have fought valiantly, forcing the mad King to dedicate more resources to the effort."

Moonbow paused again, but those gathered encouraged him to continue. "The devastating losses to the north have thinned their forces in the south. Edom had made a pact with Egypt and was beginning to turn the tide on the south front, taking back ancestral lands and resource rich areas Moab had previously taken by force."

"Thank you, Moonbow." Y'Huda patted his contemporary on the back, moving to the map. "Because of all this Moab is at its weakest, despite some form of deal made with whoever is behind the demons that keep hounding us."

Jonah spoke up at this comment, "I think we know who is ultimately in control of the creatures."

"Yes, true enough," Y'huda agreed, "but why help Moab, why specifically against the dwarves and why have they been harassing you all? The connections are still unclear, but the moment has provided us with a window to act."

Filipina and Jonah tried to speak at the same time. Jonah conceded the floor. "Thank you, Jonah. I think the Grand Templar is suggesting an opportunity to remove one enemy from the board by killing the King." Jonah nodded in agreement, everyone now looking at Y'Huda.

"Exactly," he replied flatly. "The man is evil and while fighting a war on two fronts, he is currently vulnerable."

Rake chimed in this time, "Alright, say all of what you have said is true. You're asking us to traverse a warfront to get to him. Then fight through his personal guard to get to close enough, with ten or twelve people. That's a suicide mission."

Moonbow replied, "No, we are asking nothing of the kind. This plan has been in motion for months. I have a spy embedded in Kirharseth; he has been there for six months."

Lia asked, "But isn't the King in Dibon?"

"He was," Moonbow agreed. "We spread rumors of an assassination attempt on the King in the Moabite capital, then waited for someone to take it up. Many of his generals, especially the Drow and human ones were not in favor of all of this orcish nationalism. One of them was happy enough to try to kill him, though they failed. To show you how evil this King is, he punished the attempt by murdering an entire ward of the city for the crime of being the same race as the assassin."

"Pure evil," Shay spat.

"Yes, exactly why we need to seize this opportunity," Moonbow continued. "The attempt caused him to move to his compound in Kirharseth. It is guarded by foothills and forests providing defenses impossible in Dibon. The King moved there with his wife Queen Adrosia. She was not fond of the rustic nature of the place, so he placated her with the promise of a stable and the best horses in the land. That is where our spy Mystagogue came in. The need of his dwarven skills easily overcame Bellicose's racism, as he was the best stone worker and carpenter in Kirharseth. The King demanded that a stable be built, a chamber with exterior entrance for the stable hand and a reinforced stone wall around it joining with the wall around the rest of the compound."

"Brilliant," Draco admitted. "You seem to have thought of everything."

"Well, almost." Moonbow replied. "We have no control over the timing of things. Mystagogue's work is nearly completed so we will need to move quickly."

Jonah had been mostly quiet, taking it all in, but he felt now was the time to speak up, "Ok, you said it is not a suicide mission, tell us the rest of the plan."

Elowen had decided to join the others in the training area. Azure and Gadget followed along with Madisyn as she gave her sister the tour of Haven that they had received upon their arrival. Madisyn guided them around the compound, ending the procession in the temple. Ember was awestruck at the simple, understated beauty of the architecture. She walked around the perimeter to the front which was dominated by a raised dais. Azure and Gadget had stayed back, giving the sisters some privacy, while still enjoying the tour. They felt a surge of emotion as Ember took it all in. They remembered the feeling that the Spirit of God was alive in this place when they first came here.

Gadget was distracted by the sound of soft sobbing from behind them. She couldn't see anyone over the top of the benches, so she crouched down. About three rows back she saw a woman in leather armor and blue garments on her knees. She felt empathy for this clearly distraught woman as she watched her hunched over, her face pressed against the ground, her long pink hair spreading out around her head and arms. Suddenly it dawned on her, this woman had to be Willa. She tapped Azure to follow her as they moved around two rows of benches to get to their friend. They knelt beside her laying hands on her and began to pray.

Gadget began, "Father God I can only imagine what this woman of such incredible strength must be going through to put her in such a state. We ask you to comfort her and show her your mercy."

Azure continued, "We trust you Lord in all things. We go where you lead us, and we do what you call us to do. What you ask of us is not always easy. We struggle with our own fear, doubt and desires. Grant us your strength so that we may be steadfast in serving your people, for your glory."

Soft music from a lute began from behind them as Madisyn began to sing a soothing Psalm. Ember sat there staring in awe at her sister, remembering when they were young, and she would sing to her. Her voice had improved, and the song seemed to infuse them all with a feeling of calm and safety.

Willa sat up, wiping the tears from her eyes. "Thank you, sisters."

Azure helped her up and encouraged her to sit on the bench. Gadget sat on her other side with the sisters in the next row facing them. "Are you alright?"

"Not really," she fought back tears again. "I am so afraid of losing Jonah. I came here to beg God not to separate our family."

"Did you get an answer?" Gadget was holding her hand.

Willa inhaled a long, ragged breath, "I felt his answer in my heart." She paused again, "I clearly felt that I should trust him."

"You do, don't you?" Madisyn asked. "I mean 'trust him'."

"Yes, of course," Willa admitted looking up at the two fire genasi women. "Only God could ask this of me and get a yes." She focused on Ember, "I don't think I have met you, yet."

"I'm Ember," she responded, looking over at her sister. "Is she one of the 'Coram Deo' people?"

Madisyn nodded.

She looked back at Willa, "Your family saved my life and gave me back my freedom."

Willa seemed shocked by the claim, "You must be mistaken. I have never seen you before."

Ember told her the whole story of how their actions at the war camp inadvertently freed her. She described how she followed them, hearing all of the stories of how Coram Deo had helped people from Jabesh-Gilead to Magdala. She finished with the part about how she followed the wrong group at Mount Tabor and ended up in Ever Grove where she found the others, nodding at Azure and Gadget. Tears welled up in the young girl's eyes as she told her story, by the end she was sobbing openly.

Willa wrapped her arms around the young woman, "I'm glad we could help you, even if we had no idea that we were doing it."

Ember gently pushed Willa's shoulders so they could be face-to-face, "I think that's the whole point. I'm new to this Adonai business, but you did what he asked of you and trusted him to do the rest. Maybe I am here to remind you of that in your current situation."

Willa hugged the girl tightly again, "How did one so young come to be so smart?"

Madisyn responded without even a pause, "probably genetic."

People walking by the Temple looked in to see what was happening as raucous laughter echoed down the stone hallways.

Moonbow and Y'Huda took turns relating the plan to the group. Moonbow had planned a route that took the party through Gilgal to drop off Willa, Wren and others who felt called to care for the orphans of war. They would then cross the Jordan and follow Mount Nebo east then south to Deepforge.

Y'Huda took over the briefing from there. The elder Templar filled them in on their dwarven allies who would provide safety, rest and an escort through the tunnels under the mountain that would bring them far into Moab and within a half-day of Kirharseth.

Moonbow began speaking again. He told them that Mystagogue would rendezvous with them at the tunnel exit. The dwarven monk would then help them get through Kirharseth to the compound. From there they would get inside the King's retreat to complete the assignment. Along the way they would plan several exit strategies to get out of the compound and city undetected.

Moonbow and Y'Huda answered questions, then along with Barnabas, excused themselves from the training room. The men and women of Coram Deo felt like they could do anything after their mentors finished the briefing.

"Saphic," Jonah asked, "do you mind if we stay and spar for a bit?"

The seneschal agreed, staying with them to evaluate and make suggestions. They took turns pairing up and fighting, each learning the other's tendencies, go-to moves and defenses. Elowen had returned by then. She and Rake discussed their favored wild shapes. The eladrin preferred a bear for melee with tooth and claw attacks. The shadar-kai used a strange whip-tail lizard form that Jonah thought looked like an eight-foot-tall version of Godzilla with short arms, a long tail, and jagged blue scales down its back. In this form he had a vicious bite attack and a tail swipe that could upend foes coming from the rear. Draco showed his tendencies in rogue form then switched to Shadolok form to flex his barbarian muscles. Jonah made a mental note to ask Draco how he became symbiotically attached to Shadolok. He would wait until they knew each other better, maybe one night on camp watch. Fili was built to be a front-line fighter but seemed to prefer archery. He also noted that Lia preferred stand and tank techniques where Shay favored her ranged abilities hex and radiant blasts until forced into melee.

When they finished sparring, they sat together with Saphic discussing their findings. "Jonah, you're newest to the group. What did you see?"

Jonah paused, considering his words, "Please take no offense, these are observations from one time sparring together."

They all nodded, some smiling, others wary of the coming criticism.

"Ok then, here goes," Jonah paused again. "Rake and Elowen seem to have a good grasp on their abilities due to their experience. We need to develop a signal of sorts to be ready to support you if you are knocked out of your animal forms in melee."

Rake replied, "I planned to tail swipe and retreat. I could roar first as a signal."

Elowen thought about it, "I could also roar but would probably need support to retreat."

Saphic chimed in, "Perhaps Jonah and Lia could each pair with one of you for that situation. Go on Jonah, you're on a roll."

"Filipina your style seems..." he searched for the right word, "...undecided, maybe."

"How so," the centaur asked, genuinely curious.

"You have all of the skills, size and bearing to charge in and fight, but you seem to prefer to attack at range with your bow." Jonah paused for a reply, but none came. "You are excellent at both techniques, just be careful not to get swarmed before using that charge ability."

Filipina nodded thoughtfully, "Agreed. Depending on the situation I will either charge in or start out at range. When at range I will be ready to charge in to provide backup for a retreating druid."

"Yes, excellent," Saphic stated, with everyone nodding in agreement.

"Shay," Jonah began, before being interrupted.

"Uh-oh, here it comes," she pretended to joke, but her expression belied her anxiety over the perceived incoming criticism.

"I think you have good tactics," Jonah reassured the young genasi. "You like to hang back and attack from a distance which you do well. Your capabilities as a fighter and healing skills are perfect for bodyguarding Azure and Gadget."

"Uhh, yeah, thanks," Shay managed, surprised by the compliments.

"One thing though," Rake added, "you tend to try to solve every problem. You can't. You have to stay with Azure and Gadget and trust that the rest of us can handle our roles."

"If you see something bad going down, hold your position and call it out," Fili offered.

"Yeah, that's fair," Shay admitted. "I do have some trust issues."

"I guess that leaves me," Draco was unusually quiet during this whole briefing, "or should I say, us."

"You are a complete wildcard Draco," Jonah admitted with a slight chuckle.

The halfling rogue seemed to want to be offended at first, but then thought it through and nodded. "Yeah, I guess I am."

"You should remain hidden whenever possible," Jonah began, thinking it through as he spoke. "Only reveal yourself when most advantageous."

"I'm liking this so far," he was now fully engaged in the conversation. "Continue."

"Support the entire team by taking down opponents in melee with the others from a flanking position," Jonah continued. "If someone gets overwhelmed or there are too many melee opponents for the fighters you engage as Shadolok."

Draco paused, looking down as he often did when communicating telepathically with his symbiotic partner, "We agree, that sounds good."

"Wow, you got all that from a few minutes of sparring?" Rake seemed genuinely impressed with Jonah. "You must be an amazing teacher, Saphic."

"Yes, well," the seneschal was never one to take compliments well. "Jonah had all the strategic and tactical acuity when he got here. I merely taught him how to use the weapons and armor of our world."

"I'm still a work in progress there, but I'm getting better," Jonah admitted.

Just then the door opened. Madisyn entered followed by Willa, Azure, Gadget and Ember. "I brought them back safe and sound."

Willa walked straight to Jonah and fell into his arms. He could see she had been crying so he pulled her in tightly.

"Well, we should go," Madisyn said, wrapping her arm through Ember's.

Ember flinched and pulled back, "Maddi, I want to do my part. I want to go with them."

Madisyn's always smiling face turned to concern, "Are you sure? You just got here. I just got you back."

"I will spend all the time I can with you when we are together," Ember reassured her big sister, "but I need to do this. I need to learn more about Adonai, and I need to serve him much like you do. Please understand."

"I do sister, I truly do." Madisyn embraced Ember lovingly, then she looked up at the assembled team. "Anything bad happens to her, you answer to me."

Chapter 20
The Least of These

Azure and Gadget offered to have Wren, Saraé and Leo bunk with them that night so Jonah and Willa could spend some alone time together. When they arrived back in their quarters Jonah was not surprised to see everything packed and ready for their journey. Spread out on a small table was Willa's equipment. Gideon's breastplate, Shamgar's oxgoad, Tola's rod, Deborah's cloak, Jephthah's boots, and Jair's ring were all displayed carefully.

"What's this?" Jonah knew the answer but wanted to hear it from his wife.

"These items were meant to help us complete this mission," she touched each of them as she answered. "For all we know they may be essential to the mission. They need to be given to the group."

Jonah hugged his wife from behind. She melted into his embrace. "I don't know if I can do this without you and the kids."

"You can and you will," she replied. "You will come back safely to us." She turned in his arms and they kissed. It had been a while since they kissed like that. She prayed that it wouldn't be their last.

Jonah woke early the next morning. He barely slept, his mind racing with fears, doubts, and hopes. Willa was already gone, probably to retrieve the kids from their friends. In her new Elven form she didn't need to sleep. Elves called it a 'trance'. It lasted about four hours, and they were good for the day. Jonah often thought that it was unfair that a race so long-lived also got more time out of every day. He knew well that fairness wasn't really found in worldly things. He sat on the edge of the bed savoring the memory of his last night alone with Willa for who knows how long. Then the reality of the day rushed in and overwhelmed him. He got up and got dressed. He noticed that the gear Willa had planned to surrender to the group was gone. All that remained were the travel packs for them and the kids, organized meticulously and ready to go as was Willa's way. He took one last look into the empty room and left. He had one stop to make before meeting with his new team in the war room.

The news of Xof's mission failure and the loss of his team was once again written all over Barnabas's face. He invited Jonah inside, "We received the news last night after your family left. I didn't want to burden you, so I waited to tell you the news."

"Barnabas," Jonah consoled, "I am so sorry for your loss."

The cleric seemed surprised by his friend's choice of words, "It's a loss to all of us."

"Yes, well, that's why I'm here," Jonah replied. "Please go get your journal."

Barnabas did as he was asked but he looked puzzled. When he returned, he handed it to Jonah, "This is most odd."

"I know," Jonah replied as he flipped to the most recent entry. It was for today. Jonah flipped back a page without reading it. The page before was completely blank. Flipping again revealed the day before yesterday's entry. Jonah's heart sank for a moment but then he realized the omission may be evidence in itself. "Do you write in this book every day?"

"Yes," he replied. "Why are you so interested in my journal?"

"It's not about what is there, it's about what isn't," Jonah explained. "Yesterday is blank."

Barnabas looked at the blank page. "That's odd, I could swear I..."

Before he could finish, Jonah flipped three pages back. "This one is blank too." Barnabas was looking more and more baffled, as Jonah flipped three more pages, "And this one."

"Jonah, stop." The elder man said, his hand on Jonah's. "Just tell me what is happening."

Jonah explained the time-loop theory once again. Barnabas had no recollection of the first conversation. This time Jonah had him take notes, put them in a locked box and give it to him. His friend and mentor did just that, a confused and stricken look on his face as he did.

Jonah took the box placing his other hand on his friend's shoulder, "We will fix this. I promise you."

"Can't we just warn Xof not to go on the mission?" He was grasping at any straw now.

"If we do, it might stop the time loops," Jonah mused, "but I'm afraid we could lose the Codex. That could be devastating for this world and Earth."

"Yes, it certainly could." Barnabas seemed more upset at this thought. "We can't just..."

"We won't," Jonah assured his friend. "I have some ideas, but first I need to figure out if my family are the only ones not affected by the loops. We have to find a course of action that successfully completes the mission and avoids whatever causes the loops. To do that we need to know how it fails. I'll figure this out. In the meantime, you don't tell anyone what you know. Use the time in the next three days to note anything out of the ordinary. If you find anything call me or Willa right away. You're going to forget everything again in three days but trust me, I have another plan."

The two men parted, both anxious about this mystery. Jonah stopped by his room, where he secured Barnabas's box in his footlocker. His mind returned to the concerns of the day as soon as he walked out the door.

Everyone was already in the war room when Jonah arrived, including Willa, Wren, Saraé and Leo. Willa and Wren wished everyone well and encouraged them to look after Jonah. Saraé stood quietly at the table studying the war maps, Leo at her feet.

"Good morning, all," Jonah said as he entered.

"There you are," Willa greeted him with a kiss.

"Get a room," Wren chided, prompting everyone to look at her with tilted heads questioning the outburst. "What? It's our thing." Her voice trailed off as she could see no one was buying the explanation.

"You tossed and turned all night," Willa said softly, "I thought you'd be the first one here."

"I guess I wasn't all that motivated to get this day going," he said, squeezing her once more.

This comment prompted an involuntary but audible, "Aww," from most of the group.

Willa let Jonah go, "I came to say a personal goodbye to everyone. I will likely be preoccupied on the journey and want you all to know how much you mean to us and how much we are counting on you to take care of each other. In order to do that you'll need some of these items we found while investigating the dreams."

"They are yours, Willa," Filipina replied, "you should keep them."

"Thank you, Fili," Willa was touched by the sentiment. "Jonah and I discussed this, and we agree that these items are intended to help you complete your mission. They may even be mandatory at some point. We had this identified," she handed Jair's chameleon ring, found in Kamon, to the centaur. "You can use it to pass without a trace or disguise yourself. It has three charges per day, but it should help you be more..." she searched for the right word, "discreet when you want to be."

"This is amazing," Fili hugged her too tightly. "Thank you."

"You're very welcome." Willa picked up Gideon's ephod, holding it against her own chest one last time. "Lia, I have seen you fight in a manner that is entirely selfless and sacrificial. You are a protector so you should have the Breastplate of Righteousness."

The young sea elf paladin took the ephod, looking at it in awe. "Thank you, Willa, but shouldn't Jonah..."

"I'm with her, Lia," Jonah replied before she could finish. "It's yours."

Lia removed her current breastplate and donned the new one, "It's so light, and it fits perfectly."

"We aren't sure what else it does yet..." Willa began.

"I can help with that," Ember nearly ran to the front, anxious to be of service. She focused on the ephod for a few seconds, moving a pearl and an owl feather in her fingers as she spoke a prayer. Her eyes opened, "It adds protection, and the wearer can cast bless or shield up to three times in a day. It gains power as you do but I can't see beyond what it can do now."

"Thank you, Ember," Lia turned to Willa and Jonah, "and thank you."

Next Willa retrieved a long wooden staff that looked like four gnarled branches that had grown together ending at the top in a hook-like shape, "This oxgoad was Shamgar's gift to us," Willa held it out to Ember, "can you…"

"Of course," the young genasi repeated her prayer. "This is also very powerful. The wielder must activate it using the word 'Anath.' This will cause the oxgoad to emit radiant energy that causes damage to any evil creatures in its radius, growing as they get closer. It too has capabilities I can't discern yet."

"Amazing, thank you Ember." Willa turned to Rake and Elowen. "This should go to one of you."

Elowen answered, "Take it, Rake. My sister gave me a shield that requires activation. I don't want too many things to do before going into wild shape."

Rake took the staff from Willa, "Thank you."

Ember spoke up, "I had better save some of my power for the road trip. I can use my remaining strength, to magically find what the other items can do before we sleep."

"Good idea Ember," Jonah agreed. "We also know a guy in Gilgal who can help if needed."

Willa handed the golden rod from the Tola shrine to Jonah. "We have no idea what this does. You can decide who should have it when we find out."

She then lifted the cloak, looking at it fondly as she remembered her solitary encounter with Deborah. "We believe this to be the Cloak of Prayer. We don't yet know what it does, but it isn't likely to be activated accidentally. I hear Shay will be taking responsibility for protecting the healers and other support people so she should have it. Deborah herself served in a similar role against Sisera's forces."

"Thank you," Shay replied. "I only hope to live up to her example and yours."

Willa put a hand on her cheek and couldn't help but see a little of Wren in this young earth genasi warlock, "You already do, sweet girl."

Lastly, she grabbed the leather boots. "These are clearly the Boots of the Gospel. They have served us well in our mission already. They allowed me to read and understand many languages, giving us a way to spread the word of God. A local leather worker said they can also calm heightened emotions at will. We didn't know they could do that, so we don't know the limits. Looking back over many encounters, we recalled several times that this ability was likely swayed things in our favor. They should stay with your cleric, Azure."

"Thank you, Willa," the eladrin cleric replied. "I will use them to serve the Adonai as you have."

Willa looked at Jonah, who nodded. "Before Wren, Saraé and I leave you to your planning, we wanted to pray with you."

"I do have one last item that doesn't belong with me." Jonah pulled a scroll case from his hip pack. "This scroll provides a different spell each morning. We each opened it once and it gave us a spell specific to our abilities. New spells are a rare and valuable commodity for Wizards so, Ember, you should have it."

"I don't know what to say," Ember's eyes welled with tears that seemed to evaporate on her cheeks. "You gave me my freedom, a purpose and now this! I will use this for the glory of Adonai."

"We are so glad to hear you have dedicated yourself to Adonai. We know you will continue to learn and glorify his name," Jonah agreed. "Now let's give thanks to the one who truly deserves it. Father God, only you could have done all of this to save the eternal souls of your creations. Only you could have called all of us together from so many different places to serve your people. Only you could have gotten us this far in both doing your will and spreading your word. We pray that though we may never see the fruit of our efforts that you continue to guide us to your will. We surrender our lives and hearts to your service. Tell us what you want from us, and we will give everything to carry it out. Please protect Willa, Wren and Saraé as they answer your call to the orphan and the widow. Bring them many hands to reap the harvest that your spirit will bring. We love you God, we trust you with everything of value to us. In your holy name we pray. Amen."

No one even bothered to hide their tears as Jonah finished his heartfelt plea to the One True God. Several minutes passed in silence as each of the assembled heroes gathered themselves for what would come next.

The members of Coram Deo, old and new, made their final preparations before setting out for Gilgal and beyond. Some checked and cleaned their gear, others went to the tent city to get supplies, most went to the temple one last time to pray.

Soon they were all gathered in the stables near the farming community. They left in small groups. Given the recent incursion, it was prudent to take every precaution to protect the secrecy of Haven's existence. Segen Lisal and Seren Audra had tripled patrols in the mountains around the farms and prayed that the invaders didn't see anyone enter or leave Haven while they were spying on the farms.

The smaller groups met near Ai and traveled the rest of the way to Gilgal posing as a caravan of merchants. They kept to themselves along the road, though they didn't miss an opportunity to give aid when needed. They made it to Gilgal a couple hours before dusk. What they found there was incredible.

About a half mile from the city, they began to see tents along the road and riverbank. People of all ages, families, friends, craftsmen, and even vendors selling their wares were lining the road on both sides. As the small caravan passed people began to recognize them.

Kalin and Lukas were the first to rush up to greet them, "You made it!"

Jonah hugged them, "Us? We were so worried about you after we had to split in Magdala. Is everyone here?"

"Yes," Lukas replied, "and then some."

"Twenty-two more people joined our caravan along the way including two more orphans." Kalin seemed proud of the accomplishment and even looked a few years younger, somehow renewed by this new purpose.

"Amazing," Willa replied, hugging both men. "I can't wait to see the kids. We will catch up with you later, maybe for dinner?"

"Oh, everyone knows you are coming, there is a feast planned in your honor," Lukas laughed.

Jonah blushed a bit, "We don't want all of that. The glory should go to God."

"True enough," Kalin responded, "but the effort of his faithful servants can be celebrated in his name as well."

Jonah sighed, unable to argue that point. "Thank you Kalin, Lukas. We will find you later."

The rest of the new Coram Deo members had almost reached the bridge into the main town by the time Jonah and the others caught up. People who they had steered here were greeting them fondly too, citing their efforts as the main reason for their survival.

As the group reached the bridge, Azor, the Elven teen from Shamir, spotted them. He seemed an inch taller and was wearing a uniform similar to the Mishtala. He tapped a pudgy halfling guard on the shoulder, "Coram Deo! They are here!" Then he ran to greet his friends, starting with Jonah. Awkwardly hugging the taller man, Jonah returned the embrace.

"Are Zadok and Mari well?" Jonah asked, referring to his siblings.

"They are fine," Azor replied, "they are in school."

Willa looked around excitedly, "Where is the school?"

Azor bowed at Willa, unsure if it was proper to hug her. "They are holding it in the gathering room in the mansion until the new school is built nearby."

She touched the young man's face gently, "So polite and grown up. Thank you." She looked at Jonah, "We're going to go see the school and the house. We'll catch up later." Wren, Saraé and Leo followed Willa.

Jonah greeted Amos, the halfling guard leader. He had slimmed down since their last visit and his face no longer displayed the intensity it had before.

"Welcome back Jonah," he greeted, running a hand through his messy blond hair. "I see you brought friends."

Jonah introduced the rest of Coram Deo. After greeting the halfling Filipina, Shay, Lia, and Gadget decided to go find the magic shop they had been told about. Azure wanted to see the temple. Elowen and Ember went with her. Draco and Rake stayed with Jonah.

"How are your Mishtala holding up with the influx of people?" The paladin showed genuine concern. The town seemed to have tripled in size in just a few weeks.

"Better than you'd expect," Amos answered. "I think we have you to thank for that too."

"How so?"

"Some of the people you sent have been incredibly helpful," Amos explained. "Galen, Ariadne, Joss, Brace, Marilyn and others who joined them along the way all signed up to help with patrols and defense training." Amos tilted his head toward Azor, "We even instituted a squire-like program to teach the young adults. There are seven of them in the program with three more aging in on their next birthday."

"Amazing," Jonah responded, looking around at all of the activity. "Take care Amos, you're doing an incredible job!"

Jonah led his new teammates to the Sharpened Scythe Inn, next. They were barely in the door when people recognized Draco and Rake rushing to greet them and catch up. Jonah walked to the bar. Malevor, the minotaur owner of the place, had his back to him while he cleaned. "Who do you have to pray to get a meal around here?"

Malevor turned and his facial expression changed. He grabbed Jonah around the shoulders, hugging him and nearly pulling him over the bar. "Jonah, my brother! It is so good to see you!"

"Good to see you too my friend..." Jonah paused his hearing just catching up. "Wait did you say brother? Do you mean?"

"Yes! I have seen the truth of Adonai," the smile on the minotaur's face was like nothing Jonah had ever seen before, "thanks to the teaching of Luc and encouragement of Gadrun."

"That's such good news," Jonah replied as his friends joined them. "These are my friends Rake and Draco," he said, pointing out each of them. "This is Malevor, another new follower of Adonai."

They each shook hands at the elbow, barely completing the greeting before Malevor offered them food. The trio sat at the bar talking with Malevor while he worked. "You know there is a huge feast planned in the town center for all of you tonight?"

"We heard something about that on the way into town." Jonah paused for a second, "We have some news we can announce then when everyone is together."

"Uh oh, the last time you held a town meeting things got weird," Malevor chided, recalling their earlier visit to Gilgal.

Jonah chuckled, "I promise, only good news this time."

Azure's group entered the temple. She found it to be beautiful in a simple sense. It was meticulously clean and well kept. There were several people on the benches praying quietly. Near the dais was a dwarven man with a long red beard. He had soft, kind eyes, "Welcome to Adonai's Temple, I am Luc."

"Hi Luc," Azure replied. "Willa told us all about you, we thought we'd meet you for ourselves. This is Elowen and the young wizard is Ember."

"Well met ladies," Luc replied cordially. "Any friends of Willa's are friends of mine."

"I was hoping you'd say that," Azure said excitedly. "I need a favor."

Azure explained the idea that the trio had come up with to Luc. The four of them were instantly giddy with excitement over the idea. Then terrified that they had only hours to get it done before the gathering.

Willa hadn't been inside the mansion before. They had barely got past the front gate when it was Jafan's home. This time the gate was wide open. As she walked up, her kids in tow, they could see a dozen people working on a large building to the north. A smaller group was extending the mansion fence around the new construction. Others were coming and going bringing supplies and food to both places. Wren walked Leo to a tree and told him to rest.

Willa, Wren and Saraé entered tentatively and were instantly greeted by a familiar voice.

"Willa, Wren!" Zarra, the de facto leader of Jezreel during the evacuation, greeted them fondly. "We are so glad you stopped by. Come and meet the team." Willa followed her. Wren and Saraé heard voices from the library and headed in that direction. Zarra ushered her to a small room off the kitchen where a woman sat feverishly poring over papers and books. "This is Pren. She is organizing everything from building contracts to lesson plans."

Willa recognized the woman instantly, "It is good to see you under better circumstances, Pren."

The woman's eyes welled up. The sight of Willa had brought to mind her greatest regret. She had lied for Jafan and still felt responsible for Zelitra's banishment. "Willa, yes, good to see you," she stammered uncomfortably.

Willa hugged the woman who was surprised by the act. Willa whispered in her ear, "have you repented and asked for Adonai's forgiveness?"

"Yes, every day," Pren replied, unable to whisper through a sob.

"Then you are forgiven." Willa released her and looked the woman in the eye. "It is now time to forgive yourself."

Pren took a deep breath and gathered herself. "Thank you, I needed to hear that."

Zarra continued to lead Willa around the mansion. "I knew she had something dark weighing on her, but I was afraid to ask. She has been an incredible help."

"We all struggle with forgiving ourselves," Willa said.

Zarra showed her the ten bedrooms, each had been converted into a dorm style room with three bunk beds in each room. They were simply decorated, half for boys and half for girls. Some of them were clearly still vacant but about half were at least partially occupied. She then showed Willa to the library where an elder dwarven woman was teaching a class of about fourteen children. Wren and Saraé had taken seats on the floor behind the students listening intently to the history lesson.

"That is Brulnyss," Zarra was whispering, "she came from…"

"Kamon," Willa interjected. "Jonah met her there. She helped us on our quest."

"I shouldn't be surprised," the woman replied, shaking her head in amazement. "I can't believe I doubted you when we first met."

"Hah! We doubt ourselves often." Willa laughed too loudly, catching the attention of the students and teacher.

"We are sorry Brulnyss," Zarra offered, blushing a bit. "We didn't mean to interrupt."

Several of the children recognized Willa and Wren and looked from Brulnyss to Zarra. One young girl, Mari, who Willa had connected with in Shamir leaped to her feet and hugged Willa around the legs. Netty and Oren, from Kedesh, ran to Wren who introduced them to Saraé. Once everyone was seated again, Zarra officially introduced the family to Brulnyss. After a brief chat they excused themselves so the teacher could get back to work.

"Zarra, you all have done so much here for these kids," the elven cleric paused, not sure how to say what she had to say next, or how it would be taken. "Can we talk privately about something?"

Zarra nodded and led her to one of the vacant rooms.

After eating their fill Jonah, Rake and Draco headed for the smithy. Jonah wanted to check in on Gadrun. When they arrived there, he was hard at work as always. His smithy had doubled in size since Jonah was there last. There was a second forge and anvil set up nearby. Lukas was there working on armor pieces, while Gadrun was making a set of horseshoes.

Gadrun froze for a moment when he saw Jonah, then dropped his work in the water trough and hurried to greet him. He hugged Jonah tightly. "Greetings my brother," Gadrun held him by his upper arms, "Lukas told me you had arrived. I hoped you would come by."

"I had to check in on you," Jonah replied. "Thank you for giving your testimony to Malevor. He credits you and Luc with his change of heart. These are my brothers Rake and Draco."

Gadrun turned his attention to Jonah's friends, clearly uncomfortable with the compliment. "Well met," the elder human offered with a hug for each of them. "Are there any supplies you need while you are here?"

Draco spoke up, "We are heading into the mountains. Do you have climbing gear on hand? We have plenty of rope but could use pitons, crampons, grappling hooks and ice axes."

Lukas looked up, "I made a lot of those items last week for Ramah. Tell him I will replace whatever you take."

"Let us pay you for them," Rake offered.

"Your money is no good here," both men replied almost in unison.

Jonah replied instantly, "We brought a crate of weapons that we confiscated along our travels. I will have it delivered here for you to do with as you will. Melt them down or refurbish them as needed. Please let us provide what we can to this amazing place. We all have to do our part."

A lightbulb went off in Draco's mind at Jonah's comment, "Right! I have a half dozen daggers to contribute." He retrieved them from his pack and handed them to Gadrun.

"As if you all haven't done enough for everyone here," Gadrun grimaced.

"We can never do enough for the God who freed us," Jonah answered. "We owe him our lives and more."

"Literally, in some cases," Rake agreed.

"I see we're not going to win this argument," Gadrun stated, aiming the comment at Lukas, who chuckled, shaking his head. "We will see you tonight at the feast. Be prepared, it will be all about you, you're gonna hate it, but we all have to do our part, right?"

Jonah laughed at his comment thrown back at him. Shaking the man's shoulder he replied, "It is really good to see you. Both of you."

The trio headed to Ramah's shop next, to see about the climbing gear.

Saraé was completely engrossed in the history lesson, so Wren left her with the class. The young doppelganger turned girl had a voracious appetite for knowledge. Her nearly photographic memory absorbed anything she saw or heard quickly. Wren had set herself a challenge that she was not really looking forward to but was determined to carry out before making this place her next home.

She approached the mill, unwanted memories flooding back to her of her last visit there. It was a crime scene then, eerily quiet, and somber even before they started finding evidence of poor Harvit's demise. Today it was different, vibrant, and active. People were coming and going. Some carting in crops for milling, others carting out crates for delivery. The waterwheel was spinning slowly but consistently with the flow of the El Qelt River. All seemed right in this place, as if the tragedy of just weeks ago was but a faint memory. It was neither faint nor forgotten in Wren's mind, especially after running into Zelitra again in Magdala. It was that encounter that cemented her plan to get closure with Jafan.

She told Leo to wait for her outside and entered the building through the mill side entrance. It was controlled chaos inside. A half-dozen workers placed materials, retrieved completed grain, and packed them in sealed crates for delivery, stacking them neatly in a corner of the work area. Wren took it all in and couldn't help being impressed by the organization and efficiency of the operation. The door leading into the house squeaked loudly as it was opened. Wren looked to her right at the surprising sound. There stood Jafan covered in grain dust. His small, greasy hands showed cuts and bruises clearly earned with honest but hard work. He hadn't seen her when he entered the workspace, so she stepped back behind a wall to watch the gnome discreetly. A move that was devoid of her usual impulsive brashness.

Jafan walked straight to two of the workers. She could barely hear his words, but he seemed calm. He showed them a technique for adjusting the speed at which the grain was poured into the hopper. It had been coming too fast leaving a significant amount of grain on the top stone. He seemed careful and kind in his tutorial, watching them repeat the process, then patting them on the back in acknowledgement. He reminded her of her father teaching her. She stepped back completely out of sight, a feeling of conviction swept over her as she realized that her intent for this confrontation was completely wrong. She prayed there on the spot, asking God for clear vision and a pure heart in the conversation that was about to happen.

When she had finished praying, she stepped back into the work area, expecting to see Jafan with the two workers but they were back at work taking turns using the technique their boss had just shown them. She looked to her right to see where the gnome might have gone.

Before she could turn back, she heard, "Wren?" from her left.

She turned to see the gnome at a desk attending to some paperwork. They stared uncomfortably at each other for an awkward moment, neither prepared for the surprise confrontation.

"Before you say what I am sure I deserve, please know that I am truly sorry for what I have done and determined to make up for it for the people I have harmed and for Adonai." The gnome sat on his stool hunched over in shame.

"I won't lie. I came here fully intending to chastise you..." at which Jafan slouched further, "...but I was wrong to come here with that intention." The gnome looked up at her, a glimmer of hope in his eye. "First, I want to acknowledge the change in you. You have clearly taken this job seriously. I can see that you care for your workers and from the look of you, you don't ask them to do anything you're not willing to do yourself. You have done well here."

"When the town gave me this job, I was angry," he was looking at his feet again. "I resented the punishment but was also ashamed of myself at the tragedy I had set in motion. Once I started doing the job I realized how hard it was. I had seen Harvit as just a tool to be used, but in truth he was the lifeblood of this town. He toiled here so that everyone would be fed and sold the excess, pouring the money into the community."

Wren measured her words carefully, "the lesson you are learning was earned by your actions. You do know it is not a life sentence, right?"

"How can I ever make up for what I have done?" Tears welled up in his eyes. "The lives I have ruined can never be repaired. I take no pay. I provide rooms upstairs for the workers who need one. Every gold coin that we take here goes to the workers, pays to run this place, or is going to build the school. It's just not enough."

She put her hand on his shoulder. Sitting on his stool he was nearly her height. "Have you asked Adonai for forgiveness?"

"I can't, he must be so angry with me." He began to weep.

"Oh Jafan," she said, moving his chin with both hands so they were face-to-face. "That's not how this works at all."

She noticed that the workers around the room had all stopped and were edging closer. "If you love this man and want to see him set free, come and put a hand on him." All five of them did so.

Wren turned back to Jafan, "God will forgive you as soon as you ask. You can't buy back your salvation. It is given freely by the only person who can. Don't let pride stand in the way of his glory. Just ask for forgiveness."

Jafan looked up to see his coworkers around him, "Adonai, I am so sorry for all that I have done that is against your will. I know I can never earn your forgiveness, but I ask that you give it anyway. I promise to live my life for you and your people. I will never be perfect, but I will never be the old me again."

"That was perfect," Wren replied. "Now I am going to pray for you, and your friends are going to amplify it so there is no doubt." She paused for a second asking the Holy Spirit to give her the right words. "Father God, we love you and we trust you in all things. This man Jafan has been selfish and far from you, but the man I see before me today is not that man anymore. He has surrendered to your will and relinquished his own."

Various co-workers voiced agreement with "Yes, Lord."

"Forgive him Lord as only you can," Wren continued. "Set him free of the pain of the past but not the memory of it. We learn much from our missteps. Don't let him live in shame any longer. Set him free to live in your glory. Encourage him to continue to give of himself not in recompense, but in true charity to spread your word to all who would hear it. We know you are a good God who tempers justice with mercy. Consider Jafan's plea and accept his surrender to your will. Thank you, Lord, for listening to our prayer. In your name we ask, Amen."

As Wren finished the prayer Jafan inhaled deeply pressing back into his coworkers behind him. Tears were still flowing as his friends hugged him. Wren stepped away to make room, but Jafan grabbed her hand and pulled her into the group.

He leaned his head up to her ear and whispered, "Thank you."

"You did the work, and asked for forgiveness," she whispered back. "I just got to see you being born again as a new creation. That's all the thanks I will ever need."

Filipina, Shay, Lia, and Gadget made their way to Ramah's Enchanted Items, which served as a general store and outfitter for the area. Though he specialized in gear for everything from farming to adventuring it was also known that the half-elf traded in items of magical capability as well.

Gadget approached the man behind the counter, "Hello, my name is Gadget, are you Ramah?"

"I am. Pleasure to meet you Gadget," Ramah's voice was lilting and inviting. "That's an odd name for one of such petite beauty."

"It is a name more tied to my skill set than anything else," she explained. "My name is Sapientia, but many find it difficult to remember."

"Do you mind if I use your given name?" She nodded and the half-elf seemed pleased. "What brings you to my humble store, Sapientia?"

"My friends Jonah and Willa said that you trade in items of curiosity and power," she replied hopefully.

"Ah, you are friends of Coram Deo!" His already high level of enthusiasm jumped up a couple of notches at the name-drop.

"Actually, we are part of Coram Deo now," she said proudly.

"Excellent," Ramah replied. "Their sphere of influence is growing as will their impact in the region I will wager."

"With God on our side, who can stand against us?" She offered proudly.

"Yes, well said," he mused. "Though many will try, Adonai's will shall be done. Are you buying or selling today?"

"Possibly both," she replied. "I have a couple of inventions with me. Can I get your professional opinion?" She placed a pair of goggles and a metal ball with a wick coming out of the top on the counter.

Ramah inspected both items carefully. His eyebrows raised a bit, "Impressive crafting. What do they do?"

"The goggles allow people with normal vision to see in the dark," she beamed.

"Impressive," he admitted. "Though I have seen similar items in my travels, they are rare. The ball? It smells funny."

"Yes," she replied. "I gave it a ten second fuse. The thin metal casing adds to the damage as it breaks apart during the explosion. I call it a 'boom-ball'."

"Brilliant!" Ramah was genuinely impressed. "Can I ask what provides the explosion?"

"That's a trade secret," she responded wryly. "Suffice it to say it has alchemical and divine components."

"Fair enough," he agreed. "I can get 75 gold for the goggles and 50 gold each for the Boom Balls. I will keep only 20% and give you the rest, when they sell of course."

"Deal," she responded, proud of the accomplishment. "I want my share to go to the orphanage and school."

"Is there no end to the generosity of Coram Deo?"

The gnome did not answer, assuming the question to be rhetorical as she retrieved six boom balls and three sets of goggles from her pack and handed them to Ramah.

Chapter 21
The Fruit of the Spirit

As dusk began to fall on Gilgal people began to shut down their businesses and head for the festival ground that had been set up in the center of town near the Sharpened Scythe Inn. There were tables of all shapes and sizes everywhere they could fit. One huge table dominated the front and was facing all the rest. People began milling in from the homes in town and the tents all along the road. Soon, it seemed that every person in Gilgal was there mingling, singing and praying together in community.

Malevor's voice boomed over the din of the crowd, "Please find a seat, we will be serving the food. I have asked one of our guests-of-honor, Jonah, to pray for the meal."

Jonah rose to raucous applause and even a few shouts of Coram Deo. He raised his hands before beginning and the crowd quieted. "Father God, we are in awe of your provision. We see the faces in this place and know that you are a good, loving Father who wants all his children together. We pray today that you bless our journeys wherever they may take us in your name. We ask that you give us boldness and courage to not only do your will, but to use the words and skills you have graciously given us to spread your gospel to those far from you by chance or by choice. We love you, we trust you, and we thank you for all that you have already given us. In your mighty name we pray. Amen."

The cheer that erupted after the blessing lasted minutes. People were on their faces in prayer, hugging each other, and praising the Lord in thanks for their own stories of redemption and forgiveness. Eventually everyone sat and the food was served. Several townspeople played instruments softly while the rest shared a hearty meal together. As the food was cleared away, a few people went to the front of the gathering to say a few words about their guests. Most were stories of how Coram Deo, old and new, had found them at their worst and offered them a better way. Galen, who was worshiping Bael one day and fearing God the next, spoke. Then Davel, the necropolis caretaker, shared how he had lost all hope in life until he met them. One by one the stories flowed ensuring that not a dry eye was to be found.

Azure stepped away to take a moment. This whole journey was overwhelming. She had mastered the ability to look the part but inside she was unsure of herself and her abilities. She felt dread at the thought of one of her companions dying on her watch. She knew that God's will would prevail, but she also knew that none of them were guaranteed to see the end of the mission. She shuddered at the thought as she stepped behind the inn where it wasn't much quieter, but it was more private.

"Azure?"

The voice came from the darkened back door of the inn. The lantern outside the door left only the man's silhouette visible. She had heard the voice only once before, when she used the sending stone in her pack, but she recognized it instantly. "Who's there?"

A young wood elf stepped out into the lamplight. He had short white hair that was much longer at the front. He wore a rapier and dagger on his belt and had a flute on a chain around his neck. His face was not angry but showed confusion or maybe concern. "You really don't know me?"

"No, I'm sorry." Azure's empathy made it impossible for her not to feel the pain of others in a very real way. "I may be able to explain why, but I'm not sure it will make any sense. Would you mind telling me your story first?" She motioned toward a table that the inn staff probably used to get away from the chaos for a few minutes during their shifts.

He sat, then paused briefly gathering his thoughts, "First, my name is Ayzee Blight. We are both from a town near Borsippa, far to the north of here. When I was very young a dragon attacked my people killing many including my mother. I was too young then to do anything about it, but our greatest warriors were sent every year to exact revenge and slay the beast. Every expedition failed, most of the warriors never returned. The few who did come back told the leaders that the dragon's name was Avalystra. They verified that she was the one who had attacked us but reported that she denied it vehemently. She claimed that she wanted no trouble, but she would defend her home. She never pursued those who fled her lair. Those who did make it back returned with one message from the beast, that she never hunts intelligent humanoids, only beasts and aberrations. Of course, there were many living witnesses to her attack. No one believed her claims so the expeditions to kill her continued to be sent every year."

The young bard paused to gather himself before continuing, "I grew up dreaming of one day leading such a mission. I studied all the dragons of lore but found little about Avalystra.

One writer described her as reclusive and almost motherly. This author claimed that she only killed people who attacked her in her lair and avoided people outside of her lair. She hunted for food, choosing large beasts or aberrations. There was not one mention of her attacking the cities or people of Aeramor." Ayzee paused for a moment. Azure could see the retelling was affecting him negatively. Soon he collected himself, leaving the cleric wondering if her new boots were helping him to stay calm.

He continued, "I was undeterred. I turned to the study of war and focused on bardic pursuits. After the twentieth failed mission by my people members, I began to form my own party of adventurers. My first choice was a young halfling orphan who I grew up with, named Eustace. He survived by picking pockets so the two of us moved to Borsippa and lived as petty thieves. We made some enemies, but also gained the notice of Sethrekar Mystan, a local 'gangster' whose fingers were in every criminal activity in and around Borsippa. He appreciated our skill, but he couldn't allow us to keep causing chaos in his city. He gave us the choice to work for him for an excellent wage or disappear mysteriously. We obviously chose the former, doing whatever Sethrekar asked of us. Working for him allowed us access to his network, which we used to find more members for our dragon hunting group. We met a Minotaur fighter named Zed, a Drow wizard named Veridia, a Half-Orc barbarian named Garogg, and you. We practiced tactics for months. Then one spring day we made our way into the desert to Avalystra's lair to confront her."

He took another deep breath, "She was welcoming and almost hospitable until I brought up her attack on my people. She became enraged, claiming that she had never attacked a city. The denial was too much for me, and I recklessly attacked. The plan was out the window, destroyed by emotion, and as you would imagine, the fight went poorly. Garogg and Veridia were killed almost instantly. Zed yelled for Eustace to run, not sure where the sneaky thief had gone. Then he grabbed you and me and ran out of the lair, despite our protests. We narrowly escaped and hid from the dragon's pursuit, though it never came. When we were sure there would be no pursuit, we looked for Eustace, but he must not have made it out. I refused to leave until we knew for sure. You and Zed went for help, so I gave you one of my sending stones. Help arrived three days later, without you and Zed. When the dragon finally left to feed, my rescuers went in but found no trace of my friend. I arrived in Borsippa days later to find that you and Zed had both left. I was angrier than ever, and it showed in my behavior and lifestyle over the next few years. I had all but given up on my old life when my sending stone suddenly spoke to me. It was your voice, Azure's. I had to know what happened, so I quickly called in favors and had your stone scryed upon to find its twin. The vision I saw led me to Bethel, where I found you and followed you here."

"Oh, my," she said, stunned at this revelation. "That is quite a story."

"You don't remember any of it?" He was sure hearing the story would make a difference.

"I'm sorry, I don't, but as I said I think I know why." She paused to gather her thoughts.

"Go ahead, I'm listening."

"I am certain that I don't remember any of your story because it was not me who was there," she exhaled after the statement as if it took some effort to say.

"What does that mean?" Ayzee was back on his feet, pacing.

"Please sit," her voice remained calm. "I'll explain." When he cooperated, she continued. "My name is actually Claire, I'm from a place called Earth."

Ayzee's mouth was agape.

"I know it's hard to believe, but I'm not the only one who was sent here in this way. We think that somehow when we went through the portal that brought us here, we were either swapped with counterparts here, or…" She trailed off, not sure how to say the rest.

"Or what? You replaced dead people, took over their bodies? This is all ridiculous?" Ayzee was clearly frustrated.

"We simply don't know," she explained. "All we know is our world has only humans and no magic. I don't look anything like this there."

"So, I wasted my time," he sighed heavily.

"Not necessarily," her voice was purposeful and soothing. "Come meet my friends. Maybe it is time you learned a better way to live and had a new purpose."

Azure returned to the celebration with Ayzee. No one even noticed them as they sat at the end of the table. The testimonials were continuing, and no one could look away. Ayzee sat there, largely unmoved by the stories at first. He listened in hopes of learning something about these people before they officially met.

Eventually Ramah stepped in as the stories of how God had used these heroes could go on all night. "We are told that our friend has something to say, so Jonah?"

Jonah didn't stand, he simply looked over at his wife, "I think he means you…"

"Yes," the pink haired elf agreed. "I suppose he does." Willa rose to her feet and stepped in front of the table. "First, I want to thank all of you for the kind words and stories. We are so blessed to have been called to this place and this work. We are humbled at the effect it is having. But as you hopefully know by now, every bit of the glory for this goes to God. We simply try to heed his call and live our lives before his face. We make no claim that any of this is happening by our power."

The people began to clap, but Willa quickly raised her hands and looked to the sky, passing the adoration to Adonai.

When the gathering quieted again, Willa took a deep breath and continued, "Over the past weeks I have seen a great need in this world. God has called my attention to the people most victimized by this war, widows, and orphans. We have seen horrible things happening out there in the world. War has widowed so many and orphaned a generation of kids who now have no one left in the world to care for them. We need to help them before they can lose hope. I am so proud of all of you here for coming to this realization on your own. The work you have done to provide housing and a school for these children is inspiring."

She paused again, forced by more applause. "Our family has decided to split our focus and aid in that mission, while continuing the mission to rescue and protect the believers. Jonah will be joining with these brave heroes, who many of you already know as part of Coram Deo. Rake, Filipina, Shay, Draco, Gadget, Lia, Elowen and Ember will ensure that God's people are found and protected in the name of Adonai. I will be staying here in Gilgal with my daughters to help you see to the needs of these children in any role you all see fit."

Zarra stepped up to the front, "Willa, can I speak for a moment."

"Of course," Willa responded.

"After you told me your plan to stay here this afternoon I met with Luk and Brulnyss. We discussed how the temple, orphanage, and school should work together, and we came up with a plan. We want all the children in the area to live together and learn together. We want them to pray together, praise together, and someday serve together in our places. We need someone to lead the school who will stay connected with the temple. The children need to be taught about the Lord first, but also be given a well-rounded education preparing them for the future. We agree unanimously that we need you to run the school."

"I am flattered," Willa was in tears, Jonah joined her to comfort and congratulate. "If you are sure, I will gladly accept."

Zarra continued, "We thought we might call the school **'Solus Deus bet Hammidras'** because only God could have empowered us to even get this far. Brulnyss and I will live in the manor and run the orphanage, but we don't want it called that. The children here may have lost their birth parents, but Adonai has adopted them and given them to us as our own. We were thinking of calling it **'Behth 'av'** which means The Father's House."

"That's perfect!" Willa beamed. "I am so proud to join this group in this mission. This has been such an amazing day."

Gadget and Azure approached Willa, "It's just getting started Willa, come with us, you too Wren and Saraé." The group of ladies and girls rushed the confused cleric into the inn.

Rake and Draco grabbed Jonah, "You're coming with us big boy."

Jonah looked confusedly at Malevor, who simply shrugged his massive shoulders in feigned confusion as the pair ushered him into the nearby guard shack.

As soon as they both were gone dozens of people were in motion setting up for the next event.

When Jonah appeared from the guard shack, he was wearing white and purple robes. The area where they had been sitting for dinner was completely different. There was a path of flower petals leading from the inn to a massive archway of flowers. Luk was wearing black robes and was standing in the archway. Jonah instantly knew that his friends and probably his daughter had set up a wedding for him and Willa. A wave of gratitude came over him as he looked at all the smiling faces around him. Azure and the other ladies were giddy with pride over pulling off this surprise.

Jonah looked to Rake and Draco, "You could have warned me."

"I don't know about Rake, but I would have told you," Draco admitted., "probably why they didn't tell me."

Jonah and Rake chuckled and agreed with the halfling's assessment.

Suddenly the music started again followed at once by a wave of fear through Jonah as he reached the archway. Jonah recognized the words to Psalm 128:1-6 as many in the gathering sang it softly.

"Blessed are all who fear the LORD, who walk in
obedience to him. You will eat the fruit of your labor;
blessings and prosperity will be yours.
Your wife will be like a fruitful vine within your house;

your children will be like olive shoots around your table.

Yes, this will be the blessing for the man who fears the LORD.

May the LORD bless you from Zion;

may you see the prosperity of Jerusalem all the days of your life.

May you live to see your children's children — peace be on Israel."

The psalm had never moved Jonah more than in this moment. Tears welled up in his eyes as his two daughters, both sent to his care by God himself, walked out of the inn. They threw flower petals as they walked, stopping in front of the women of Coram Deo, opposite Jonah at the archway. As soon as they arrived the music changed, the singing stopped. Jonah was transfixed by his wife, who appeared to glow as she walked to the archway, led by their friend Barnabas.

When they arrived Jonah hugged his mentor, "Thank you for this."

"Thank your friends," Barnabas whispered back, "they arranged all of it. I wouldn't have missed it for the world."

As Barnabas stepped in line with Rake and Draco, Luk cleared his throat and began to speak. Jonah couldn't take his eyes off his wife as he realized that this wedding was more like the ones at home than the ones they had seen in dreams or in Pirathon. Luk spoke words that Jonah assumed were traditional at a Hebrew wedding.

The dwarf introduced the couple out of tradition, not necessity. Then he quoted Genesis about man leaving his parents and cleaving to his wife. Willa beamed as Luk sang the words of Psalm 133:1-3 to bring things to a close.

"How good and pleasant it is
when God's people live together in unity!"
Many began to join in the song as the verse was repeated.
"It is like precious oil poured on the head,
running down on the beard,
running down on Aaron's beard,
down on the collar of his robe.
How good and pleasant it is
when God's people live together in unity!
It is as if the dew of Hermon were falling on Mount Zion.
How good and pleasant it is
when God's people live together in unity!
For there the LORD bestows his blessing,
even life forevermore.
How good and pleasant it is
when God's people live together in unity!"
This song was repeated three times, once for the groom,
once for the bride and finally for the God who had made
them and brought them together.

As the chorus faded Luk finished the ceremony and
announced that the couple was now one in the eyes of the Lord.
A cheer erupted that may have been heard in Heaven itself.
Jonah had always loved the lyrics about the 'sound of Heaven
touching Earth'. He couldn't help but wonder, in this moment,
if this could be the sound the writer of that song was describing.

The celebration went well into the night. People danced,
sang and gave praise to the God who made all this possible.
Old and new members of Coram Deo were swarmed with
people offering congratulations and thanks for all that they had

done to get them to safety during their evacuations. Ayzee was awestruck by story after story of how these people overcame grave circumstances to help strangers escape certain death. The weightiest testimony came from an older man, a young woman, and a twentyish boy. They spoke of their service to Bael and a confrontation with Jonah's family that should have been the end of their lives. The man, Galen, thanked them for this second chance and the opportunity to get to know Adonai. They attributed their service to this community to the family's obedience to God's will.

Ayzee, whose heart had only known rage and anger for so many years, began to feel hope. As if on cue the horrific memory of the dragon swooping from the sky breathing fire on his home returned as did the anger that it wrought. He sat on a bench, his head in his hands, shaking with anger and despair.

A hand touched his shoulder. Ayzee looked up through tears to see Azure standing there, her eyes closed in prayer for him.

"I don't deserve it," he sobbed. "I have done terrible things."

"God will forgive you," the eladrin cleric assured the young wood elf, "when you are ready to ask." Azure stayed with this man who she had met only today, though he had known her for years, as he struggled to give up his idol of rage.

Jonah and Willa were sent off to the 'honeymoon suite' of the Sharpened Scythe Inn. It was just another room but decorated just for them with rose petals on the floor and scented candles to cover the smell of food cooking downstairs. It was also private as Wren and Saraé camped with the rest of Coram Deo near the river. They enjoyed precious moments together, knowing that at best they were the last they would have for a while. They didn't even want to consider the worst-case scenario. They would trust God and continue to do his will to the best of their ability.

Sleep took all of them easily that night. There were no dreams or visions, nor were there fears or anxiety, despite the questions looming and the mission ahead. Nothing penetrated their hearts or minds that night, God had seen their efforts in his name, and he had given them rest.

Chapter 22
To The Mountain

Morning found the entire group rested and revitalized. They were physically ready for the next leg of the journey, even if some of their minds and hearts were breaking. The rest of the team, leaving soon for Mount Nebo, finished preparations for the journey, allowing Jonah some final moments with his family.

Jonah took advantage of that time. They had breakfast together, then brought the girls' belongings to the rooms in the completed part of the school intended for the new administrator. The builder was going to adjoin the rooms on either side to accommodate the small family. They had offered more space, but Willa declined. The three of them and Leo didn't need much space. They were happy just to be together. Jonah and Willa discussed plans and contact schedules though they knew, by now, that Jonah's ability to reach them would be inconsistent. As they brought their gear into the rooms and separated Jonah's there was a knock at the door.

"Good morning," Azure greeted the family with a smile. "I Hope you two had a good rest, or not..." she teased.

"Gross," Wren feigned retching. "Children in the room." She was covering Saraé's ears but the look on the girl's face made it clear she had no idea what was going on.

Azure laughed, "Fair enough. I sometimes forget your true age."

"Is it time for him to go already?" Willa looked stricken.

"No, but soon." Azure paused. "I'm not sure if you caught any of the story last night, but the man on the other end of the sending stone I found in my pack, tracked me down."

Jonah shifted, instantly going into protector mode.

"It's ok," Azure assured the paladin. "We talked. He doesn't really understand that I am not the Azure he knew but he accepts it. He told me this morning that he was going to come with us. He's still angry over his past but he recognizes a need for change in his life."

"That's good news," Jonah agreed. "We'll take all the help we can get, but you didn't have to come here to tell us that."

"I know, that's only part of the reason I am here." Azure reached into a pouch on her side retrieving two smooth stones. She held one out to each of them. "Ayzee gave me his and Xof brought me mine. We wanted you to have them. We thought it might make this situation a tiny bit less awful for you."

They each took a stone, unsure what to say in the moment. Willa looked at it then at Azure. Her eyes were full of tears that dropped onto the eladrin's shoulder as they hugged.

Willa whispered, "Keep him alive. I know it is a lot to ask but keep them all alive."

"I will do my best," Azure assured her friend. "As long as I stand, they will too." They broke the embrace, "I better get back, we leave in an hour. Do you need me to carry any of your things to the group?"

"No, I can get it," Jonah replied. "You have done more than enough. Thank you."

Jonah, Willa, Wren, Saraé and yes, even Leo made the most of their last moments together for a while. They prayed, each taking a turn asking God to protect the others. Forty-five minutes later Jonah kissed his wife, surprisingly to no protest from his elder daughter. He hugged each of them not wanting to let go. Then he took a knee by Leo. The wolf sat before him face-to-face. "You're the man of the house now buddy, you know what to do."

Leo nuzzled his head up under Jonah's chin. Jonah knew this was Leo's way of saying, "I've got this."

With one last kiss and a group hug Jonah was off.

Coram Deo was ready and packed when Jonah arrived ten minutes early. As he greeted his new group, he spotted a man nearby who he recognized. "Kenath?"

The man looked at him with a concerned look on his face upon hearing his name. That look changed to a smile when he saw Jonah, "I was glad to see you made it here," Kenth offered. "I didn't want to bother you last night on such a festive occasion. I take it you found what you were looking for in Tola's tomb?"

"Yes, we did, thanks to you," Jonah replied as he hugged the man. "It would have been no bother to see you last night. I am happy that your family is here safely."

Kenath's face grew serious at that statement, "This place is as wonderful as you said. It has been a welcome respite on our journey, but we cannot stay."

"I'm sorry to hear that," Jonah admitted. "May I ask why?"

"This is just not our mission," Kenath explained, turning so no one else could hear his next words. "We of the Unseen are sworn to go to the most difficult places and spread the word through shared work and community."

"I understand," Jonah agreed. "I am leaving my family behind to help with the children orphaned by the war, while the rest of us continue our original mission. We all do what we are called to do, even when it seems impossible."

"I knew you would understand." Kenath leaned in closer, "We are heading south through Jerusalem, then northwest to Joppa. We are going to seek passage to Ebreyon. Many have gone before and have made homes in Lyon, Valinor and even the Freelands. It is time the rest of the world heard about Adonai."

"That's a truly amazing mission," Jonah beamed. "I wish you safe travels and God's protection. If there is anything we can do for you…"

Kenath didn't let Jonah finish. "You have already done enough," he replied, tilting his head toward the tents along the river. "You spread the word to Israel and Judah, we will do the same in Ebreyon."

Jonah rejoined the group, who were waiting for him patiently. He had said goodbye to his family in private because he didn't want to cry in front of the entire town. It was an issue of pride that he was still working to overcome. The journey would be several days, barring problems, and most of the group were anxious to get started. Jonah was less anxious. The people of the tent city lined the river road heading east, cheering and waving. They promised prayers for the group and protection for those left behind. Jonah took up a position at the rear of the formation. Soon the crowd began to thin. Jonah spotted young Azor waving at him in his Mishtala trainee uniform. Jonah wagged a finger at him that stopped his waving. Jonah turned, squaring up his body to face the young man, then saluted him, fist to chest, as was the custom here. The boy's smile nearly reached his ears as he returned the gesture with pride. With a slight nod the elated Elven boy disappeared into the crowd heading back toward town. Jonah caught back up to the group and fell in line as they walked.

Shortly after crossing the Jordan, they stopped to eat. Rake, Fili, Lia and Jonah gathered to check the map and make sure they were on the right path. Jonah was still noticeably quiet.

Fili was never one to hold her tongue, "You gonna be ok Jonah?"

Jonah was elsewhere until he heard his name, "Huh, yeah, I'm good," he lied.

"Ok everyone, get focused," Rake addressed the group, always the diplomat. "We need to continue due east," he looked up to point to a split in the mountains in that direction. "When we get to that pass we should find a river. Then we simply keep to the south and east faces of Mount Nebo until we hit Deepforge."

Lia spoke up, "We should rest near the river, either before or after the pass."

"Yeah," Rake agreed.

"Before the pass is better," Jonah replied to everyone's delight. "That gives us the night to recon what's ahead."

The trio nodded in agreement. They had begun to understand some of Jonah's strange earth words.

Shay brought them some jerky, bread and water, which they decided to eat while they walked.

As the sun lowered in the sky behind them and they neared Mount Nebo, Draco and Elowen had gone ahead to scout for signs of trouble.

Elowen came racing back from the southern side. "We have potential trouble ahead," she was a bit breathless from the sprint back. "I saw a demon portal and several demons waiting in a clearing with a woman in robes. She had blue skin and blond hair." Elowen looked at Lia, "She looked a lot like you, but older."

Draco hadn't returned yet, but the rest of the group spread out in pairs and approached the clearing in a half circle formation. Elowen and Rake both prayed for sure steps and quiet, each keeping a couple of the more heavily armored teammates near them. Rake led Jonah to the far right. Gadget and Ayzee went to the near right. Ember and Fili went to the far left, with Shay and Azure to the near left. Elowen led Lia straight up the middle so she could get a look at the face of the ambush leader.

As soon as the woman turned from the portal to face the surrounding trees Lia knew her face, "Aunt Qiné," she mumbled under her breath as she broke cover and began walking directly toward her.

Jonah had just informed Rake that the woman exuded evil when he saw Lia appear from the woods.

Rake knew that he and Jonah were the flanking squad, so he reached for his sending stone, "Fili you and Ember give support. Draco we are half a mile southwest of where you left us, get here now. Everyone else, stay hidden and ready."

No sooner had he stopped speaking he saw the centaur with Ember on her back join Lia, who was still intent on getting to the woman by the portal.

Draco responded, "On my way at top speed."

As Lia approached her target it was clear, from the look on the woman's face, that she knew the young paladin.

The winged bone demon stood by its mistress, despite the approaching enemies. A chain in his right hand led to an unseen object inside the portal. The various imps and two barbed demons spread out, some looking toward the woods while the others watched the approaching trio.

"Aunt Qiné?" Lia stopped about twenty feet from the other woman.

Fili leveled her spear at the bone devil, while Ember dismounted and watched their backs.

"Oh, you are ready to accept family now?" The elder sea elf asked accusingly.

"What does that mean?" Lia asked incredulously.

"You left nearly twenty years ago, Liathana," the woman responded matter-of-factly. "Now you think you are owed something?"

"I was kidnapped, brought here and sold into slavery," Lia was furiously yelling now. "If you are working with these demons back off and leave us alone!" Her hand was on the hilt of her sword.

"You'll get one offer from me, 'niece'," that last word dripping with sarcasm. "Give me the halfling who has stolen from me and walk away, or you die with the rest of the faithful idiots hiding in the woods."

"Draco? What are you talking about?" Lia replied, struggling to understand any of this.

Just then Draco burst from the woods, directly behind Lia, and inside Qiné's line of sight. He looked around taking in the scene, quickly realizing that he should have stayed concealed.

As soon as Qiné saw him, her facial expression changed to what can only be described as her 'game face'. "There he is, take him, kill the rest." All the demons on the field rushed toward Draco, Qiné turned toward the portal to watch what was coming next. The bone devil pulled the chain and a creature stepped through the black and red swirl. It seemed to resist the pull but upon seeing Qiné it complied. It was eight feet tall, with deep blue skin and thick muscles. It had a massive scimitar in its left hand and wore a cloth headdress of sorts. It was lightly armored, and its right hand crackled with blue energy.

"If you separate the Aetherian, contain it in this," she handed him an ornate container. "Bring me the box, the halfling and his belongings. Kill anyone who gets in your way."

With nothing more than a slight nod, it locked its eyes on Draco. The bone devil released the chain, leaving behind an odd metal collar with lines of greenish light running throughout it. The Djinn looked at the devil and its master with clear disdain then at Draco with a softer look, almost showing pity, before it began walking toward the halfling with purpose.

Draco had gotten himself into plenty of scraps over the years, so he was always ready for something he had done to come back to haunt him. He knew the blue woman and she was right, he had stolen from her, several things in fact. One of those things was not a thing at all. It was a person, Shadolok, who had become part of him in these past weeks. Determination crossed his face as the Djinn approached. It was at least four times his size and looked angry. Daggers of pale blue light appeared in Draco's hands, which he threw at his assailant.

They both found purchase in the barrel chest of the creature, its face tensing with the psychic pain of the attack.

The battlefield erupted into chaos at that point, the front-line fighters charged, the druids wild-shaped and the rest did their best to provide support to the widespread group.

Jonah emerged from the trees with black pools for eyes and spectral wings flapping. He swung straight down on a surprised imp cutting it in two. As the creature turned to dust, he swung backhanded at the barbed devil now to his right. He prayed for divine power against the demon causing his sword to radiate as it hit the creature's ribs. Jonah could feel the energy of Adonai release pushing the creature further to his right, but it managed to clamp its arm down over Jonah's pinning his weapon to the creature's side. As Jonah tried to pull free, Rake, in his bipedal lizard form, hit the demon full force. It toppled to the ground taking Jonah with it. Rake-zilla nearly tripped over their now prone bodies but managed to regain his footing as he passed.

Filipina and Lia were also ready. Lia ran for her aunt, but Qiné saw her coming. She retrieved a vial and began moving her hands to cast a spell. Before Lia could get to within five feet of her aunt a blast of cold energy hit her. Ice formed in all the crevices of her armor and around her feet. She could move her upper body a bit, but her lower legs were locked in place. Qiné looked at her one last time, shaking her head in disappointment, before turning and going through the portal. The black and red swirl closed behind her. Fili had charged at the bone devil using her go-to move. She hit the creature at top speed with her front hooves then speared it while it was recovering its balance. She could feel the exposed bones crack under the force of her hooves, but the spear had found spaces between its ribs, doing little damage.

Ember was suddenly alone on the field. She surveyed the situation around her. To her right she saw two imps, one had gone toward Jonah and Rake further to her right, but the other had made eye contact with her. It smiled and drooled a little in expectation of its next meal then vanished. The young mage prayed and moved her hands sending a loud thunderclap sounded in the direction she assumed the imp would take. She was off target by a bit, but the edge of the blast hit the creature enough to reveal it. As it became visible it lashed out with its tail hitting her on the shoulder. Almost instantly she swooned from the poison in her veins.

Shay had seen the imp head for Ember from her position. With an encouraging "Go!" from Azure she was already on her way to her injured companion. Her face focused as she used her telekinetic ability. The imp felt an invisible shove moving it back ten feet. As Shay took a protective position over her friend, a crossbow bolt appeared in the chest of the imp, turning it to dust. Suddenly, Ayzee appeared at Shay's side playing his flute. Wisps of light flowed from the instrument to Lia, still frozen in place.

Gadget, the problem solver of the group, didn't even wait to see if her crossbow bolt had hit the imp she fired at. She was already running full speed on an intercept course with the Djinn. Something had caught her attention, and she was not to be deterred.

Azure had followed behind Shay, she barely avoided Elowen in bear form crossing the field. When she arrived at the group she grabbed Ember, whose weight was heavy against her, and dragged her back to the tree line.

Elowen-bear rammed into the other barbed devil hitting with tooth and claw. An imp joined the fray, lashing out at the distracted bear with its poisonous tail, but missed, barely. As the Djinn passed by her it had a painful look on its face. Never taking its eyes off Draco, it swatted the imp. Lightning arced from its hand into the small demon causing it to disappear in a poof of dust. The two remaining imps on that side split up, one heading toward the immobilized Lia, the other to replace the downed imp on Elowen.

The Djinn bore down on Draco with a singular purpose. The halfling did what he usually did when faced with melee combat. He deferred to his symbiotic counterpart. Black smoke poured from his mouth and nose trying to engulf him. Before the process could complete the halfling was hit with a thunderous blast from the hand of the Djinn. Draco flew twenty feet back into the thick trunk of a tree. The wisps of smoke evaporated into the air as the halfling fought to stay conscious, the wind knocked from his lungs. Unleashing the thunderous blast did not even slow down the djinn's advance. It grabbed Draco off the ground, turned on a heel and headed back toward the bone devil, where the portal had been.

Rake-zilla lashed out with his tail killing the last imp near them while biting viciously at the barbed devil still wrestling with Jonah on the ground. Jonah had rolled over slamming the demon with his shield allowing him to pull his sword arm free. Using the momentum of his roll and Rake's distraction the paladin was able to straddle the creature, driving his sword down into its face. It stiffened then turned to dust. The pair gathered themselves and ran to aid Fili.

Fili hadn't had time to wonder why she was still alone fighting the most powerful of the demons in this fight. She dropped her spear and drew her matching hand axes. She crossed them blocking the creature's tail sting, but it managed to hit her with its claws, raking them across her ribs on both sides.

Lia could feel the power of Ayzee's song coursing through her. She reared back with her sword and drove the hilt into the ice at her feet, it shattered, freeing her legs. Seeing Jonah and Rake heading to Fili's aid she ran to her left to help Elowen.

The bear was holding her own against the barbed monstrosity. Each was doing damage to the other. Despite her powerful bear form she wondered how long she could keep this up. If her wild shape faltered, she would stand little chance against this demon. If a bear could smile, she would have as she could see the rocks, leaves and debris on the ground began to swirl behind the beast. She knew this was Azure's spiritual weapon. As it formed fully it began to pummel the creature, distracting it from Elowen's assault.

Gadget had seen Draco get blasted then throttled by the Djinn. She was concerned for her friend but couldn't take her eyes off the collar. Every fiber in her being was saying that the mechanical device, seemingly powered by magic, was the key to stopping the strange being. As the fight raged around her, she ran up behind the Djinn not sure how to even get to the contraption five or six feet above her.

Two more claw strikes had Fili on the ropes. She had connected a couple of times with her axes, but she was in much worse shape than her opponent right now. Its tail hovered above her, about to strike, as Jonah and Rake arrived. Jonah's sword shattered the tail above Fili as Rake-zilla barreled into the creature, knocking it to the ground. Fili retrieved her spear with her left hand, while her right was pinned to her side to staunch the bleeding. She drove her weapon into the ground between the bone devil's ribs pinning it in place.

Lia dispatched another imp on her way to help Elowen. She prayed for divine aid as she ran causing her blade to light up with a spectral flame. She drove it into the barbed devil causing it to screech in pain and defiance. Elowen used the opening to strike again, slashing it with a heavy claw and tearing at it with her teeth. After another barrage from Azure's conjured weapon the beast's demeanor changed. It became desperate, lashing out recklessly. Seconds later it was dust.

The final imp charged at the restrained Draco, driving its tail spike deep into the halfling's back. The Djinn did not seem pleased, driving its scimitar up into the demon. It too turned to dust. The portal began to open again, as the djinn got near the bone devil. Gadget knew it was now or never. She ran and jumped up, using the creature's belt and crossed harness, she scaled the creatures back. Straddling one of its shoulders she began to examine the collar.

The Djinn, scimitar in one hand and Draco in the other, couldn't do anything about his unwanted rider. He looked at the halfling for a second, then threw him into the growing portal. Elowen-bear saw Draco fly into the portal and raced in after him. Gadget, now with tools in hand, began to dismantle the collar. She knew the halfling was in trouble in whatever place the portal led to, but that would have to be someone else's job. She had to stop this blue monstrosity.

Lia was heading toward the djinn to help. Gadget saw her and managed, "No, stay back. I've got this… I think." Just then the collar popped open. The Djinn stopped walking just short of where Fili, Rake and Jonah were fighting the bone devil. All eyes were on this huge blue humanoid including the bewildered demon.

The djinn looked over his shoulder at Gadget saying something unintelligible to any of them. The gnome jumped down., hands raised to show that she wasn't a threat. The Djinn nodded, then looked at the bone devil, lightning sparking from his eyes. He grabbed the devil by the neck. Looking it in the face and said something only the devil understood, causing it to thrash wildly in an effort to escape. The Djinn's other hand drew a circle in the air causing a hole to open beside him. Through it those nearby could feel a warm breeze. There were many clouds in this other place. Thunder could be heard, and lightning could be seen through the new portal. The Djinn stepped through still holding his prisoner. He stood on a cloud, looking down at Gadget for a moment. He nodded in thanks once more as the portal closed.

Almost on cue the demon portal flashed. A brown bear, blood pouring from many wounds, ran from the portal dragging an unconscious Draco by the cloak. Seeing her friends she dropped her cargo and face-planted into the ground among them.

The party healers and medics patched up their gravely wounded friends as the demon portal once again dwindled into nothingness. Azure took Filipina behind some trees for privacy while she wrapped her ribs. As the centaur sat in the grass she felt a strange tingle in her leg, almost like when a limb falls asleep. The tingle traveled up her leg and dissipated into her torso.

Suddenly she heard a voice in her head, "Filipina, it is me Shadolok."

Filipina winced, unused to the mental contact, though it didn't hurt.

"Am I hurting you?" Azure asked, concerned about her friend's injuries.

"No," the centaur replied, "I'm fine."

"I was cast out of Draco by the blast," the Aetherian explained psychically. "It is not our way to return to a host that couldn't keep us both safe. Besides, he doesn't seem...right."

Filipina replied with her thoughts, "Its fine, as long as you agree to leave my body if this gets weird, or weirder anyway."

"Of course," Shadolok replied silently. "Can we let everyone think I'm gone for a while? Maybe they will stop pursuing us, at least that evil blue woman."

"Yeah. That is probably for the best," she agreed.

"You're awfully quiet," Azure prodded, having no idea about the mental conversation happening.

"I'm just frustrated," Filipina admitted, though she left out some of the reasons. "This was our first fight together as a group and we got smacked around."

"I understand," the elf agreed. "We will get better."

Rake, Jonah and Lia decided that it would be best to move away from this area before camping for the night. They all walked in silence for several miles, no one ready to confront Lia and Draco about what had happened just yet. The night's campfire conversation was sure to be interesting.

After a couple hours, the last one in darkness as the sun had set, Elowen found a defensible cave near the river in the pass between Mount Nebo to the south and Mount Gilead to the north. The cave was up in the foothills and offered a concealed high-ground view both east and west. There was little conversation outside of setting up camp, cooking, or cleaning wounds. Once everything was prepared, they sat together. Jonah prayed over the food, and everyone ate.

Filipina, never one to hold back said, "Are we all going to keep quiet about what just happened?"

Rake replied, "I was trying to gather my thoughts and not be reactive, though it's getting hard to keep learning things about each other by the surprise method."

"Before we get started dealing with the surprises, I would like to say something positive," Jonah interjected. "You all did well looking after each other. Everyone did their part to deal with enemies while watching someone's back. That said, Gadget, you were amazing. Your quick thinking saved Draco's life and probably several others."

"Just trying to do my part," she replied humbly, as she systematically dismantled the collar, she had removed from the Djinn, to learn how it worked.

"Still pretty cool," Ayzee added with his mouth still full.

Everyone agreed, each thanking her in their own way.

Azure spoke next, "I am in no way judging as I brought my own surprise revelation to the group recently," Azure said, motioning toward Ayzee.

"That would be me," he responded, still eating. "You guys are good, and care about each other. I'm still going to kill that dragon, but for now, I'm with you."

"Thank you Ayzee," Azure replied. "Lia, what happened back there? You saw that woman and broke cover, putting people at risk."

"I'm sorry," she said. The response was meant for everyone, though she didn't look up from the ground. "It was foolish, but it had been so long since I had seen any family."

Shay reached over and threw an arm around her friend, "I'm your family now, we all are."

The blue-skinned elf smiled and nodded, "I know, and I feel the same way about you. She was quite the piece of work, wasn't she?"

"Do we think there's any significance to her being one of our adversaries, or at least working with them?" Gadget always saw sides of the equation no one else had noticed yet.

"Clearly Draco has something to add here," Filipina said matter-of-factly. "What do you know about her aunt?"

Draco had been unusually quiet. No one except Filipina knew it yet but Shadolok had been torn from him. He was confused and lost without his psychic partner. Now he was being confronted by his past, again. He dreaded the potential backlash, but knew it was time to come clean.

He cleared his throat and stood. The halfling had a hard time sitting still especially during stressful situations, "It won't surprise any of you that I wasn't exactly a productive member of society before I met you. My dad was a thief and a scammer all his life. He made it seem glamorous in a way, though we lived in poverty. When he disappeared on his last big score, that was going to set us up for life, my mother gave me some money, this pendant," he touched the flower shaped item pinned to his chest, "and a few necessities and she sent me away. Later she wrote me a letter explaining that my father's bosses would make us pay for his failure, so she got me out of the picture." He rummaged around in his bag retrieving a couple of items. He held them out to the group. One was a beautiful, ornate dagger with a curve in the blade and a ring in the pommel for added grip. The other was a small silver pendant in the shape of a beetle. "I found these…"

Lia was on her feet, her hands over her mouth and nose, her eyes wide in horror. "S-silver scarab," she gasped.

"What?" Draco replied. "I guess so. Are you ok?"

"No!" She yelled, tears now running down her face. "That is the symbol of the Silver Scarab Trading Company. They are the slavers who took me and sold me as a child."

Draco touched her arms gently, "I'm so sorry Lia, I had no idea. I found these hidden in my father's room. I have no idea where he got them but knowing him, he stole them."

Azure and Shay calmed the young paladin, vowing to help her through this. When she had regained her composure, Lia said, "Please go on Draco, maybe more information will come to light."

"Thank you," he wanted to know more about her connection to the scarab pendant, but he soldiered on with his story. "I headed south stopping in cities to rest or make a few coins to continue. I scammed and stole until I reached Jericho. When I first got there it seemed like a paradise for a guy like me. The combination of people of vast wealth, rampant crime, and a corrupt justice system more concerned about punishing people's faith than ensuring their safety, provided plenty of targets for a clever thief like me. I found the biggest mansion in the city and broke in and I stole this cloak."

Several of the group members were struggling with these admissions. They were clearly not ok with his thieving past, but they had seen a different person in their time with him, he had changed in many ways.

He took a deep breath and continued, "Right away I knew I had made a big mistake. Even the most corrupt system has people it protects without question. Apparently, the person I stole from was one of those elite people. As the heat mounted,

I knew I had to hide my items of value, including the cloak, until it died down. I thought that the best place to hide something was the last place they would look so I went back to the mansion and hid the cloak and my personal items in the basement among many other boxes and crates in storage. The next day I was arrested."

The others recognized that this was where they had met the halfling, "They threw me in a cell while they searched my quarters. Of course they found nothing. I was thrown into a cell with Rake, Filipina and a woman named Kendra, who you may have met in Haven." A few of the party members nodded. "In the middle of the night we woke to find our cell door open," he continued. Everyone was riveted by his words. "We heard a massive commotion coming from below. I found out later that the noise was from your wife and daughter making their escape."

Jonah nodded, "Yes, the monstrosity they accidentally unleashed."

"Right," Draco agreed, "When the guards left their post to investigate, we went right out the front door. Kendra told us about Haven, and said she would lead us there, but I couldn't leave without my things. I told them I would meet them in the skids at The Weary Traveler Inn by dark, or in the woods, northwest of the city by morning. They agreed to the plan, thinking it best if they didn't move much in the daylight."

Draco realized he had hardly eaten anything while telling his story, so he took a few bites and had a drink before resuming. No one spoke during his break, anxiously awaiting the rest of the story. "Once again, I broke into the mansion but this time it was much more heavily guarded. I managed to get into the basement again but just as I found my stuff your aunt and a woman with green skin, called Pandora, showed up. They went into a secret chamber near the stairs. I was able to get close enough to listen without being seen. They talked about prophesied ones arriving, being captured, and escaping. They mentioned that someone named Vixyn had made contact and was trying to follow them. The sea elf mentioned two names, Cairncross and Greed, who she clearly didn't like. She told Pandora to head to Philistia with a minotaur to secure alliances. After the green woman left, Qiné used a crystal ball to contact Greed. When he answered he called her Envy. They threw barbs at each other. I lost track of their conversation as a portal opened near my hiding spot."

Draco took another bite of his food and a drink, "Two imps appeared and began looking for something in the crates. One of them found an ornate box that seemed heavy by the way the small demon was holding it with two hands. I couldn't resist so I sprung on them burying my dagger deep in one of them. It instantly turned to dust. I turned to the other, but it had disappeared, I stabbed in the direction it had been, and luckily, my dagger found it. The box rematerialized as that imp too, turned to dust. I caught it before it hit the ground and made noise, but I was careless, and it opened. A smoky mist swirled around my hands before I could get the lid closed. I didn't know then, but it was already too late, Shadolok had claimed me as his host." He ate some more before continuing again.

Filipina thought that moment would have been a good time for him to mention losing Shadolok, but he didn't.

He continued his tale, "Envy, or Qiné as we know her now, must have heard something because she came out shining a light around the basement. I hid behind some odd smelling casks until she closed her secret room and left. The sulfur smell reminded me of fire magic, so I grabbed one of them and went out the window. I needed a distraction to get past the guards, so I lit the cask and rolled it toward the corner of the mansion. It exploded with enough force to damage the house, light it on fire, and knock down the adjacent wrought iron fence. While the guards put it out, I escaped through the broken gate."

"Why would my aunt be called 'Envy'?" Lia mused aloud. "It is fitting though, she always competed with my mother and rarely measured up."

"Envy and greed are both mortal sins in our Bible on earth." Gadget explained. "Pride, greed, lust, envy, sloth, wrath and gluttony."

"Are they really being that obvious about their intent?" Filipina was flabbergasted.

Rake, never the one to speak about faith before his recent near-death experience, replied, "Which of those sins do we not run toward willingly, despite knowing the cost?"

They all nodded in agreement, some unable or unwilling to even look at the others in shame of the many sins that came to mind.

Jonah spoke up, "Let's not dwell in the negative. Thank you for sharing that Draco. I'm not sure the rest of the story gives us any more about Lia's kidnapping, but it does explain Qiné's obsession with you."

"The pendant my mother gave me shields me from location and scrying spells, which has held her at bay," Draco shared. "She clearly knows we are together, so she must be tracking me through the group now. I understand if you think it best for me to go on my own."

"No!" Rake's volume and forceful tone made his intent clear. "You all saved my life, helped Elowen and her people, and even aided Shay's clan without question or complaint. I hope everyone agrees, but I don't think we can call ourselves 'Coram Deo' if we're not willing to stand with each other and for each other."

Everyone nodded in agreement. Lia and Draco thanked everyone for their understanding. Soon the watches were set, and the party went to sleep. Weather and conditions allowing, they should reach Deepforge sometime after midday. They had no idea what to expect as they trekked through the mountain caves and warrens, so they knew they needed a good night's sleep tonight.

৩৶৶

Sleep came easily as their minds were calm following the revelations of the evening. Once again, a dream comes to the believers among the group. This time it is a mild summer day in Israel. The sun is bright, but the cool breeze moderates the heat. Your vision bird is on a tree branch, through its eyes the dreamers are looking down on another wedding. Some of the people at the wedding fade away and disappear as other younger ones appear. Leaves fall from the trees, withering as they gently float to the ground. As you look back up the young guests have aged and faded away, replaced by young guests again just as new sprouts form and grow on the trees. The sun rises and sets in fast motion starting each new cycle with a different bride and groom. You aren't sure how, but you know the man to be Ibzan. He is the only constant throughout the dream. He sits in his chair of judgment, aging slowly as he presides over the weddings of his sons, thirty of them in all. During each event Ibzan hosts the ceremony then sits and judges his community.

After the **thirtieth wedding** time slows. The trees stop shedding and blooming, freezing in place. Only the vision-bird is free to move. It lifts off from the tree. Looking down there is a procession moving from Bethlehem to Jerusalem. The procession ends at a necropolis under the Holy City. You see Ibzan's wife, thirty sons, daughters-in-law, and many grandchildren attending the internment of their patriarch. The bird lifts off back into the sky. You see only the brightness of the sun for a moment then the dreamers awaken to a new day.

❧

The mood was completely different when the party members started to awaken. Jonah and Filipina had taken the last watch. When the others began to stir, the paladin and the fighter went to get firewood. Upon their return Lia and Shay had started cooking breakfast. Everyone else packed up camp. Draco was nowhere to be seen. Each team member took a few minutes to check on Lia, who seemed to have regained her resolve after the shocking revelations of the previous day. She had endured so much in her still young life, she would endure this too, this time with Adonai in her heart and Coram Deo at the side. She did pray boldly that she might find the slavers responsible for her kidnapping and stop their evil ways. She trusted that God would hear her prayer. Gadget tinkered with some scraps and components, while Ember studied her spell book as was her habit during any downtime.

Draco returned to report that no one was behind them for at least a few miles. He asked Elowen to scout forward with him. They finished eating quickly and left ahead of the main group.

After a hearty meal the rest of the group set off to the east through the pass separating Mount Nebo and Mount Gilead.

They stayed along the river until the face of Mount Nebo turned south. The temperature rose noticeably as the mountain now blocked the wind from the west. The scenery was beautiful. From the edge of the tree line, they could see the vast desert wilderness to the east with mountains rising in the distance in every direction. They were up in the hill country that met the mountains and extended south as far as they could see through the trees. They took a zigzag path through the hills enjoying the protection from both the sun and from passers-by on the road below. Even with this large of a group they would be nearly impossible to spot from the road.

Around midday they had stopped for food when they heard the sounds of shouting and battle below by the road. Elowen took to the skies while Jonah, Draco and Rake crawled up a hill and looked down using the spyglass they had found in the war camp. Everyone else paired up and circled the hill to provide support from the flanks if necessary. They could see a small caravan of people, possibly halflings, being harassed by goblins and orcs. The adults had formed a circle and were brandishing weapons in defense, as their attackers advanced.

The druid in bird form was diving to help but pulled up when a female dwarf suddenly appeared in the middle of the halflings. She spoke some words and a glimmering force field appeared around the small caravan. "Not one more step, foul creatures. My companions have ya dead to rights. Ya move and ya sprout a crossbow bolt from yer ear." Her voice bellowed, echoing off the nearby mountains.

The orcs and goblins looked around nervously for the hidden snipers. Jonah's group on the hill and the bird in the sky could see the dwarf was bluffing, but the brigands bought it. They mounted up on their camels and rode off to the east. Jonah led the trio down the hill while Elowen continued to circle above making sure the attackers didn't circle back. She noted that they went east about a mile before turning southwest. She thought they may cross paths with them again before Deepforge.

Everyone met at the caravan. The dwarf was instantly on guard but relaxed a bit and breathed a sigh of relief when she saw the group and their insignias. "Thank Adonai, orcs and goblins are so gullible," she offered. "Me name's Audhilda, ye must be the group from Haven?"

"We are," Filipina answered. "So, the snipers were a bluff?" The centaur fighter smiled, impressed with the dwarf's boldness.

"I suppose ye were my snipers," she mused in reply, "though I didnae know it at the time."

Azure, Shay, Lia, and Jonah were all seeing to any injuries incurred by the halflings. They were pleased to see the family was unhurt. Draco and Rake looked over the caravan and were surprised to see children hiding among the stores.

Azure checked some facial bruises on an adult male, "Where were you heading?"

"We were bringing supplies west, to Gilgal," he replied, still a little shaken from the assault. "This road is usually safe, patrolled by the dwarves, at least through the pass."

"Apologies Harwick," Audhilda offered. "We're spread a bit thin with all the raids in the south. We're down to solo patrols north of Deepforge. I slept up on that ridge last night or I'd have missed yer situation."

"You know he wasn't complaining," the female halfling offered. "We were just scared, especially with the kids in the cart."

"No offense taken Aida," the dwarf replied. "We're all doing our best. I'm sure these folks need to get on their way. I'll escort ye to the pass. Ye should be good from there."

Jonah had been furiously writing something on a piece of parchment. He gave it to Aida, "When you get to Gilgal, find a woman named Willa, she will be at the orphanage or the school, please give her this note."

Aida nodded in agreement and the two groups parted ways.

Draco and Elowen went out ahead again, followed by the rest a mile or so behind. After a few more miles the pair of scouts knew they had to be getting close to Deepforge, so they moved back up into the foothills and forest along the base of Mount Nebo. They probably didn't need to as they approached a friendly city, but it had become a habit. After another few miles Elowen saw smoke down below by the road.

She whispered to get Draco's attention as she pointed down from behind a tree. "The two guard towers by the road are on fire," her voice was getting a bit frantic. She moved to the other side of the tree to get a different vantage point, "and look there are bodies down there. I think Deepforge is under attack!"

The young druid barely felt the dagger slip between the ribs of her back as Draco leaned in and whispered into her ear, "Yes, right on schedule."

She turned, warm blood soaking the back of her tunic. She leaned back against the tree, "D-draco, wh-why?" She found it difficult to speak.

"You really are slow on the uptake, elf," he spat back at her, his voice was different. "Did you think you could destroy Samael's keep without repercussions?"

Her vision began to blur. She wondered if it was from loss of blood or if he had poisoned her. Her mind was fuzzy, but in a moment of focus she saw her betrayer's face waver and change. It was older, wrinkled, and scarred. His hair was mostly gray, and his eyes were as dead as a shark's, without a hint of the playful joviality of her friend. "Who are you?"

"Why, I am Draco's father Merrick, of course," his voice held a lilt of pride at the admission. "You can call me Greed." A portal opened behind him but before he stepped in, he looked back at Elowen, her face white now, her brow covered in sweat. "If it makes you feel better, wherever you are going Draco will be right behind you as soon as we retrieve the Aetherian. Then maybe we will go after your grove again. Either way, you won't be alone for long." With that he stepped through the portal, and it closed.

Elowen lay there bleeding, unable to speak. She prayed, in her clouded mind, for her death to be painless and her trip to Heaven to be swift. She also prayed that her friends would find a way to succeed where she had failed. Her final thought was for her sister and the grove. A single tear ran down her face as she slid to the ground beside the tree and lapsed into darkness.

The rest of the party saw the smoke from a mile away. Wondering why Draco and Elowen hadn't warned them, they ran that mile as fast as they could. To their left they could see two guard towers ablaze, siege engines propped against them, also on fire. There were bodies of fallen dwarves, orcs, and goblins littering the landscape. It was eerily quiet until they got close enough to hear the low moans and cries of the injured and dying. Everyone who could heal ran to a dwarf clinging to life, healing them and instructing them to help their brothers and sisters on the field and then get up into the foothills for safety.

Filipina had seen a lot of death in her time, but this was overwhelming. Shadolok must have felt her discomfort through their psychic connection, but he resisted replacing her remembering their bargain. While her friends tended to the fallen, she noted, "The front gate is breached, we need to go help."

"Agreed," Jonah replied. "Filipina, Lia, and Gadget take the left side. Rake and Ayzee with me on the right. Shay, you're with Azure and Ember in the back for support. Watch out for Elowen and Draco, they may already be inside."

With the orders given Jonah prayed aloud, "Father, your children are in need. You have equipped us for such a time as this. Lead us into this battle and give us the strength and skill to aid your faithful dwarven people. May all the glory go to you today and if any of us should fall, bring us home to thank you for the opportunity to give our lives in your name. It is for your glory that we fight, only through you can we be victorious…Solus Deus!"

As one the group that had come to be known as Coram Deo, for living their lives before the face of God, repeated Jonah's final oath, Solus Deus, Only God. With that, the nine heroes took a deep breath and moved with purpose toward the sounds of battle echoing from within the great halls of Deepforge.

To be Continued…

Epilogue

Willa had struggled to calm her mind enough to even trance the first night Jonah was gone. She had prayed all day for peace, calm, and acceptance of God's callings on their lives. She overcame her exhaustion the next day by immersing herself in her work. She walked through the construction of the school. It was progressing beautifully. Solus Deus bet Hammidras was going to be a literal godsend to this community and Judah in general.

After assuring herself that the project was in good hands, Willa headed over to the Father's House. Classes were still being held there and at the temple until the school building was completed. She checked in on Saraé who was enjoying every minute of learning. She saw value in every piece of knowledge and especially enjoyed learning about Adonai from Luk and her mother. Wren was apprenticing under Brulnyss, while serving as the blind dwarf's teacher's aide. She enjoyed the work and was looking forward to teaching her own classes soon. Willa checked in with Zarra while she was there and was assured that everything was under control.

Willa was both impressed and relieved that there were no emergencies though it did provide room for thoughts of her husband to return. She walked across the now busy main street of Gilgal toward the temple where her class would meet in an hour or so. Completely distracted by thoughts of Jonah she never saw the petite, white haired half-elven woman until they collided.

"Oh, pardon me," Willa offered as she helped the woman pick up some fruit she had dropped. "I was lost in thought and didn't see you. I'm Willa, I don't think we've met."

The woman chuckled, "people rarely see me coming, Willa. I'm Nicole, thank you for the help. Have a nice day."

Willa walked away almost completely distracted again instantly.

The young half-elf turned into an alley. Leaning against the side of a house she shook her sleeve. The key she had stolen from Willa dropped into her palm. She looked at it and smiled, then tucked it into a pocket on her dress.

That evening, Willa, Wren and Saraé prayed together, then ate. They were mostly quiet until Willa asked about school. Both of her daughters went on and on about how much they loved it. Willa smiled listening to their words, but her mind was far away, hoping that Jonah was safe.

The face of Nicole, the half elf from the street, appeared in the darkness outside their window. She stayed well back so the light from inside wouldn't give her away. As she watched Willa interact with her daughters she smiled deviously. Her facial features began to shift and change until right outside Willa's window stood Vixyn. The real face of the changeling woman, or at least the one she used most, was a like blank mask. It was devoid of emotion as she watched the mother and daughters interact. Lines began to form between and beside her eyes. The more they enjoyed each other's company the angrier Vixyn's face became. Finally, she took a deep breath and held up the key she had pickpocketed from Willa, "Enjoy yourselves ladies, with the half-celestial gone, you'll never see me coming."

Voices rang out from nearby pedestrians as they passed the alley outside Willa's window. It was empty, Vixyn was gone, for now.

That night Willa felt calmer. God had given her some peace in her dual roles as mother and teacher. When she focused her mind and fell into her trance she dreamed again. This time she saw an older man resting by his tent in the heat of the day. He wiped sweat from his brow. As his vision cleared, he saw that three men were standing in front of him. He gave them a spot to sit in the shade by a tree while he got them water and bread. He ran to the well for the water and to the flock for milk then returned. The three men asked about their host's wife.

When she was within earshot the Lord spoke through them, "I will surely return to you about this time next year, and Sarah your wife shall have a son." Sarah was listening at the tent door behind him. She laughed to herself, saying, "After I am worn out, and my lord is old, shall I have pleasure?" The Lord spoke through the men again to Abraham, "Why did Sarah laugh and say, 'Shall I indeed bear a child, now that I am old?' Is anything too hard for the LORD? At the appointed time I will return to you, about this time next year, and Sarah shall have a son."

Willa awoke. She found the verses she had dreamed about in her Bible. She read Genesis 18:1-21 over and over. She couldn't help fixating on the line in the scripture where the Lord asks, "Is anything too hard for the Lord?"

The
End

Coram Deo will return in

Heavenly Places 3
Gracia Dei

In

2025

Also available
in the
Heavenly Places

The story begins here. The mage and the rabbi have come from earth to the mage's home world. They brought with them the story of the One True God. Adonai heard their prayers and decided to reveal himself. The region changed in a day to a version of Israel before the exile to Babylon. Not everyone is pleased with this change. Can the heroes called from Earth and Aeramor decipher God's will, spread his word of salvation, and fend off the forces of evil?

Available on Amazon.

www.ingramcontent.com/pod-product-compliance
Lightning Source LLC
Chambersburg PA
CBHW061423150726
47987CB00001B/78